BREAK THE SPELL

Mages and Mates Book One

ANDY GALLO

BREAK THE SPELL

Copyright © 2022 by Andy Gallo

Cover Art © 2022 Alexandria Corza

www.alexandriacorza.com

Published by Gallorious Readers, LLC

P.O. Box 1654 College Park, MD 20741, USA

This is a work of fiction. Names, characters, places, and incidents either are the product of author imagination or are used fictitiously, and any resemblance to actual persons, living or dead, business establishments, events, or locales is entirely coincidental.

This book contains explicit sexual content.

Cover content is for illustrative purposes only and any person depicted on the cover is a model.

All rights reserved. This book is licensed to the original purchaser only. Duplication or distribution via any means is illegal and a violation of international copyright law, subject to criminal prosecution and upon conviction, fines, and/or imprisonment. Any eBook format cannot be legally loaned or given to others. No part of this book may be reproduced or transmitted in any for or by any means, electronic or mechanical, including photocopying, recording, or by any information storage and retrieval system, without the written permission of the Publisher, except where permitted by law. To request permission and all other inquiries, contact Andy Gallo, P.O. Box 1654, College Park, MD 20741, USA; visit www.andygallo.com; or send an email to andy@andygallo.com.

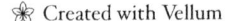

❦ Created with Vellum

Break The Spell: Mages and Mates
Book One

Bartholomew Hollen, professor of defensive magic at Utrecht University, just wanted a no strings, no feelings, no attachment hook up. Nothing messy like when his ex-boyfriend tried to feed him to a demon. Bart's heart, however, has other ideas. But when he has a vision of the future and sees his hookup dying at his feet from yet another demon, Bart does the only sensible thing – he sneaks out like a thief in the night.

Not like he'll see the guy again.

Caelinus Reinhold has done something no elf has done before – become the professor of creative magic at Utrecht University. His first day should be magical, except Cael can't stop thinking about the hot mage he hooked up with the night before who then snuck out while he slept. Whatever. His loss.

He'll never see the jerk again, anyway.

Things get awkward fast when the department assigns Bart to be Cael's mentor. Despite their rocky start, neither can deny that Fate wants them together. But Bart's premonitions all end in tragedy for the pair. No matter how he tries to change the future, Cael is *always* a casualty. How can Bart follow his heart when Cael's death is sure to break it?

Like everything I write, this is dedicated to my husband Mike and my daughter. You give me the courage and freedom to write.

Forever will not be long enough.

Chapter One

❧

BARTHOLOMEW

Declan: Can you come to my classroom?

Setting my phone down, I pressed the heels of my palms against my eyelids. What now? This was becoming a daily thing, and I was over it. And him. He broke up with me. Why did he keep asking to see me?

Worse, not one time had it been anything remotely important.

I grabbed my phone and angrily typed a response.

{**Bart:** I'm busy. Can we talk later?}

Five months since our last date, and you'd think *I'd* ended our relationship. To be fair, when the head of the Ocular Society reads the signs and says you're not each other's forever person, it takes the zing out of things. That, however, still wasn't my fault, so why was he torturing me?

Deep down, we'd both known we weren't a long-term thing. It was mildly fun, the sex was good, and we mostly got on fine, but we lacked any real chemistry. Hearing it in such stark language, however, burst the illusion. I didn't blame Declan for breaking it off after Gran told us—on New Year's Eve in front of my entire family, no less—we wouldn't be together long. The timing was shitty, and she probably picked that moment on purpose because she'd never liked Declan. Which, in his mind, made it my fault by association.

Fair enough, but it was the hot and cold treatment since then that made it hard to be around him.

For most of the semester, he'd kept his distance. Even in staff meetings, he sat as far away from me as he could. And if I took the seat at the far end of the table, forcing him to sit next to the head of the department, it wasn't meant to be spiteful.

Not much at least.

The last three weeks, however, he'd found excuses for us to talk. Not that he was friendly when we did meet. I think he just wanted to see if I'd respond.

I tried to get back to my research, but now I was waiting for him to reply and say it was important. It never was, but he'd text me until I caved just to make him stop. That *was* my fault. I never liked parting on bad terms—unless one of us had done something shitty, like cheat or lie about something important. We'd been friends once, and that should have survived.

Everyone disagreed, but I didn't give in to group think.

Today, however, I needed a new approach. It was almost five p.m., and I had another hour of work to do before I left for the weekend—if I could save myself thirty minutes of distraction . . .

Sighing loudly, I locked my screen and pushed back from the heavy oak desk I'd found in the attic of Hollen Hall. I'd moved out of my ancestral home the first chance I could, but that didn't mean the place wasn't a treasure trove of antiques I could appropriate for my personal use. The thick Persian rug, ornate bookcases, vintage Victorian chairs, and mahogany side table had all been liberated from the same dusty attic banishment.

Declan said it made me stodgy at twenty-eight, and I'd owned it. I liked old things. They had more character and style than modern pieces.

Pulling my door shut, I dropped my hand to the mage stone in my pocket, running my fingers instinctively over its outline through the cotton of my slacks. I touched the tiny indent where my index finger rested and remembered how big it felt when my grandfather gave it to me for my twelfth birthday. Now I felt naked if it wasn't in my pocket.

My footsteps echoed in the empty hallway of the applied magic department. Not many students came to the third floor after four p.m.. It was a gorgeous Friday in May, and most of the rooms were empty. Philadelphia generally had pleasant spring weather, but today was perfect. Warm enough for shorts, almost no humidity, and hardly a cloud to be seen. The kind of day that begged me to leave the campus and go for a long run before dinner.

I turned onto the creative magic wing. Only one classroom had its lights on—Declan's. When we dated, I'd spent a lot of time there, but the familiarity had worn off. Magic hummed from inside the room. Declan was using a lot of power. Why wasn't the door warded closed?

Shaking out of my daydream, I pulled my stone and walked faster.

"Declan?" I called as I entered. "What are you . . .?"

The desks had been moved to the perimeter and a giant series of glyphs covered the floor in a large circle. Declan knelt at the back of the room, working on a smaller circle of symbols. He looked up in surprise and then snapped his gaze back to his work.

"Shit," he muttered, and worked faster.

"Declan, what the fuck are you doing?" I glanced over the big series of runes. "Are you out of your mind!"

He never took his eyes off his work.

I stepped into the room.

"No!" He held up his hand. "It's not ready!"

Power hummed under my foot when I triggered a completed spell. I froze and studied the glyphs covering the floor. Declan was toiling furiously. Fear, the deep paralyzing kind, swallowed me in its icy grip; there was more dark magic in Dec's classroom than I'd ever felt. This was meant to kill, and it was clear who he wanted dead.

The symbols of the larger pattern thrummed, and light pulsed up from the stone floor. I snapped out of my terror-induced stupor and realized the pattern.

Declan was still feverishly trying to finish the other circle. Everything came into focus, and anger roiled inside me.

"Fuck that." I pointed my stone in his direction and sent a narrow blast of magic toward the arc of his circle. A small sliver of stone flew up, breaking the continuity of the pattern.

"No!" His wide-eyed look of horror morphed into a glare of pure hate. I didn't need a cipher to know it was meant for me. Hell was about to break loose, and I'd destroyed his only chance of survival. With my proximity to the door, he'd be the first to die.

Except, I wasn't a killer. At least, I wouldn't kill Declan. I released a second spell before he could attack, the force of my magic sending him flying backward. He struck the wall hard, dazed from the impact. His mage stone fell from his fingers as my enchantment pinned him to the wall.

The barrier I'd created was strong enough to hold him—for a time, at least. It was the best I had on short notice.

Light swirled inside the circle, and the floor turned a translucent yellow. I was running out of time. As soon as the energy expanded to the edges of the pattern, his spell would be active.

Without taking my eyes off the circle, I extended my left hand and called for the Orme Seax. I'd bought the ancient Viking short sword as a curiosity. It was very old and strikingly beautiful; the brilliant blue sapphire wedged between golden serpent fangs in the pommel and the gilded hilt meant it must've been a valuable piece, for an important person. It also reeked of magic, so I'd dug deeper. It was more than an ordinary weapon.

It had taken a year to decipher its purpose and another six months to unlock how to use it. I thanked the old gods I'd made the effort.

The crash of wood splintering in the distance meant I'd need a new door. A small price to pay for my survival. Assuming I survived.

The sword slapped against my outstretched hand. I wrapped my fingers around the cool hilt and activated the magic inside. The jewel pulsed once, and blue fire shot along the blade. Energy sped up my arm until it covered me in its protective embrace. Alone, it wouldn't be enough, but it allowed me to divert magic from my defenses into offense.

With all the dark magic Declan had used, he should have set off the school's detection spells, but they were silent. I didn't have time for that mystery. I needed to warn school security.

The amount of power needed to do this was insane. Where did Declan get such magic?

Shaking off the question, I grabbed the thread of the detection spell that ran through the building and yanked it into the classroom. A shrill alarm screeched through the campus. Hopefully that was enough—the yellow energy had reached the edges of the circle. It was impossible, but it was coming. No demon had breached the Great Ward since it had been erected, yet a demon was about to appear. I needed to give it my full attention. I raised the seax, pointed it in the direction of the circle, and touched my mage stone to the gem in the pommel.

There were two ways to bring a demon into our world: summon it or open a portal. Theoretically, at least. No one had done it in twelve centuries. Summoning any demon was crazy, but using a portal was *really* insane. It was like opening a door and inviting anyone who happened by to enter. You couldn't limit the number or strength of the creatures who came through.

Thankfully, this was a summons; only a single demon of a

certain size and strength could answer. Unfortunately, given the size of the circle, that single demon would be big and strong.

The light flashed, and I released my spell even before my vision cleared. I needed to keep its attention on me, so it didn't consume Declan. My survival improved exponentially if I prevented that.

The demon roared and I felt the power in its voice. Windows rattled and desks shook, but my blast served its purpose. I had the creature's full attention.

Wonderful.

It wasn't as big as I'd feared, but it was big enough. The horns on its head almost touched the ceiling and its arms were as thick as my body. Good thing we weren't going to wrestle. Its blue-black skin shimmered an iridescent orange, the same color as its eyes. Naked from the waist up, it had cloth wrapped around its hips, clasped by what looked like the skull of some poor creature. The hem was tattered and hung down in strips.

I didn't see a weapon, but its massive hands ended in claws that could easily peel the skin from my body. Around each wrist, it wore a metal brace with some etching or writing I couldn't see clearly. It was as fearsome as the legends suggested.

I specialized in defensive magic and had sparred numerous times with other mages, but that'd been controlled, and I'd had time to prepare. Fear bubbled inside me.

This was nothing like those fights. Lose, and no one helped me to my feet and taught me how to do better next time. Death was a very real possibility.

Confused, the demon watched me. Why had I summoned it, only to attack? Beating it down wouldn't bend it to my will. Subjugation required the right containment spells, not brute force. It bared its teeth and growled.

"You have not summoned me!"

My first combat magic teacher taught me never respond to an opponent. Failure to answer usually led to anger. Anger led to mistakes, and I needed to be ready to capitalize if it made any.

The Orme Seax throbbed in my hand. I'd studied this weapon—it had been made to fight demons. The magic forged into the blade burned a demon's flesh.

My hands shook as I tapped my stone to the weapon's jewel, feeding it magic, then slashed the air. A thin line opened on the creature's chest and orange ichor seeped out. Its roar was louder than the first.

"I will rend you apart and feast on your flesh while you watch."

It took a step toward me, but I hit it with another blast of magic, aiming for the wound I'd inflicted. The brunt of my attack struck true; the creature flailed its arms to ward it off, and in the process its head whipped around. It stared at Declan, dazed and tethered to the wall.

Adrenaline coursed through my body, counteracting my barely controlled terror. I couldn't let it consume Declan's power or I'd be fucked.

I slashed the blade again and the strike cut deeper and wider into its back. Spinning to face me, it snarled and belched fire from its mouth.

The old lore taught that hellfire was a staple in a demon's arsenal. I expected this, but I still flinched when the flames hit my wards. Years of magical combat training kicked in, and I directed a blast of mage fire into the demon's open maw. At the last second it blocked my attack with a metal bracelet.

We watched each other warily across the remains of Declan's classroom. The thoughtful look scared me more than the previous attack, but time was my ally. Utrecht Academy boasted more than a dozen alpha mages on staff. One or more would answer the alarm. In addition, Utrecht only hired beta twos or higher for security. There was enough mage talent here to help me if I could keep the beast occupied a little longer.

If I'd had time to prepare, and if Declan wasn't nearby, I wouldn't need help. Declan's presence, however, complicated things. Keeping the demon from Declan without freeing my ex in the process was hard. Why the fuck had he raised a demon? *How* had he raised a demon? The Great Ward was an incredibly powerful spell; it kept creatures like the one Declan had raised out for good reason. The last time demons crossed into our world, they nearly killed everyone. What sane person . . . what *insane* person would want that?

My enemy snuck a glance at Declan, finally deducing who had summoned it. It was bound to this room as long as Declan lived. The classroom, however, wasn't a safe space for the demon. It needed to feed on Declan, but it knew I'd kill it if it ignored me. The lack of good options would make it desperate, which made it a very dangerous enemy.

The next fiery attack lasted longer than the first, and the demon inched closer to Declan during the exchange. It couldn't break Declan's bonds without exposing itself to attack, but I didn't want to let it close enough to make the attempt. Preparing my spell, I waited.

I released my counter the moment the demon opened its mouth. My magic redirected the fire, making it swirl around the creature. I wrestled control of the flames and fed it more energy. The demon tested the swirling fire and snatched its hand back upon contact. It wouldn't hold it at bay for long—the flames would soon consume my magic—but I was ready.

"What the fuck?"

Anton Brador, head of Utrecht's security. He and I had a mutual dislike going, but I could work with him. Which was good, because he was an alpha mage, and I needed his help.

"Declan summoned it," I said between clenched teeth, not taking my gaze off the demon.

Brador eased into the room and pointed his stone at the nightmare in front of us. "Holy shit!"

My thoughts exactly. Thankfully the man had been a mercenary before he came to Utrecht and didn't lose his nerve.

"The flames won't last much longer." As if on cue, they flickered and grew dimmer. "We don't want to fight it if it takes Declan."

"Fuck, no," Brador said, as he slipped behind me and crept closer to Declan.

The seax shook in my hand. An image—myself, throwing the blade at the demon—formed in my head, as if the sword sent it there. Was it . . . sentient? Something to explore another time.

"Not yet," I whispered. "I need a better opening."

A pulse of blue light quieted the blade. If I survived, I needed to examine it more closely. The weapon jerked and I heard an old teacher's voice in my head. Fear was the killer. It clouded the mind and led to poor decisions. I stared at the seax, waiting for it to communicate again. It didn't, and I cleared my thoughts.

The demon followed Brador's movement with quick glances but kept its attention mostly on me. Good acting, but I wasn't buying. The way it shifted its weight telegraphed its next move. I forced myself not to let on I knew what it planned as I readied my counter.

The flames died with a puff and the black nightmare lunged toward Declan. Brador hadn't been fooled, either, and he hit the demon hard enough to stunt its momentum. Using the opening Brador gave me, I loosened my grip on the seax and fired energy from my stone.

Blue light bathed the room and the Orme Seax shot forward. The point embedded itself between the creature's shoulder blades, and the demon's shriek shattered the classroom windows.

A flaming blue aura crept slowly from the blade, crackling as it inched out in a circle. The creature strained to reach the hilt, but it was futile. The seax was in the perfect spot to evade removal.

Fire expanded evenly from the blade, and the pace quickened

as the area grew. Once it spread across most of the demon's back, the gem pulsed once, and the flames charred the rest of the body.

The carcass slammed face down, kicking up soot and ash on impact. Brador and I exchanged glances, and he edged closer.

"Hold up," I said, raising my now-empty left hand. "The summoning circle is still intact. It might be able to call up another."

Without waiting for an answer, I dropped to a knee and carefully directed mage fire from my stone onto the nearest glyph. Working as quick as I could in case the demon wasn't dead, I erased the symbol and created a gap in the circle.

Standing, I nodded to Brador. "It's safe now."

With my stone pointed at the creature, I touched its charred body with my shoe. The tiny contact caused a cascade of ash as the form collapsed in on itself.

The Orme Seax kept itself upright, as if it had imbedded itself in the stone. I reached down and it flew into my hand. It was cold now, and the blue light in the heart of the stone was gone.

"Interesting weapon," Brador said.

I ignored him. I didn't fully understand it myself.

My ex had revived enough to glare at me with a hatred I didn't recognize. Something was off. Declan had his faults—we all do—but he'd always had a spark of mischief in his eyes. It was part of why I'd been drawn to him.

This Declan had none. His expression was cold and vacant.

I kept his gaze for another second before I picked up his mage stone. The place would soon be swarming with inquisitors, and I needed time to sort out my thoughts. Brador stepped beside me; he turned his hand over, and I placed the yellow orb in his hand. Without a word, I spun on my heel and headed out of the ruined classroom.

Chapter Two
FOUR MONTHS LATER

※

BARTHOLOMEW

The detection spells went off as I pulled my tray of cookies from the oven. *Crap*. What the fuck was he doing awake at 8:47 a.m. on the last day of his vacation? Baking was my Zen time, and I needed that before my scheduled guest arrived.

I'd tried several times to get my siblings to come over at the same time, and one or both always made an excuse. The one time I didn't want them here together, it happens.

The universe clearly hated me.

Ignoring my shitty luck, I placed the cookies on the cooling rack and slid the sheet of apple strudel in to bake.

"Oh my god," Jannick said. "This place smells like heaven. Are those peanut butter?"

My brother had a knack for showing up whenever I made something he liked. It had to be more than mere coincidence that one of the only times I didn't want him to come by, he appeared.

I stitched on a happy face. "I bought a new brand of organic peanut butter and thought I'd try it on cookies."

He eyed the cookies greedily. "I'd eat your baked goods anytime."

I snorted at the overused joke. "You need new material."

"Why?" He plunked himself on a stool at my breakfast bar and nicked a warm cookie. "It still gets a rise out of them."

We were seventeen when he first said it and half the assembled family hissed in a breath and clutched their pearls. Given we're half-brothers, their reaction was fucked up. It spoke to a larger issue we'd spent most of our lives battling.

And bonding over.

"You're up early." I tried not to sound too probing.

"I need to get an early start so I can take a nap this afternoon."

Jan *never* wanted an early start on a day he wasn't working. It took me a moment to connect the dots.

"Ah right. Maintaining traditions requires work. We could always pass on it this year."

He snapped a bite of cookie and shook his head. Strands of brown hair flopped onto his face; he swept them aside with his free hand. "Part of the tradition is we stay out all night."

That part of our ritual I could do without. When we'd moved up to the university level of Utrecht Academy, we left behind the strict rules and curfews of the high school side. To celebrate our newfound freedom, we'd gone to the Trade Den, Philadelphia's trendiest and hottest club. The Den always held their "College Welcome Night" party the Friday before the start of the new term. Teachers and legal age students got a discount and priority admission. Jan had talked me into magically altering our IDs so we could go.

I'd been so scared we'd get busted and our pictures would be plastered all over the news, but I did it anyway. When we were kids, he'd talked me into crazy stunts all the time. Most of them were harmless, but some . . . Dad almost sent him to a different school after we got caught sneaking off campus at fourteen to see a Black Veil Brides concert. Which might have been one of the few times I was *totally into* one of Jan's schemes. I mean, Andy Biersack set my teenage hormones on fire.

"What's that amazing smell?" Jan asked. "And why are you smiling?"

"Thinking about the BVB concert you took me to for an early fifteenth birthday present."

He frowned. "We remember things differently. I *remember* us being booked and sentenced for wasting Mage Council resources. I *remember* being sent to build houses for a summer."

I remembered all those humiliating things, too, but they didn't dull the shine of the concert. "You also got to see the world, and *I remember* you and a cute guy hooking up half the summer."

"Titus was hot." He smiled and took another bite.

Thirteen years later and that night was still the best gift anyone had ever given me. Jan and I were practically twins. I was born six weeks before him, and he came to live with us when he was five. He knew me so well he had no trouble finding the right gift.

"See, it wasn't so bad."

Jan nodded toward the oven. "What are you making now?"

He also never let me avoid a hard answer. Turning on the oven light, I peered into the glass opening. "Apple strudel."

"Seriously?" He put the cookie down. "And you didn't tell me?"

And sometimes we were so close, he forgot I didn't need to clear everything with him. Especially when I didn't invite him to join me and the sibling he didn't want to spend time with. I turned around and busied myself moving the cookies off the baking sheet.

"Come on, Jan. When was the last time you were up this early on a day off?"

"You thought you could sneak her in and out without me noticing?"

I hated their stupid feud. They were both so stubborn, neither would budge. "First this is my home, so I'm not hiding anything. Second, I didn't invite you to come over. And last, she's *our* sister. She's welcome to visit any time she wants."

My sensors went off again. Great. No time to get rid of him. Not that I wanted to. I just wanted peace.

"She's here."

"Fuck."

My sentiments. Now that she was here, Jan wouldn't give her the satisfaction of leaving. "Be civil."

"Easy for you to say—every time. She likes you."

If he didn't take every chance to needle her, she'd like him, too. I didn't need this today. "Try for me, please?"

"One day you'll learn we can't all just get along."

"Bartholomew?" Avelina called.

Jan made a face and mouthed my full name. I snapped an angry finger at him. "Kitchen, Avie."

Our oldest sister, all five feet three and one hundred pounds of her, swept into my kitchen and took over the room. Next to Jan, she was my favorite sibling. If only they could do more than tolerate each other.

"How did I know you were baking?" She smiled and opened her arms.

"Probably because your big nose could smell the aroma from Hollen Hall." Jan said under his breath, and Avie and I tensed.

Ignoring him, I bent into the hug and kissed her cheek. "Good to see you, Avie."

She glanced at Jan. "I didn't think you'd be here this early in the day."

"Hoping to avoid me?"

I didn't get Jan's bitterness. Enough of the family treated him like a bastard child, which technically he was, but she wasn't one of those relatives. It was his flippant, snarky attitude that rubbed her wrong.

"I don't avoid you, Jan. That would mean I cared enough to take action."

And it was her uptight, all-business attitude that drove him to needle her. The worst part was, they weren't so different at their core. Kind, loyal, and compassionate were words I used for both.

"Stop!" I held up my hands. "I know you're never going to be great friends, but could you *please* not snipe at each other in my house? For me?"

The last bit was my trump card. They both loved me as much as I loved them. It wouldn't last forever, but I only needed a couple of hours of peace.

I directed my gaze at Jan. Getting him to stop usually calmed things; Avie would be cool but polite as long as he didn't toss grenades at her.

Fortunately, much like I usually went along with his crazy plans, he usually did what I asked. "Fine."

I turned to Avie. She nodded. "Of course, Bartholomew. I'm sorry I disrupted the energy of your home."

If you didn't know my sister, you'd hear that as condescending. But it wasn't. She understood their constant bickering sucked the life out of me.

The buzzer went off and I grabbed my oven mitt. Through the glass, I saw the strudel had the right golden color; Avie stepped back so I could whisk the tray out of the oven and onto the cooling stand. She scanned the kitchen as I shut the door and turned off the heat.

"Is there more?"

Avoiding her gaze, I moved to the stove where I had the milk in a pan and the sugar in a bowl. Because I had *my* issues, too, I pretended I misinterpreted her question. "Don't worry, I'm about to make the icing."

"You know that's not what I mean. You made my favorite and Jan's but didn't make anything you like."

It wasn't about making things for myself. Baking calmed me. And I'd been under more stress than usual the past four months. Plus, Avie and I needed to have a serious discussion. If making something she liked put her in a better mood, I wasn't above plying her with goodies to make her happy. "I like them both."

"No," Jan said. "You're okay with peanut butter cookies, but you like chocolate chip or white chocolate macadamia. And you don't like apple turnovers, you like cherry."

The morning was not going well. I hadn't told Jan about Avie's visit because I didn't want him to bicker with her. It never occurred to me he'd take her side against *me*. The day had two strikes already, and we hadn't gotten to the craptastic reason Avie had come to see me.

"I can't make everything, so I make what my guests like."

"Except you didn't know I was coming this morning," Jan said. "But you made my favorite cookies anyway."

Avie stunned me when she nodded. If the two of them could agree on something, maybe there was hope for them. At that moment, however, I gave them an annoyed expression. This was my house, and I could bake whatever I wanted.

"Do you ever think of yourself first?" she asked.

"All the time, just not when baking. I'd gain too much weight." My small laugh didn't change their sour moods. I turned on the burner under the pot and added the vanilla extract. "Jan, if you're staying, make coffee while I finish the icing. Avie, you know where I keep my tea so find what you like, and I'll put the kettle on."

Jan shoved the rest of his cookie in his mouth and took a second one as he got up. "What am I staying for?"

Avie stiffened next to me. She'd asked to meet early because she expected Jan wouldn't be awake, much less at my house. Now that he was here, she wouldn't suggest I exclude him. I loved Avie and most of my siblings, but Jan and I had a special bond. Losing his mother at age five and coming to live with a father he never knew had been hard. He'd been so petrified when my father brought him home. Half the family hated him on sight because of family politics. I promised him that day I'd always be there for him, and I'd kept my word.

My conversation with Avie, however, wasn't about him. I should've given him a to-go bag and said I'd see him later; I didn't, because I didn't want to hurt him. "She wants to talk about the incident at the end of last year."

He pulled his head from the cabinet. "Did something else happen?"

Jan knew we were going to discuss Declan. What he really wanted to know was why I'd tried to have breakfast with Avie without him. "No. Avie wants to discuss . . . protocols."

"Right, because you woke up early to bake for Miss . . . our dear sister to talk *protocols*."

"This is why I don't include him." She turned her back on us and pulled out my teapot.

As much as I loved Jan, there were times I needed him to stop being himself for a few hours. Not everything was personal and not everyone saw him as a bastard trying to get something that wasn't his. "She's not wrong. Snark has its place, and then there are times when you need to stuff it."

"Sorry." Shockingly, he sounded sincere. "What's really going on?"

"That's what we're going to talk about," I said. "Still want to stay?"

Jan grabbed the coffee filters. "Where's your regular? I don't do decaf in the morning."

Once the coffee and tea were ready, we moved to my sunroom. Despite the early hour, the dog days of August had a grip on Philadelphia. Even with the air conditioner and the ceiling fan running on high, the room would be too hot to use in an hour. The trade-off was it faced east, so it was cooler in the afternoon when I was usually home.

Compared to the ancestral Hollen Hall where I grew up, my house was tiny. Not that I cared about size—words I couldn't voice in Jan's presence without him derailing the conversation with middle school, locker room quips. It had been built in the late nineteenth century, just outside the Philadelphia city line. I'd bought the house because it had retained almost all its Victorian details. The dumbwaiter still worked, no one had taken away the servant's staircase, or converted the small, third floor live-in staff rooms into a loft or other horrible concept. It also had a library *and* a solarium. Well, not a true one. Who wanted a glass roof?

An awkward silence followed as we sipped our drinks and nibbled our food. Since I had things to do before Jan and I went out, I set my cup down to signal we should start.

"Did the investigation finally uncover something useful?" I asked.

"It's not finished. I made the mistake of assigning the case to Kleinman. He's thorough, but sometimes painstakingly so. He's still gathering evidence and identifying witnesses."

As the Deputy Inquisitor General, Avie technically reported to the Minister of Public Safety. In reality, she answered to our father, the Chancellor of the Mage Council. He trusted her more than any of his ministers.

He also set the rules.

Avie wanted to handle the case, but Dad said she was too close to me to be objective. She might be salty about the decision, but it was the right call.

"Has he found out who was controlling Declan?" I asked.

"Bart." She frowned. "There's no evidence someone manipulated him. I spoke to the forensic examiners personally. They did a thorough check."

This was the same response I'd gotten for months. They were wrong. Dec and I might have ended badly, but he'd never willingly raise a demon. They were too dangerous, and he had a healthy respect for his own being. "He wouldn't have done this if he wasn't under a spell."

"Right, because he had no reason to want to harm you." Jan's lips twisted into a half sneer, half frown. "Granny P. telling you and him in front of the entire family that you won't be together long wouldn't make him resentful."

Jan might have been a dick in how he said it, but he wasn't wrong about Declan having a motive. The annual Hollen New Year's ball was a big deal in the mage world. Nothing made you bitter quicker than being embarrassed in front of every important mage in the country.

That didn't, however, mean he was stupid enough to raise a demon. "You never liked him, so you're hardly unbiased."

Jan's face softened. "You need to stop feeling guilty and see the facts."

It wasn't that simple.

Dec had been drinking before he asked her. I knew what Granny Pederson would say without having to ask. She'd never talked to me about my future, which was a clear sign she didn't have anything good to say. I was sober enough that I could have . . . should have stopped things. Granny wouldn't have said anything if I'd objected.

So why had I let her answer him?

Declan had been my first—and only—adult relationship. I never got the feeling he thought I was his forever person, and I knew he wasn't mine, but we were still having fun. I could've laughed it off and pulled him aside, but I didn't. Granny even paused to give me a chance to object.

"I can't believe I'm going to say this, but Jannick is right." Avie set her strudel down like she'd lost her appetite. "You won't see the truth because you feel like this is somehow your fault. It's not."

I'd spent months wondering the same thing, and while I might blame myself for letting Granny answer him, this wasn't about that. Dec knew he couldn't kill the demon he summoned and wouldn't have taken the risk. "No one willingly raised a demon like that."

"Bartholomew, please. There's no proof he was manipulated." She locked her gaze on mine. "The Council is putting him on trial."

Why was everyone so eager to assume Dec had a dark side? He'd tried to kill me, not them. I should be the one screaming burn the witch. "I thought they wanted to keep this under wraps."

"They're going to have a closed tribunal." Her face told me how she felt about that arrangement. "The safety of the world demands he be punished."

Anger boiled inside me. It was wrong, and Avie knew it, too. "When?"

"You can't, Bart." She put her hand on me and a calming sensation flowed into me.

Shutting myself from her, I pushed her out. I hated being manipulated, especially over this. Guilt didn't cloud my judgement. Something wasn't right. The Council didn't care about the truth, they just wanted a quick resolution.

That let the real threat walk free. "Watch me. When's the trial?"

"You have no proof." Avie's voice had more steel in it now. "Testifying will destroy your career."

My career didn't matter if they continued to ignore the truth. Declan was being used. Proving it, however, might be impossible. "There's more here than just my career. We're prosecuting the wrong person."

"You're being stupid, Bart. This is a classic case of revenge." Jan held up a hand. "I know you're going to tell me he ended it, but that was in response to what happened. What else could he do?"

We'd had this discussion a dozen times since the attack, and neither of us was going to budge. I might usually be the peacemaker in the family, but I didn't compromise my principles.

"God help me, I agree with him again." Avie faced Jan. "Who are you and can you make sure my real brother never returns."

My eyebrows went up at this unexpected sibling bonding. If only they weren't connecting over their shared dislike of Declan. I hummed in disapproval. An uneasy silence followed, and we all took a drink. They knew ganging up on me wasn't going to change my mind.

Avie took a bite of her strudel. "This is so good, Bartholomew. I'm still amazed you can bake this well."

Her phone rang and she put her plate down.

"It's not that hard," I said as she dug out her phone.

"You can't testify at the tribunal, Bart. They'll ruin you," Jan said.

Jan always had my back, but this time he was wrong. It had nothing to do with my feelings for Declan. "I'm right. Someone else is behind this, and no one's looking for that person."

"There's a mountain of tangible evidence against him," Jan said. "You won't sway the judges with a gut feeling and telling them you're right."

"Jan, think about it. There are *much* safer ways to kill me. You weren't there. The stupid protection spell he'd woven wouldn't have stopped that demon. Whoever is behind this planned for him to die with me. This wasn't the actions of a bitter ex."

"This also isn't him being manipulated," Avie said, setting her phone down. "They found evidence Declan had been practicing for months before he attacked you. Kleinman *finally* tracked down those leads you gave him on Declan's past addresses. The remnants of glyphs designed to contain a demon were all over his previous two apartments. They go back at least two years."

When we'd met, Declan had just moved into his new place. I slumped back in my chair. "Both of them?"

"And the one he was living in the year before that." She glanced at Jan before adding, "I'm sorry, Bartholomew."

She wasn't, but at least she didn't gloat.

Chapter Three

❧

CAELINUS

Traffic flowed briskly as I approached the main gate. Having just signed the lease on my new apartment, I wanted to experience the walk I'd be taking every day. The stone walls surrounding the campus were as impressive as I remembered from my visit. Not that rocks and mortar could change much in three months. The sights behind them, however, were far more amazing.

Hidden in plain view where the city met the suburbs was the premier school for mages in the country and possibly the world. As a young elf it had been my dream to study magic at Utrecht, but I fell victim to the class system that kept most beings from the upper echelons of power.

I should have been admitted by virtue of my talent. My earth magic was strong even for an elf, and I was an alpha class, tier two mage. No one in my race had tested that high in four centuries. If anyone deserved a place at Utrecht, it was me.

The board of admissions, however, didn't agree. Human or elf, who you were counted more than talent. I never had a chance. My family wasn't rich, or important. No one had a seat on the Elven Conclave, and we didn't number any well-known wizards in our lineage.

I'd expected the same stacked deck when I applied for the Professor of Creative Magic opening. My application was a fuck you to the system that said I wasn't good enough without giving me a chance. Utrecht University had never hired an elf to teach one of the four primary disciplines.

Talk about a shock to the system when the first camera showed up to interview the prodigal elf who'd just been offered the position. My time in the spotlight, however, was brief. I didn't fit the story they wanted to tell. I wasn't an orphan or a poor elf who pulled himself out of poverty with his talent. I was a middle-class being whose parents were professionals. We lived in a nice neighborhood, in an above average public mage school district. I worked hard but I wasn't Bartholomew Hollen, wunderkind alpha one mage. Not the stuff that sells papers or brings in page views.

The school grounds were something I expected to see on a fancy estate far from a major city. Once this was the home of a powerful wizarding family. When Philadelphia grew around them, they sold it to the Mage Council, who moved Utrecht Academy from its humbler environs.

I reached the front gate and checked my watch. Seventeen minutes for my leisurely, imbibe the surroundings walk. I could easily make it in under fifteen, ten if my long legs took up a good pace.

Life was pretty perfect for one Caelinus Eoghan Reinhold.

Soaking in the moment, I stepped onto campus for the first time as the new professor of creative—

A siren blared and a stasis spell hit me—my heart jack hammered, and my adrenaline-fueled self-defenses flared into action. Only my practice of keeping my wards up at all times saved me from total paralysis.

I shored up my defenses and edged them away from my body.

The shrieking alarm grated on me, and I nearly panicked when I realized it wasn't *just* an intruder alert. Mumbling a spell, I kept the harmful effects of the sounds out of my head.

Next, I tried to step back. I couldn't move. My wards kept the effects of the stasis spell off my person, but the attack latched onto my defenses. I couldn't leave the grounds.

If I wasn't fighting to save myself, I'd have admired the cunning of its creator. I dug into my pocket and pulled out my power sphere. The shiny sapphire orb radiated agitation to match mine. Tapping into its energy, I reinforced my protective spells and waited to counter the inevitable attack.

Each second that passed without me being pummeled left me more anxious. Immobilization spells rarely held anyone with any talent for long. I could have banished it long ago, but the effort would have left me exposed.

Which, if I were designing the defenses, was when I'd launch an offensive strike. More props to the mage who designed the trap.

"Mr. Reinhold," a dusty old voice said with a mixture of amusement and annoyance. "We weren't expecting you until Monday."

A distinguished mage walked slowly toward me. His white hair, parted on the left, spoke of his age, but his posture was erect, and his blue eyes were shrewd and appraising. Two armed guards flanked the man, their crystal tipped staffs glowing with energy. A third man, his red power stone held to one side, stood a pace ahead of the mage who'd spoken my name.

"Dean Blackstone," I said. I could barely meet his disapproving gaze. Not the impression I wanted to make before my first official day. "I was timing the walk from my apartment. I didn't realize . . ."

He raised an eyebrow, and I swallowed my thought.

"Didn't realize, what, Mr. Reinhold?" He flicked his hand, and I could move again. "We protect some of the most precious mages in all the world. You didn't think we'd employ extreme measures to keep the students and faculty safe?"

My shoulders sagged as he ticked off my stupidity. In my defense, I'd walked onto campus for my interview. How was I supposed to know they'd made an exception for me that day?

"I did, sir, but I wasn't thinking like an intruder." I stared at the concrete between us. "I was excited."

"Indeed. You can put that away." He pointed toward my gem. "Unless you want to measure your skills against the rest of the school's defenses."

My stone still glowed with energy. I drained it and shoved it back into my pocket. "No, sir. That's one test I don't wish to take."

"No, you don't." His slightly snarky smile didn't help me relax. "Mr. Brador, would you please see that our eager new professor is given his security credentials? I'd prefer we not have a new incident should Mr. Reinhold decide in his exuberance to come back over the weekend to take in more of his new place of employment."

Dean Blackstone turned on his heel and left me to stew in the worst start ever to a dream job. So much for my pretty perfect life.

The guards with the staffs followed the dean. The third man had to be Mr. Brador. He gestured for me to follow. I'd never met him in person, but when we spoke about my security clearance on the phone, he didn't leave me warm and fuzzy. The silent, clinical way he carried out the dean's orders didn't change my opinion.

He was a finger shorter than my six feet two inches, with short, dark brown hair. The fluid way he moved reinforced my impression I didn't want to spar with him. Like all mages, his age was impossible to tell. Most retained their youthful appearance for centuries. Where Dean Blackstone was clearly centuries old, Brador was probably a hundred or less.

Silently, we moved farther onto the property. It was bigger

than I remembered. The only time I'd been here had been for my in-person call back. I'd been so focused on my interview, I barely noticed anything until my ride dropped me off at the administration building. It was dark when I left, and the five-hour inquisition left me bleary eyed and pessimistic about my prospects. I hadn't wanted to make memories to remind me of what I couldn't have.

Today, however, I gawked like an elfling at Disneyworld.

Under the warm, late August sun, the buildings gleamed, and the grounds were immaculate. The school was ready to welcome back the scions of the mage world. Eager young minds, destined to be the next generation of leaders, would invade the silence with their energy. Voices would fill the open spaces with debate on magical theory or gossip about who shagged who.

All of which was a romanticized version of what would be a rowdy, chaotic, hormonally fueled clusterfuck.

"You make quite an entrance." Brador's voice broke the silence and sapped some of my good vibes. "I haven't seen Blackstone move that quick in years."

It wasn't a good idea to admit to being an idiot when hired to be a professor at an elite university. Someone could have warned me I needed to call ahead to enter campus. "I'm sorry. I'm . . ."

"You were excited," he said. I expecting to see a sneer or some mocking expression, but he smiled instead. "You're allowed. Teaching at Utrecht is a great achievement, especially at your age. Before you beat yourself up too much, I've told Blackstone we need to credential new hires when we make the offer or alert them about not arriving unannounced. He forgets not every great mind was trained here."

There was a message there I needed to unpack when I had time. "It was the open gate. In Chicago, the schools are always locked."

"Different worlds. Chicago is known for the Wild West, anything goes attitude of its mage population. There's a lot more order in Philly. It would be unseemly if the council couldn't keep its home safe for visiting mages."

The emphasis on "unseemly" made me smile. The council was known for its staid rules and insistence on archaic decorum. Utrecht had some of that, too, but kids were still kids. They softened the edges of proper.

Based on the videos I'd watched, we were on the high school side of Utrecht. The lower and middle schools had a separate campus across the street. Keeping the high school with the university had been controversial. Progressives called the academy board beholden to medieval times. They missed the point.

Utrecht used the university professors to enhance what high school students were taught. Little surprise Utrecht seniors scored well above the average public-school attendees who were segregated from any affiliated university.

The security building was a massive, foreboding edifice. It was the second oldest building on campus after the main admin building, which came with the estate. Power radiated from the walls, a testament to its ability to contain even the strongest mage.

Brador placed his hand on the door, and it opened. "Once you get your amulet, it will be keyed to every building you'll have access to. If you forget to wear it, you'll have a hard time getting around campus."

I followed him up a grand staircase. There were four doors on the second floor; Brador led us to the one to the north. I stared at the emblem resting over the rounded point of the door. A dragon, its head draped over a mage's shoulder. The wizard held his stone to his left and their eyes were trained on me, as if they guarded the room.

"The North Guardians' seal," I whispered. Rotating clockwise I confirmed the other doors were marked with the other three Guardian pairings. My gaze returned to one closest to me. "It's so lifelike. Is it an original?"

Brador craned his head toward the seal. "I can't say. Whoever made it—and the other three—is a master craftsperson. First time I saw them, I swore the eyes of Hro and Eldwin Hollen were watching me from their citadel."

His description was spot-on, and it creeped me out a little. I studied the medallion closer, searching for a hint of magic.

"Are they? Watching us?" I asked.

"No. It's just a stone carving." He opened the door and motioned for me to go first.

A beehive of activity blending technology and magic assaulted me when I stepped inside. Video screens and monitors were stationed beside scrying crystals, telephones sat next to communication gems, and control boards had been paired with what looked like seekers.

The staff used tech and magic interchangeably. Like most elves, I struggled to use the two in tandem. Either I used magic, or technology—rarely both together. Good thing I didn't apply to work security.

People glanced up but didn't spare me much attention. We wove our way to an office at the back of the large room and Brador shut the door behind us.

His office was not the shrine to over-the-top testosterone I'd expected. There were pictures of Brador, another man and two kids, photos of just the kids, crappy drawings, some ugly macaroni art, and a lopsided clay bowl on a wall cabinet. This was the office of a man who prized family over everything.

As I took the seat he offered me, something hit me. "How did you and Blackstone get to the front gate so quickly?" I'd been too flustered in the moment, but it was impossible they'd happened to be in the area at the exact moment I arrived.

"Just figured that out? The stasis spell slows down everything it touches. You were there for almost seven minutes before we arrived."

"Holy . . ." The assault I'd been waiting for never happened, because they didn't need one to incapacitate me. "That's genius. Whatever they pay you, it's not enough."

Brador belted out a laugh, and it softened his chiseled features. At first glance, he was unremarkable; someone who easily faded into the background. But when he relaxed, his square jaw and full lips were far more attractive.

Not that I was crushing on the head of security—who was happily married, based on his personal effects.

"Those spells are as old as the school. You can fawn over Beornraed Hollen for that bit of defensive magic." Brador was less intimidating in his office than standing next to the dean with his power stone ready to blast me.

He crossed the large room and stopped in front of a glass cabinet. The stylish piece of office furniture shimmered and changed as soon as he touched it. The mahogany and glass case with books and personal effects disappeared, leaving in its place a hulking, blocky hunk of steel with no handle or visible way to open it. Utrecht wasn't just superior for its students. My face would be shouting newbie a lot in the coming days and weeks.

Brador touched his ruby mage stone to the metal box, and a small door in the upper middle part popped open. He grabbed something and shut the door. The bookcase returned, and he came back to his chair.

I couldn't see what he'd retrieved until he laid it on his desk in front of me. A flat piece of silver, carved in the image of a phoenix, sat on the wooden surface. It glistened for an instant and I flinched before I realized the sun was shining on that part of the desk.

"It should be worn around your neck." Brador leaned into his large, burgundy leather chair. "As long as it's touching your skin, no one will see it. Do you have a silver chain?"

I blinked, still processing. "Um . . . no, but I'm sure I can get one."

He slid open a drawer, removed a small box, and held it out.

"No need. I figured you wouldn't, so I made sure I had one on hand."

"Thank you." I accepted the offering and inside was coiled a thick silver rope chain. From the weight, it was easily worth more than anything I owned. "I'll need a couple of paychecks to pay you back."

He shook his head. "It's a welcoming gift from the school. As you surmised, they're not cheap, but it's more cost effective if we provide one. Left to their own, staff almost always bought lower quality, unsuitable chains. The number of 'emergency' requests from professors whose talismans stopped working dropped to almost zero once we gave them one. If you lose it, however, we'll charge you to replace it."

Carefully, I threaded the chain through the loop on my silver phoenix. Holding the ends apart, I dangled it in the open space between me and the desk. It was a beautiful piece of jewelry, even it if was really a magical key card.

"If you touch the ends together, they'll link and make a solid connection." Brador pinched his index fingers to his thumbs and brought them together. "If you want to separate the ends for some reason, you will need to pull the chain over your head and tug it apart once it's free."

Smart. It could never be yanked off me or break without my knowing. "Thank you."

"You're welcome." He slid a sheet of paper from the corner of his incredibly neat desk. "This has your office assignment, and the building where you will have classes. The head of your department, Dr. Gretchen Hollen, will give you your teaching schedule. The handbook has a guide to all buildings on campus, but your talisman can be linked to your stone and will act as magical GPS if you like. Those instructions are on the back."

I nodded, trying my best to keep up with the information. All I'd wanted was to time my walk and see the campus before it was crammed full of students and teachers. At least the list would help me acclimate quicker.

"One last thing." He paused until I looked up from the paper. "You may hear comments comparing you to the professor you're replacing."

Great. I didn't know I was replacing an icon. I'd have to prove myself before I began. "I take it he was well loved."

"Hardly. He summoned a demon to kill another professor."

I paused, waiting for the punchline, but he'd delivered the news without a hint of humor.

"Holy shit!" I clapped a hand over my mouth. "Sorry."

He smirked. "I said worse when it happened. You need to know the context in case someone says something."

Was there any context for trying to raise a demon to eat a coworker? It was one of the bright line rules. Don't do it. Ever! "Okay. What happened?"

"Professor Declan Guthrie had dated a colleague. After they broke up, he lured his ex into his classroom—your classroom—and summoned a demon. Fortunately, Professor Hollen is one of the world's foremost experts on dark magic. He trapped and killed the creature."

I raised an eyebrow. Talk about handling a breakup badly. How had I not heard this? Raising a demon was bigger news and using it to try to kill the chancellor's son was *the* news story of the century. "A real, actual demon?"

"Yes." He raised his eyebrow and nodded. "I was there when Professor Hollen killed it. Thing was bigger than an angry grizzly and twice as mean."

How that didn't make the news was incredible. A demon hadn't breached the Great Ward since it was erected. "I hadn't heard that."

"The academy and council managed to keep it out of the press, for obvious reasons. But this is a school. Everyone saw Professor Guthrie hauled away, and his classroom looked like there'd been a big mage battle. Kids talk, and things take on a life of their own. No one can confirm anything, so the press won't run with it."

No journalist, human or being, wanted the Mage Council—or worse, the Hollen family—to come after them. "Understandable."

"Most remarks you'll hear will be harmless, so you should ignore them. But if anyone sounds more interested than they should, or asks you about it, let me know."

The shine was quickly wearing off the new job. "Do you think he had help among his students?"

"There's no evidence he did, but we have a lot of smart, ambitious young adults on campus. Short of using inquisitors on everyone, there's no way to be completely sure."

Stepping into a viper's nest of dark art practitioners hadn't been part of my vision of my first year at Utrecht Academy. "Right."

Brador rounded the desk and sat on the end in front of me. "I didn't tell you that to worry you. There's a good chance it won't come up, but in case it does I wanted you to understand."

There was a better than good chance someone *would* ask me about it. Not only was I the new guy who replaced the rogue mage, I wasn't human. Teaching creative magic at Utrecht was one of the most prestigious jobs in academia. The fact an elf held the position would invite comments without my predecessor's actions.

"Thanks, I appreciate it."

"Now . . ." he crossed his arms and gave me a genuine smile. "Let me give you some recommendations for where to go on your last weekend of freedom."

Chapter Four

BARTHOLOMEW

The magic dampeners pressing against my wards were giving me a headache. Which, of course, was their function. The Trade Den advertised itself as a safe, magic-free, gender-fluid dance club, and either you let them inhibit your powers, or you suffered the effects.

I scanned the crowded dance floor for Jan and spotted him dancing with a tall, muscular guy with thick black hair. Probably a bear shifter. The dude couldn't dance, but he was giving it a good try. Good thing neither was focused on the how well the other danced.

I scoped out the room, hoping to find a quiet place to stand and people watch. Jan and I had gone clubbing enough times that I knew I'd be on my own while he decided if he wanted to hook up with his dance partner. My money was on yes. If not, Jan and I would be done for the night because Mr. Bear was definitely interested.

The Trade Den was hopping, making it hard to find a spot where I wouldn't get constantly jostled—or fondled. Not that anyone could get past my defenses. A throbbing temple beat someone squeezing my ass or cock.

The presence of someone very close to me snapped me out of my daydream. I glanced over, intending to put some distance between us, but instantly decided my little patch of wall was perfect.

Tall; fair skin; long, light brown hair pulled back in a ponytail; lean, but not skinny; chiseled jaw; perfect Grecian nose worthy of a marble statue—I don't think I could have ordered a more perfect man. And that was before he smiled. I'm not easily swept away by anyone, but this guy was beautiful.

"Hi," he said with an awkward half wave.

I must have given off a "not interested" vibe because his confident posture waned. That was the opposite of what I wanted, but I was so good at being distant it came naturally. I quickly smiled and held up my free hand. He stood taller, and his eyes twinkled with excitement.

It was rare anyone I wanted to meet approached me. Jan said I gave off an arrogant twatwaffle aura when clubbing. I didn't mean to, but I was terrible at telling people I wasn't interested so I tried to avoid being noticed.

Predictably, our inept waves were followed by that uneasy moment when you got a positive reaction from a guy, but didn't know what do next because you didn't really think he'd say yes. Then you both stare ahead while you think of something interesting to say.

That was us.

I pulled up my big boy boxers and faced him. The moment I moved, he shifted and angled himself to look at me. We smiled sheepishly at each other again, and he dropped his gaze, shaking his head.

I leaned closer to introduce myself without shouting and felt his magic. It was restricted, something I would never allow to happen, but it meant he'd know the name Bartholomew Hollen.

Pivoting mentally, I used the fake name I used when meeting strangers.

"I'm Barry."

Not original, but when in doubt go with simple. I tentatively held out my hand. Would he think I was stiff, going for something so formal? I was about to pull it back, when he clasped his hand to mine.

"Cael. Nice to meet you." His awkwardness didn't go away, which wasn't totally bad. I didn't like players.

He was close enough I could smell a hint of peppermint body wash. "Having fun?" Okay, that was pathetic. "Sorry. I suck at this."

He laughed nervously. "That makes two of us."

We stood together. Neither of us spoke, but we didn't walk away either; I didn't know what kept him quiet, but for me, it was the past. I hadn't had a date, hooked up, or done anything remotely sexual with anyone since Declan. Having the person you'd dated try to feed you to a demon gave you trust issues.

I snuck a peek and damn, he was hot. Hot enough that I should say something and see what happened. My stomach staged a revolt as I leaned closer. "Do you want to go somewhere quieter?"

His dimpled cheeks ended my angsty moment. "Yes."

Nervous excitement replaced anxious gut fluttering. One of the things I'd learned when clubbing: Bartholomew Hollen was more attractive than Barry. When I first used Barry, it hadn't been meant as a test—it was to avoid being on the gossip page the next day. Once I'd realized it helped weed out those only interested in my family, I stuck with it. Knowing they were attracted to me and not my name always felt good. I smiled widely as I pulled out my phone. "Let me tell my brother I'm leaving."

Tapping quickly, I sent Jan a message. I'd get shit for it in the morning, but who fucking cared. Cael was beautiful, and I wanted him.

"All set," I said, pocketing my phone.

He led the way, and I had a chance to admire the way his perfect ass filled his khaki shorts. The legs attached to said ass were long and toned. I pried my eyes off and looked up. Sporting wood while walking out screamed booty call.

We cleared the door and I led us across the street to escape the dampeners. Away from the magical restraints and under the bright streetlights, we could *see* each other better. Cael's talent, released, swirled around him in earthy tones. He pulled it in a half second later and shielded himself from my magical sight.

If I hadn't resisted the dampeners, I'd have been wrestling with my own magic flaring back to life and missed seeing his true power. Or his hidden nature.

"Ah yes." He filled his lungs with only slightly cleaner city air. "I hate magic dampeners. They make me feel naked."

Talking about himself naked had the predictable effect. I stopped thinking about his magic and considered what other talents he had hidden. "I know what you mean. It's odd not having magic hovering at the edge of my senses."

"Yeah?" He eyed me up and down. "I figured you were a mage."

He might have wondered, but he didn't know. I was the only mage in the club who'd kept their power. It wasn't an ego thing, it was fear. After the demon attack, I kept my shields up all the time.

"I thought you were a mage, too."

"What gave it away?"

Only very advanced mages could thwart the dampeners without a charm. And since the club did a thorough search, if I admitted I'd retained my power, he might guess Barry was really Bart. *That* might be my ego talking, but I didn't want to find out if he found Bart hotter than Barry. I pointed to his pocket.

"Power stones are hard to hide."

He dropped his gaze to his right leg. The outline of a gem was clearly visible. He smirked when he looked up. "You didn't think it was something else?"

Even a non-wizard could tell the difference, but pointing that out would ruin an obvious attempt to flirt. Most normal people would fire off a witty response without any effort, but I sucked at small talk. Ask me to talk about magic or ancient weapons and I'd ace that test. Talk to someone I just met? My brain switched off. Jan tried to teach me how to be less stiff, but I was a lost cause.

"I'm pretty certain I'm right, but is there really any downside to being wrong?"

He paused, and I wanted to smack my forehead because even for me that was mind-numbingly dull. In my defense, I didn't flirt often. Most people heard my name and didn't care about anything else. I could bore them to the point they'd consider stabbing out their eardrums and they'd remain polite. Cael, however, didn't know my real name. Needing to wow him with my wit might make it a short evening.

Standing in the uncomfortable silence, I waited for him to hitch a thumb toward the club and tell me he'd prefer the magic dampeners to my company.

"Such a loaded comeback." He grinned. "I don't know you well enough to call you a size queen, which, in a roundabout way, I just did."

I let out the breath I hadn't realized I'd been holding. All I needed to do now was keep his attention long enough to get him to go home with me.

"Not gonna touch that." I smirked. "Would you like to grab coffee? I know a few places nearby."

"Too much caffeine at this time of night makes me jittery." His lips quirked and his eyes danced. "Sugar, on the other hand, is fine. Any of these nearby places serve milkshakes?"

My brain stalled as it tried to shift gears. At first, it sounded like he'd decided to go back into the club and find someone else; when he rotated, it took me a moment to remember what coffee shops were around. The fact he was incredibly beautiful didn't help my gray matter work at a high level. After an eternity, I finally remembered the surrounding area.

"There's a place on Walnut that has above-average diner food. It should be safe to get a milkshake."

He smiled like he'd snagged the brass ring. I wasn't good at intimate social settings with someone I barely knew, but Cael's happy acquiescence made me want to do better. Or maybe I just wanted him. "Walk or drive?"

"How far away is it?"

"More than a few blocks, but probably quicker to walk than wait for an Uber."

"Sounds like you think we should walk."

The idea of sitting hip to hip in the back seat of a car was hot if we were going to his place or mine. I still wanted that, but there was a spark between us. It had been a while since I'd felt that; I wanted to see if we could be more than just one and done. For that, I needed to be able to communicate and walking made that easier than sitting inches apart.

"It's what I'd normally do."

"Lead the way." Cael swiped his hand to his left.

I laughed at his theatrics and pointed the opposite way. "Walnut is that way."

He grimaced sheepishly and turned in the right direction. "That didn't scream new to town, did it?"

Now I knew why I'd never seem him before. I might not go out much, but given Cael's talent, I should've run into him professionally.

"Just a little." I smiled. "Where did you move from?"

"Chicago. New job."

This wasn't how my night should have unfolded. My job was to be Jan's wingman, warn him if he was beer goggling, and make sure he got home safely. It wasn't supposed to be for me to meet someone, leave first, go talk over milkshakes and coffee, and maybe hook up. But things don't always go as planned.

We started walking and I banked my budding interest. Guys you meet at places like the Trade Den were rarely keepers. Cael felt different, but didn't they all when you first met? If we had breakfast together in the morning, I'd let myself consider more. Until then, I hoped to get naked and enjoy the hot body I was certain lurked beneath the clothes.

"What can I tell you about the city? I'm sure you have a lot of questions."

Chapter Five

❦

CAELINUS

What was wrong with me? Ninety minutes chatting about nothing over milkshakes and cherry pie with a guy I picked up in a bar. Nightclubs, like hookup apps, were all about gratuitous sex and nothing else. Talking before we fucked took the anonymity out of the equation. Made it more . . . intimate.

I didn't do intimate when I hooked up.

We turned left onto Spruce Street, and I remembered that the Franklin House Hotel was closer to a one-star place than a five. It wasn't a seedy, rent-rooms-by-the-hour dump, but it wasn't the Ritz-Carlton.

"It's in the next block," I said, hoping he wouldn't bail on me when he saw the building.

The fact I cared intrigued me. Normally, I didn't worry what people thought. To reach my personal goals, I'd delayed earning a living wage. If someone couldn't see past my finances, I could do better. Even in a one-night stand.

"No worries. It's a nice night for a walk." Turning toward me, he smirked. "Especially given the company."

Heat rushed to my cheeks. By nature, I'm not one to blush. It took a thick skin, going through public mage schools. Even the best of them, like mine, had rough edges. Being the top student—and an elf—pasted a bullseye on my back for discontented peers who recognized the inequity of the system but didn't have the skills to break through.

Barry, however, was amazing. Tall, athletic, and intellectually engaging. I spent half our time admiring his beautiful blue eyes and chiseled jaw, and the rest swooning inside as he talked about magic like he was describing fine art.

My first thoughts were he was married and cheating on his spouse, but from our conversation I'd gleaned he didn't go out much. It still seemed improbable that someone who looked like him would be single, but I'd worry about that if we had more than a one-night stand.

"The company I'm with makes it a great night for me as well."

Color transformed his fair skin and he smiled shyly. "Thanks."

It was incredibly hot how he reacted to compliments. Barry didn't seem to have image issues, but he didn't act like I should be grateful he was talking to me either. Instead, he listened when I talked, asked questions about me, and hadn't turned any of my comments into something about himself. Part of me thought I was dreaming.

It also left me nervous. "I'm going to apologize in advance. The Franklin House is an older building and isn't five-star accommodations."

"It's sad how much this part of Philadelphia declined. These were grand buildings in their day. I'm sure there's a lot of character left in the hotel."

I paused before answering. He sounded sincere, but who cared about a run-down hotel? Was he patronizing me?

"Not in my room. They've modernized away any charm."

He shrugged and didn't seem uncomfortable. "That's a shame, but if I remember the building, it probably needed a facelift."

The conversation had a surreal feel. I worried he'd find it a shabby turn off, and he'd turned it into a conversation about restoring old buildings. It might be an act, but who cared?

"It still might."

"How long are you staying there?"

Too long. Leaving Chicago was a big step. I'd left my family and friends to chase my dream. Change wasn't so bad, but the transition phase sucked. I wanted to begin my new life but couldn't just yet.

"I pick up the keys tomorrow and the movers will be here on Sunday with my stuff."

"Exciting, although moving in can be a pain."

I thought—hoped—he'd offer to help, but that'd be weird. We barely knew each other.

"Yes, and a bit nerve-racking."

"I understand that. New beginnings are exhilarating and terrifying at the same time."

He bumped my shoulder and our hands touched. My skin sizzled where we'd made contact. Maybe the thrill of starting my new life threw my emotions off kilter, but I was insanely attracted to Barry. I craved more. I wanted to push him against the building and tongue fuck his mouth.

I tried to curb that. "Exactly."

I leaned to my left and pressed against him. We took a couple of steps bonded together. My cock, already hovering on the edge, stiffened from the contact. I heard Barry suck in air.

"How much farther?" he asked in a clipped, husky voice.

He pushed his fingers between mine and squeezed before inching away. We weren't touching but I could feel the movement of his hand. It jacked my arousal up another notch or three. "Block and a half."

"Thank God," he whispered. "I was about to suggest we run."

The part of my brain that pointed out how out of character this was for me, was smothered by my hormone enhanced libido.

I didn't really care how I acted in the past; this was now. I'd have gladly raced him to the door.

After what felt like an eternity, we reached the Franklin House Hotel. I keyed us in and my lust cooled a bit. The lobby wasn't awful, but it had a highway motel feel. Everything felt old and used. I'm sure it wasn't as bad as I thought, but I wanted to impress Barry, not show him my humble roots.

Swiping my card to call the elevator, I brushed against him. I felt addicted to his skin. I smelled chamomile and sage and wanted to bury my nose in his hair and breathe deeply. The elevator arrived and we stepped back to let a couple exit.

I punched ten and all but willed the door to slide shut. We hadn't started our ascent when I rounded on Barry and pressed him against the wall. Our lips met the same instant the car moved. His were soft, and he parted them, inviting me to explore. Our tongues touched and I moaned into the kiss. He cupped the back of my head and made sure we didn't break apart. I loved making out with someone who enjoyed it as much as me.

The car slowed and reluctantly I moved away. The doors slid left, and Barry motioned for me to go first.

My dick led the way, straining to get out of my pants. The key card worked the first time, which was good because I'd have blasted the lock if it didn't.

Barry followed me into the small room and shut the door the moment he was clear. This time he stepped up, resuming our elevator kiss. He reached between us and rubbed my cock.

He hummed. "We have too many clothes on."

"We do." I shrugged out of my coat and let it drop to the floor. Barry did the same and pulled the hem of my shirt up. I raised my arms, and my top found its way to the floor.

Barry didn't give me a chance before he added his shirt to the collection littering the carpet. In the dim light, I could see the tight corded muscles of his arms and chest and wanted to run my hands all over him. I wanted to lick his nipples and taste every bit of him.

Pulling us together, he tilted his head, opened his mouth and captured my lower lip between his teeth. Our tongues tangled and fuck! I pulled back so I didn't cum in my pants and gasped for air.

"Pants," I managed before crushing my lips back against his.

He kicked off his shoes, and at the next break he asked, "Top? Bottom? Both? Neither?"

"More top than bottom," I said as I tugged my jeans over my heel. "You?"

"Entirely versatile."

"Nice." I tossed my pants behind me. Turning around, I walked us to the bed and heaved the duvet back. "I . . . um . . . had my preventive spell before I left Chicago."

"Had mine last month." He shucked his boxers, and his dick stood straight up as he climbed onto the bed next to me. "I love oral, please tell me we can 69 or at least you want me to suck you."

In answer, I leaned over and sucked in as much as I could manage. Barry dropped to his right and captured the head of my cock in his hot moist mouth. He pulled my foreskin back with his lips and teased my sensitive head, then plunged down, pressing his tongue against my shaft.

Rolling him onto his back, I straddled him and fucked his face as I bobbed up and down his dick and he put his hands on my butt cheeks, encouraging me to fuck faster. He caught me off guard by pulling me in on a downstroke, and I sank part of my cock into his throat. Holding me down, he gagged on my dick, his throat tightening around me with each spasm.

Taking his actions as a challenge, I worked my way down his long, thick cock until the head hit the back of my mouth. Pulling up, I took a deep breath, angled my head, and slid down. I inched lower until the head of his cock pushed into my throat. He bucked up, and my nose was buried in his sack. I breathed in his scent; it was clean, with a hint of musk.

We stayed pressed together, until he let go and pushed me up. I pulled my cock out of his mouth with a wet slurp and he gasped for air. "Cael, you need to fuck me before I blow."

Someone that hot didn't need to ask me twice. I rolled off, pulled out the lube, and squirted some in my palm; he took the bottle and squeezed some onto his fingers. Reaching between his legs, he spread the slick liquid around his hole before sliding a digit into himself. He moaned loudly and added a second.

My dick twitched as I coated it with lube. I watched, mesmerized by his fingers moving in and out.

"Don't watch, Cael. Fuck me," he said with an urgent need that matched my own.

I crawled between his legs and moved his hand out of my way. He pulled his knees to his chest and I rubbed my cock against his hole. "This what you want?"

"Fuck yes."

Pressing forward, I inched slowly into the warm, tight space. "Oh fuck." My self-control fled and I pushed all the way into him.

He hissed and slammed his head back. "Oh, shit!"

"Sorry." I tried to withdraw, but he pulled my head down and pried my lips open with his tongue. My body tingled like he'd sent a thousand watts coursing through me, and I could only focus on the kiss. It consumed me to my core. I felt so connected, I could live off the energy we generated.

We broke the kiss, and my heart galloped as Barry clenched his thighs on either side of my hips. His fingers grazed my cheeks, leaving a trail of heat in their wake. "Fuck me."

In the dim light I saw a sinful spark in his eyes. He needed me as much as I needed him. He tweaked my nipple and I jerked deeper into him. He grunted, but he gave me a filthy leer. "Found a spot, did I?"

"Fuck yeah." I pulled back and thrust in, forcing a grunt from

Barry. He dragged my head down and assaulted my mouth with his. Gasping for air, I put my hands on the backs of his thighs and fucked him harder. "Like that?"

"Yes!"

He slid his hands up my chest and I growled at the light pain when he pinched both nubs. I ground my hips and crushed our lips together. Barry poured himself into the kiss, begging for my tongue with his. I wanted more. I wanted everything.

I thrust urgently and each time our eyes met, I saw the lust I felt staring back.

"Yeah, Cael. Give it to me."

"God, you feel so good," I whispered in his ear. Scraping his prostate with every stroke, I watched with satisfaction as he writhed under me, hands clutching the sheets.

"Keep that up and I'm going to shoot."

"Yeah?" I pulled out slower and slammed down. "Come for me."

"I'm so close." His breath shuddered out of him as he fisted his cock furiously. A few strokes later, the first shot painted his chest and abs. "Oh God. Oh God. More."

With every shot, Barry's muscles squeezed my cock, pushing me toward my own release. I kept fucking him even after he stopped coming.

"Come for me," he panted. "Shoot it in me."

He pulled me back into a deep, passionate kiss. The muscles in his ass tightened each time I hit bottom. My balls tingled and I fucked him harder, leaning back to angle my cock for maximum friction.

Barry ran a finger through the cum on his chest and pressed it to my lips. I sucked greedily, wanting more of him; my body was flooded with wild energy, and I hit my tipping point.

"Oh fuck," I said, tossing my head back. "I'm gonna come."

"Give it to me." Barry urged me on. "Don't stop."

Slamming my groin against him, I buried myself as deep as I

could just as my cock erupted. Barry clenched tightly around my shaft and I crushed my lips to his. We moaned into each other's mouth, our tongues tangling together. With short, hard thrusts, I pounded until I stopped shooting.

I collapsed against him, his legs still circling my waist. He threw his arms around my neck and kissed me softly.

"That was amazing," he whispered. "I've never come like that before."

"Me neither."

We lay together, panting to catch our breath.

One of my rules of hooking up was tricks didn't spend the night. Not them with me or me with them. It was just about fun, getting off.

Me and Barry had our fun, so it was time for him to go. "Will you stay tonight?"

Barry looked at me, and I could see the same calculus going through his head. "Do you really want me to?"

He'd given me the chance to think with the big head, not the one still buried inside him. I needed to take the out he gave me and remember what we were doing. I stared down and saw the contentment I felt. Fuck my rules.

"Yes." I kissed him softly. "Let's go shower first."

Chapter Six

❦

BARTHOLOMEW

Holding hands, Cael and I made our way through the press of people trying to check out. I felt a little guilty we'd stayed up so late, given all he had to do before the movers arrived. But when you and the smoking hot guy you're in bed with wake at the same time, going back to sleep isn't always on your mind.

On second thought, I had no remorse. At least not for the great sex we'd had.

"Are you sure you don't need help moving?"

That salved my not guilty conscience. Moving boxes wasn't the most fun way to spend my day off, but I'd gladly pay that price to spend time with Cael.

"Thank you, but I'll be fine. My employer paid for the movers, and I don't have that much stuff." He squeezed my hand and smiled. "Ask me if I want to go out with you tonight, and I'll have a different answer."

My dick hardened like I hadn't come three times in the last eight hours. Normally I had impeccable self-control, but Cael broke that. It should have scared the crap out of me, but it left me warm and happy. Ridiculously happy.

"Hmm, that's a tough one. I mean, I can't decide if I want to see you *without* helping move your things." I squeezed back and winked. "Where's your new place?"

"Pembrook Arms, on Overbrook Ave." He smiled happily. "Apartment 4F. In case you were in the neighborhood and wanted to stop in."

Cael got better with every sentence. We lived a fifteen-minute walk apart. Images of us walking together down the tree lined sidewalks of City Line Avenue, or through the quieter neighborhood that led to my house, filled my head.

It reminded me I needed to come clean and tell him Barry was Bartholomew Hollen.

A harried couple tried to corral three kids toward the exit. I freed my hand from Cael's and pushed the door open. The father nodded as he and his wife herded the children onto the sidewalk.

"Do you help old ladies cross busy streets, too?" Cael bumped my shoulder. "I'm kidding. Manners are totally sexy."

Heat warmed my cheeks, and I reconnected our hands. I had no idea what we were doing, but I wasn't going to overthink things. Cael felt like a missing piece, and I liked feeling complete.

"I happen to know a great Italian restaurant within walking distance of your place."

"I love Italian food." A smile lit up his face. "Where is it?"

I liked happy Cael. I liked it even more when I was the cause of that joy. But I wasn't *that* easy. "Agree to have dinner with me and I'll take you there."

"Wow," he said with mock surprise. "Withholding valuable information unless I agree to go out with you? That's cold."

I laughed at his accurate summation of my motives. "I like to think of it as monetizing my information."

"Oh?" He raised his right eyebrow and closed his left eyelid.

"You'd see me starving and desperate rather than share the location of this mecca of great food?"

I rolled my eyes at his theatrics. It was cute, and it wore away the edges of my tension.

Mimicking his expression, I peered at him with my right eyelid closed. "Only if you deprive me of your company."

I expected another witty comeback, but he grinned instead.

"Does this offer to take me to dinner include spending the night together?"

Mentally, I stuttered for a moment. A small dollop of fear formed in my gut. What if being a Hollen was a deal breaker? Mages who came from the public school system usually resented the major mage families. It wasn't without merit, but I worked hard to be the best mage possible so I wouldn't have to play on my name. Hopefully, he'd give me a chance to prove it.

"Consider that an ongoing open invitation."

"In that case, I'd love to have dinner tonight."

He leaned over and pressed his lips softly against mine. A tiny peck, something almost chaste, but wow, it froze my brain. My plan to tell him my last name stalled. I stared at him, hoping for another. Finally, neural activity returned to normal.

"Awesome." I hoped it stayed that way. "I know you never asked, but I probably should tell you that my full name is—"

A scream pierced the calm morning. I turned, hand digging for my stone, and—

The bustling street and bright morning sunlight were gone. No more taxicabs, buses, or cars. All the people walking by, talking to each other or on their phones, had also vanished.

I was alone.

Then I recognized the small grove of trees and knew I was on the east side of Utrecht's campus. The night air was crisp, almost cold, but I didn't feel its bite. I was too scared.

Something dark and vast loomed in front of me. Arcane energy crackled, sizzling on my still intact wards. To my left, Jan lay crumpled inches from my feet. He didn't move; I couldn't tell if he was alive. Cael moaned, fingers clawing the dirt. Whatever attacked us was insanely powerful.

The demon snarled and I snapped my attention back to it. My anger boiled, and I summoned Jan's gem with my left hand. It was cold, confirming my fears. I tightened my fingers around the stone.

Something formidable hit my wards, but they held. Barely. Cael groaned like he'd been struck. The blow hadn't been strong enough for Cael to feel it through my shield. Could he be reacting to me?

None of this made sense, but I didn't have time to sort it out. An angry, powerful demon wanted to make late-night snacks out of the three of us.

I steadied my defense and connected to Jan's lifeless stone. I glared at my enemy; I might not survive, but neither would it.

It roared and brought its fists down at the same moment I fired a double blast of energy, using every bit of strength I had left.

※

My eyes flung open, and I desperately tried to settle the frenetic activity in my brain. The disorientation quickly gave way to fear.

I'd had a premonition.

The burst of adrenaline gradually dissipated, and my heart rate slowed when I realized I was still in the Franklin House. Cael slept with his arm resting on my chest. He was so beautiful. I reached over, moved a lock of hair from his face, and smoothed it back. We hadn't talked about what was next, but the first part of my dream was exactly what I wanted. I suspected he felt the same or he wouldn't have asked me to stay the night. His steady breathing and peaceful expression should have thrilled me, but instead, a sense of doom tightened its hold around my heart.

Settling back, I shook off the lethargy of being woken abruptly and focused on what I'd seen. Premonitions were not welcome events. Someone I knew always died in them. Just like in this dream.

It had been more than a decade since I'd had a prophetic vision, but they'd all followed a similar pattern. I saw a recognizable event, closely followed by the fatal incident. The key was piecing it together before tragedy struck.

This time, however, the two parts weren't close in time. Leaving the hotel together was only a few hours away, but the fight was weeks in the future. It had been cold in my dream, but Philadelphia wouldn't see a temperature under sixty degrees as far as the forecast predicted.

I also didn't see how Jan and Cael had died. Of course, the demon killed them, but I'd always seen the exact action that caused someone's death. Without that information, I couldn't save them.

Staring at the ceiling, I tried to convince myself the last bit was true. It wasn't. Leaving with Cael in the morning was connected to fighting the demon in the future. The solution was obvious. I just didn't like it.

Gently, I lifted Cael's arm and slipped out of bed. I surrounded myself with a tiny wisp of magic to deaden any sound as I moved around the small room.

My boxers were at the foot of the bed where I'd shed them, eager to feel his body against mine. The jeans were a tangled mess from the frenzied stepping up and down to get them off without taking my lips from his. Our shirts were puddled together near the door, entwined just like we had been seconds after we dropped them.

An ache that shouldn't be there grew in my heart with each button I fastened. It had been a fling, some fun to blow off steam before the new semester started. I didn't do attachments. I tried it once and the ending wasn't pretty.

Pulling on my socks, I watched Cael's torso rise and sink with each peaceful breath. He was still enveloped in the joy of the connection we'd shared. I hated knowing the happy glow would shatter when he woke up alone, and the betrayal would grow at how I'd slunk off as if he'd just been a good fuck.

I wanted to crawl into bed and go back to sleep tangled in his limbs. To wake up and smile at each other like we'd been lovers for more than one night. I wanted that happy radiance I'd had in my dream of us, walking out hand-in-hand making plans for a real date.

Those feelings had to be part of the vision. I didn't fall for anyone after one night. More reason to end this now. Closing my eyes, the image of the powerful dark entity looming over me strengthened my wavering resolve. I would sacrifice everything I had to prevent that future, and that started with walking away from Cael.

I'd seen paper and a pen on the small desk across from the bed. Leaving a note might take the sting out of waking up alone. On the other hand, I wasn't going to leave my number or suggest we do it again.

Manners counted for something, so I scribbled a note. It was short and final. There wouldn't be another time.

I set the note by itself on the desk and then drank in everything I could to preserve the memory. It wasn't enough, and even knowing he'd survive didn't ease the inexplicable feeling of loss accumulating in my stomach.

My fear returned, and I quietly let myself out without looking back. It was the right decision. Maybe one day I'd believe it.

CAELINUS

I tested the drawer, but it still refused to close. "Fuck!" I stopped myself before I slammed it into place. Breaking a cabinet my first full day in my apartment was not the way to start my new life. Stupid drawer.

Okay, so this wasn't about a wooden spoon getting stuck, although after three attempts I could legit be salty. I'd been off since I woke up alone Saturday morning. Nothing gets things off wrong like going to sleep with a guy you'd hoped to see more of but waking to find he'd snuck out during the night.

> Thanks for a fun night. Best of luck in your new career.
>
> — BARRY

A fun night.

I was just another fuck. How did I get him so wrong? I wouldn't have gone back to the hotel, much less asked him to stay the night, if I hadn't been positive he was better than that.

Which was the root of my irritation. I didn't do players. My empathy allowed me to sniff out bullshit. Barry had been sincere when he said he wanted to stay. Yet he still slithered out while I slept.

Nothing fake about that.

Centering myself, I moved the spoon to a new spot and the drawer closed smoothly. Too bad every problem wasn't so easily solved.

"Time to explore," I said to my empty, half-furnished apartment. I wanted to check out some restaurants around me. "Definitely no more ramen."

Laughter filled my apartment. It felt good.

Peeling my shirt off, I shook my head. What was wrong with

me? Barry and I had one fucking night—make that one night of fucking. It shouldn't have left me a mopey mess.

If only it hadn't felt like more than a hookup. Checking again, I didn't find any trace of magic that didn't belong. Not that I expected any, but it would've been a better explanation than I'd reverted to a hormonal teenager.

My phone rang. Checking the caller ID, I wished I'd remembered to assign ringtones. Not that I had to answer it, but no one did guilt like my mother. She couldn't know I'd seen it was her, but I'd feel wrong if I ignored her.

I exhaled and almost achieved calm. "Hey, Mom."

"Caelinus, how are you dear? Did the move go okay? Are you set up yet?"

That was Mom. Why ask one question when three at a time kept her kids back on their heels. "Good, fine, and mostly."

She laughed. "I did it again."

Smiling, I shrugged. "Yes, but it gave my adolescent side a free pass."

"Hmm. There went my hope you'd grow up once you became a professor."

Mixed into that pretend complaint was the pride I'd heard from my parents since I got the offer from Utrecht. It had been my dream for sure, but they had it first. Maybe not Utrecht, but certainly a better job than the typical public-school-educated mage obtained.

"You started it this time."

"Guilty," she said. "How are you?"

Talk about a loaded question. Barry took the shine off the brilliant glow arriving in Philadelphia gave me. I'd chafed all summer waiting for school to start, and once I arrived, I'd been so excited I set off Utrecht's defenses.

Then Barry showed me the City of Brotherly Love was just as crass and sordid as any other place.

"Tired. The movers were in a rush. They figured it'd be a

quick stop because I didn't have much, but the one elevator's slow and they didn't want to carry my stuff up four flights. I ended up making a few trips to float some boxes up to my apartment."

She *hmphed* softly. "You should've made them do their job. The school paid good money for them to move you. It's their fault they didn't plan better."

I hadn't been in a good mood—the whole Barry thing—and I didn't want anything broken. "I only took the boxes with the most fragile stuff."

"You always were more practical than me. So, do you love your new apartment?"

Like my other answers, my exuberance was tainted by a bruised ego. Barry thought he was so much better than me that he could slip away like smoke on a breeze. How did I miss that?

"Yes. It's exactly what I wanted. A grand old building that retained most of its charm but updated so it has all the amenities. The kitchen looks mostly new, the shower is awesome, and I have hardwood floors and radiant heat. You and Dad need to visit. I'll have the guest room set up soon."

"I can't wait to see it," she said. "Other than tired, how are you doing? I assume you're excited."

Beneath the shame of being played, I was thrilled. Which was what she wanted to hear.

"Yeah, a bit. I feel good about the new job."

"It's such a wonderful achievement. We're so proud of you."

I smiled. She'd always been my biggest supporter. "Thanks, Mom."

"Anything else? Did you go out Friday night like you planned?"

We'd come to the reason I didn't want to talk to her. She knew I'd been lonely. Chicago wasn't my forever home. It was the steppingstone to my future. I'd been too focused to get involved with anyone during school, and after graduation, I spent my time finding the perfect job.

"I did. It was nothing special. The Trade Den could've been any club in any city."

With the exception of one hot guy I couldn't flush from my thoughts.

"Did you meet anyone?"

Shit. Clearly long distance didn't blunt her powers. "Yeah, but it didn't work out."

"How so?"

It sucked having an empathic parent. Even if she didn't actively scan me, she knew me better than I knew myself. Or it was that whole parent thing.

"I thought we were good, but he wasn't interested."

"You slept together, he left before you were awake, and you're pissed off he didn't say goodbye. Got it."

"Jesus, Mom. We're not talking about that."

"I know that you know that I know you had sex. Get over it."

Another annoying thing about my mother: she didn't believe in filters. Tiptoeing around issues or sugar-coating things didn't work in her world. You confronted things head-on, even if it was embarrassing.

"I hate you."

"Actually, you don't." She laughed.

She was right. I loved her so much, but she was also an expert at making me squirm. "It's not him leaving—I mean *yes* I'm pissed he's a cowardly asshat who snuck off, but I can't stop thinking about him. I keep thinking if he'd stayed, I'd have asked him out again."

"That's different. For you, at least."

On the other hand, Mom usually helped me work through my issues. As a mage psychologist, she helped beings with great power stay mentally healthy.

"Exactly. We only talked for a few hours. I've dated people for weeks and thought less about them after they were gone."

"There's no formula to why we like someone. Sometimes we

connect based on things we don't recognize we like. And if you two had good chemistry, that only makes it more intense."

I blushed furiously, which was stupid because . . . phone? Talking to your mother about your sex life was always completely awkward. "That could be it, but I don't like it."

"Unfortunately, that's how feelings work. We can't make ourselves like or unlike someone."

I knew she didn't have a spell to cure me, but she could be more sympathetic. "You're so helpful. Do clients actually pay you for this stuff?"

"Hush up before I really embarrass you and remind you how you were conceived."

"Lalalala, I'm not listening to my evil mother."

"You still do that?"

I smiled because I could see her shaking her head. More than a few of our conversations ended that way. Usually, she understood it was time to stop psychoanalyzing her child.

"Only with you. I was about to go exploring for a place to eat when you called." *Alone.*

"Once school starts, you'll make new friends and won't need to eat by yourself."

I hated when she read my feelings. Being alone wasn't the worst thing but having someone special wouldn't hurt. I liked being social. I grew up with two brothers; our family always had each other. This was the first time I'd lived alone.

"That's the plan. But I don't want company tonight. I want to find food, take a hot shower, and go to bed early so I'm ready for the morning."

Which was a lie. I'd gladly have company, but the person I wanted to have dinner with couldn't get away fast enough.

"Of course, dear. First impressions."

"You're such a bad liar but thank you for not calling bullshit."

"All kidding aside, I don't like hearing you so unhappy. If this doesn't pass, let me know and I'll find you someone nearby who can help."

That was a gigantic nope. I was not going to a shrink because of Barry. He wasn't *that* great.

"Let me know when you're coming."

"I'll talk to your father and get back to you. Love you, Caelinus."

"Love you too, Mom. Thanks for calling."

She knew that last bit had dragged me down, and praise the heavens, she let me work it out myself. I found a clean shirt, grabbed my wallet, and headed out. Tomorrow was the first day of the rest of my life. I had better things to focus on than dickwad Barry.

Chapter Seven

BARTHOLOMEW

The plastic containers teetered precariously as I used one hand to open the door to Haeger Hall. I'd baked way more than I needed for our staff meeting—twelve of us wouldn't eat a quarter of what I carried.

Two dozen coffee cake muffins expanded when I didn't want to think about Cael. The blueberry bran muffins were a nod to eating healthy. Shortbread cookies with icing and sprinkles took time to make so I did those next. And finally, I remembered Avie's admonishment and made two dozen cherry turnovers, for myself.

Predictably, staying busy hadn't worked.

No one had gotten into my head as quickly as Cael. Even my first love, Grayson Hewitt, had needed a few face-to-face encounters before I thought about him obsessively.

Cael did it in less than eight hours. Granted some of that time involved amazing sex, followed by three hours of cuddling, but I'd had great sex before. It never turned my kitchen into a commercial bakery.

I neared the conference room and shoved thoughts of Cael aside. Declan's replacement would be there, and I wasn't sure what to expect. For obvious reasons, the administration kept me out of the hiring process. I took the hint and didn't ask.

Now I regretted that.

Happy voices floated into the hallway from the open door. Typical. Unlike some departments where rivalries and feuds were common, we had great camaraderie. The collegial atmosphere came from our chairwoman, who happened to be my great-aunt, Gretchen Hollen.

Aunt Gretch used a lifetime of avoiding the Hollen family tradition of infighting to set the tone for our department. Teaching, not a seat on the Mage Council, had been her dream. I aspired to be just like her, if my family would let me.

I toed the door open wider, made sure not to bang the tubs against the frame, and slipped into the large conference room. The conversations stopped, and all eyes focused on me.

"Oh, Bart. Thank goodness you remembered," Aunt Gretch said as she crossed the room. She plucked the top container off the pile and eyed the others. "It seems you made a bit more than you promised. Bad weekend?"

When I first joined the department, we acted like we weren't family, but it didn't last. Aunt Gretch didn't play favorites, not even for the nephew who'd saved her life, so we stopped pretending.

"Not really. I'll tell you later."

She frowned as she opened the first container. "Must be serious if you made cherry turnovers."

I laughed and waved her off. This was a personal problem that had no place at work. I wasn't going to start the new year on a bad note.

"No. Avie suggested I make my favorites occasionally. I thought I'd listen to my big sister."

She smiled in a way that said she didn't buy my bullshit and we'd talk about it later. Opening the second tub, she moved it to the end of the table. "And like a good nephew, you remembered your auntie loves your coffee cake muffins."

"You have to share." I slid it closer to the center. "They're for everyone."

The affirmations from my colleagues earned me a fake sneer. "Fine." She moved it back to where she'd set it. "They can each have one. But I'll be keeping a close eye on them."

Aunt Gretch was only half joking. I'd just set the cookies on a plate when I felt someone join us at the table.

"Bart," she said. "I'd like you to meet our new professor."

I brushed the crumbs off my hands and turned. "Hi, Bartholomew . . ." My eyes opened wider, and I caught a glimpse of Aunt Gretch's eyebrows going up. "Hollen."

"Caelinus Reinhold." Cael looked as shocked as I felt. "Nice to meet you."

"Well." Gretchen shifted her gaze between us. "Everyone get something to eat, and we'll get started."

༄༅

Cael sat across from me because, of course, Aunt Gretch had appointed me his faculty mentor. Under normal circumstances, it would have made sense. I was the youngest member of the staff by at least three decades. Cael and I were the same age. Under these not-so-normal circumstances, this was a slow-motion train wreck.

I expected him to ask for someone else, but he politely thanked me for agreeing to help him. Then his jaw hardened, and his posture stiffened. Yeah, he was *thrilled* with his mentor.

I didn't hear a lot of what we discussed. My aunt could fill me in on the details when we talked. And we *were* going to talk. She'd caught enough that she'd want details. I dreaded that conversation, but not as much as the one I needed to have with Cael.

As the meeting adjourned, Aunt Gretch suggested I give Cael a tour of the building. There was nothing subtle about her request, and everyone grabbed a last treat before scampering off.

Wonderful. The entire department knew something was up between me and Cael.

"Are we still meeting for lunch, Bart?"

Aunt Gretch's question caught me off guard.

We didn't eat together unless she had something to discuss. The last time she "suggested" we have lunch it was to tell me I couldn't teach my high school class and had to accept speaking requests. That had sucked.

This would suck worse.

"Sure." My attempt to sound eager missed by a mile. "I didn't have time to make mine today."

"Maybe don't bring so much next time." She pushed up from the table. "You're going to make us all fat."

True to her word, she lifted the tub of coffee cakes and left. In the silence that followed, neither Cael nor I spoke. I glanced in his direction, and he turned his head before we made eye contact. Expected, but it still stung.

I stood and collected the leftovers. "If you'd prefer another mentor, I'll give Gretchen an excuse."

"Giving a reason before you leave? How polite of you, *Barry*."

Ouch. I'd caught hints of his biting wit during our time at the diner, but it hadn't been directed at me. "About that."

"Nope." He shook his head. "Don't want or need to hear your apology."

My snarky side almost told him I had a table for bitter, party one, but sniping back wouldn't make things better. I'd agreed to stay, and I left with only a "thanks for the sex, have a nice life" note.

He had a right to be angry, but he needed to get over it fast. If we didn't get along, the university would fire him, not me. Arrogant, yes, but also true. Not only was my great-aunt the department head, my grandfather chaired Utrecht's board of trustees, and my father was chancellor of the Mage Council.

I focused on the leftover pastries to collect my thoughts. Four of the six cherry turnovers, one muffin, and a few cookies went in the tub I was keeping. Two muffins, one turnover, and six cookies went into the smallest of the three plastic tins, and everything else went into the biggest.

No answer I could give would make him less salty. He wouldn't believe the truth, no one did. Snapping the lids shut, I turned. "No problem. I'll go tell Gretchen to assign you someone else. Take care."

The words left my mouth before my brain stopped me. Fake well wishes were a staple of the Hollen family, and I'd perfected the art. This, however, wasn't the time.

"You're such a jerk." The chair scraped back, and he approached. "You don't get to walk off without an explanation."

That did it for me. He was itching to lay into me, and I wasn't in the mood to oblige. I'd tried to be understanding but leaving wasn't *that* big a deal. I also didn't do demands.

Setting the boxes down, I faced him. "I'm going to have her to assign you someone else *because* you clearly don't want me. Seems pretty straightforward."

His eyes narrowed. It wasn't his best look. "Correction, you're an asshole, not a jerk."

My guilty feelings were rapidly disappearing. If he couldn't control his outburst, working together wasn't going to be possible. "Why are you so upset? It was a hookup. Neither of us asked for or promised anything else."

He flinched at "hookup." It was shitty of me, but it was also true. "As if I wanted more with you."

Even without my vision, I knew that was a lie. We both wanted more, but he'd never admit it given how it ended. "Then chill the fuck out. I'll tell Aunt Gretch I don't want to mentor you. She'll blame me not you, and then we stay out of each other's way. End of problem."

"How magnanimous of the almighty Bartholomew Hollen."

My feelings had blinded me, but I finally saw clearly. Cael's anger was more about my name than what had happened. In his mind, I left because I thought I was too good for him. We could continue to bicker about this, but it wasn't going to change anything.

"I'm sorry I handled it badly. If I'd known we were going to be colleagues, I wouldn't have gone back to your hotel with you." I waited for the broadside to come, but he stayed silent. "I'll go talk to my aunt now."

I collected the tubs and left before he could continue the argument. From Cael's reactions, my vision accurately showed how our morning would've gone. Which, more than anything, required I not be his mentor. We needed to avoid each other for a while.

My chat with Aunt Gretch was going to be awkward as fuck, but I'd manage. She'd cluck her tongue, remind me to be more careful in the future, and assign someone else to Cael.

Chapter Eight

❧

CAELINUS

Standing outside Gretchen's office, I still hadn't cleared my head. The triumphant rush that filled me when Bart left the conference room didn't last. I thought I'd won, but I quickly realized I was the only one playing.

Bart had been right to ask why I was mad. He and I hadn't agreed to anything other than hooking up. I didn't like that he'd left while I was sleeping but waking me up first would have been worse.

I'd told myself it was typical of a Hollen, except that wasn't true, either. I only found out this morning he was Bartholomew Hollen. I'd been mad the moment I realized he'd left.

Which brought me back to his question. Why was I so angry?

The answer was obvious, I just didn't want to listen. I'd asked him to stay for a reason, and I thought he felt the same. When he said "yes," we were in sync. Something changed after we fell asleep, but it wasn't his interest in me.

Even today, I'd been a jerk to him, and while he'd sniped back a little, he also tried to be decent. My empathy picked up very little from Bart. He had great control, but it wasn't perfect. The hint of regret I understood, but what had him conflicted?

Not having a full gift sucked. I couldn't drill down like my mother. I had enough, however, to know my initial assessment had been right. He wasn't an asshole, even if I called him one when I was upset.

I expected Bart to go straight to Gretchen's office after he left the conference room, but instead he stopped to give pastries to the support staff. There was nothing phony or fake about the way he spoke to everyone. He'd baked for the staff meeting, and they weren't surprised he made enough for everyone.

So why had the nice guy, who wasn't an asshole, and who'd genuinely been interested, snuck out in the middle of the night?

I shook my head to kill that thought, and then quickly looked around to be sure I was alone. Arguing with myself on the first day wouldn't make a great impression.

There wouldn't be a Bart and me. Not only were we colleagues, but I'd torched that bridge in the conference room. My angry, jilted lover schtick wouldn't earn me a second chance.

I sighed, checked my watch, and knocked on the door.

❧

Gretchen slid the paper with my schedule across her desk. She paused as I scanned the document, and then leaned back in her chair.

"Let me cut to the chase," she said. "I need to discuss you and Bart."

My stomach clenched. Was she about to fire me? I glanced at the schedule in my hand and took a calming breath. She would've fired me before going over my assignments. I was still mulling how to respond when she continued.

"To be clear, I've already had this conversation with Bart. I don't know the particulars of what happened, and I don't care.

That's your business. If, however, it negatively affects the department, then I'll have to act. If Bart's the cause of the disruption, any discipline will fall on him, not you. The reverse is equally true."

It sounded entirely fair, but the devil was in the detail. Who decided the cause of the disruption? Could I really expect her to be impartial where her nephew was concerned? My limited empathy wasn't picking up anything from her I could use.

"I'll do my best to not let our past disrupt the department."

She raised her eyebrows a fraction. "I appreciate your candor. Most beings would have promised it wouldn't be a problem."

Living with a fully empathic parent trained me to stick with honesty. "I can't control what he does, but I won't cause a scene."

Her gaze never left me, and her serious expression didn't fill me with confidence I'd given her the answer she wanted. I didn't know what else to say, so I kept quiet. Finally, she sighed.

"Bart said the same thing. He asked me to find you a new mentor. I assume that's your wish as well."

Gretchen leaked disappointment. She'd honor the request, but she didn't agree. I didn't either, but my motivation was slightly suspect. "I . . . I don't know."

"Really?" Her emotional control was excellent, but I detected a glimmer of hopeful surprise. "He seemed to think you wanted someone else."

Given my lack of response, that was reasonable, and from how our conversation went, it was more likely he didn't want to work with me. The real question was, why didn't I accept his decision?

"It was unsettling, seeing him today. I don't think either of us fully thought this through."

"Indeed." She steepled her fingers, pressed them to her lips, and leaned back. The way she watched me was unnerving. After a few more seconds, she lowered her hands. "Bart is a brilliant mage, but you're also quite extraordinary. My hope in pairing you two together was to push you both to achieve great things. Your prior involvement complicates things.

"As Mr. Brador told you, Bart dated your predecessor. To say that ended badly would be an understatement. While I doubt either of you would resort to raising a demon, the last thing I want is another semester of awkward staff meetings."

The easy thing would be to ask her to assign me someone else. The problem was, I couldn't stop thinking about him. I spent half the morning remembering the easy way we got along. I envisioned us walking around campus talking about students and having academic discussions about the finer points of magic. I saw other things as well, but this wasn't the time for those thoughts.

Gretchen's warning was clear. She didn't want any drama. I didn't either. "If you want to assign me to someone else, I'm okay with it."

Her smirk said she saw through my answer. "Too easy. Tell me what *you* want."

※

I closed Gretchen's door and leaned against the wall. Talk about a first day from hell. Nothing that happened since I set foot on campus went how I pictured my first week.

Everything cycled back to Friday. Brador's advice to go to the Trade Den seemed solid at the time. It *was* time to step out and start my new life. Hooking up with "Barry" had been the pot of gold at the end of the Lucky Fucking Charms rainbow.

Mom always said, "If it's too good to be true, it's a shit sandwich." I hated when she was right.

Gretchen hadn't made things easier when she tossed the grenade into my lap. Had she asked me during the staff meeting, I'd have said "yes" without hesitation. I was still pissed. Having cooled off, I didn't have an answer for her. How could I when I didn't know what I wanted?

My head thunked against the wall.

I had trouble wrapping my head around sleeping with Bartholomew Hollen. He wasn't the pampered prince of the mage world I expected. My new colleagues all said he was a super-nice guy who did thoughtful things like bake for meetings and remember the staff on their birthdays. Going by our conversation at the diner, I wasn't surprised. He'd even handled our surprise meeting with more class than I had.

Proof the world wasn't fair. No one should be that hot, that nice, that rich, and that powerful a mage.

The smart move would be to have Gretchen assign me someone else. Forget we were colleagues, and mixing business with personal rarely ended well, Bart had dated the guy I replaced. It wasn't hard to imagine the gossip we'd generate if we dated.

Backing down from a fight, however, never worked for me. We'd had a connection. Whatever made him leave, it wasn't lack of interest. Before I let go, he needed to explain what happened.

Plan in hand, I pushed off the wall. Gretchen had the corner office in the north side of the building. Bart's office was the second to last one in the south wing. My heart thumped hard as I checked the room numbers, which was ridiculous. I wasn't sixteen on my way to ask Greg Blocker to junior prom.

The corridor seemed shorter than I remembered because I was outside Bart's office before I was ready. I stood there for a few seconds, sucked in a breath for confidence, and knocked.

"Come in."

Bart's casual tone suggested he welcomed his colleague's visits. Would he feel the same if he knew it was me? Too late to back out. Exhaling, I opened the door and stepped inside.

It felt like I'd been transported back centuries. Bart sat, book in hand, behind an old wooden desk with ornate chairs in front. Neat stacks of papers covered most of the surface, and he had an old sideboard that was probably older than the room. The dark wood paneling and wall-length bookcases had the air of a long tenured professor, not the twenty-eight-year-old, third year professor in front of me.

"Hi." I gave him a ridiculous wave and mentally cringed at my awkwardness. "Can we talk?"

"Cael." He said it as if he only just realized who I was. Setting down his book, he pushed back and stood. "Ah . . . sure. Come in. Please."

Knickknacks and curios dotted his personal space. I wanted to examine them, to learn more about this man who captured my thoughts like no one else, but it wasn't the time.

"Can I get you something to drink?" He pointed to a high-backed mahogany leather chair in front of his desk. "Coffee? Water? I might have a diet soda—Gretchen drinks them."

I'd been sure Bart had fooled me that night we hooked up, but now I could see he hadn't. He was every bit the hot, handsome, intriguing man I thought. Until he left. "No. I'm good. Thanks."

Nodding, he sat and regarded me with guarded eyes. "I didn't expect you'd want to see me."

I liked his confidence to address the issue head on. "To be honest, I wasn't sure I wanted to see you again, either. Certainly not when you first walked into the conference room." He cocked his head and raised his eyebrows. "Right, so why am I here?"

Nodding, he didn't say anything to fill the silence. I was going to have to do all the work.

"Gretchen asked me if I wanted her to replace you. I said I wasn't sure. She told me to figure it out before I answer her."

Bart's lips twisted in a scowl. He recovered an instant later and shook his head. "I don't know why she did that."

He probably didn't. Gretchen told me he was the least assuming person she knew, and from my few interactions with Bart, I agreed. I couldn't tell if he was genuinely a nice guy or if he'd developed it over the years to deflect criticism. "Like everyone else in this department, she thinks very highly of you."

He gave that impish grin that turned my insides to jelly. "Crumb cake. Talk to her next week, and she'll be less complimentary."

I never liked people who downplayed their achievements. It diminished the reward for hard work. Having spent my life toiling to reach my goals, it felt like a slap in my face. With Bart, however, it didn't rankle me as it should have.

"No. I think she'll say the same thing." Our gazes met and I dug deep for my courage. "Why did you leave?"

Bart's eyes widened for an instant before he averted his gaze. His aura changed. The easygoing, almost happy vibe flipped into fear and regret. "It'd be best if you tell Gretchen to find you someone else."

Spoken in a vacuum, Bart had just rejected me. Viewed through the lens of past, it was something else. I needed him to tell me why.

"What if that isn't what I want?"

He lifted his eyes and sat straighter. "Then I'll tell her I don't want to be paired with you."

The answer fit the arrogant dickhead I thought was Barry. My mother would have a litany of explanations for what he was doing, but I didn't need psychobabble. I needed the truth. "Please don't."

"Cael . . ." He exhaled loudly. "There are things . . . It's better if we stay away from each other."

If he thought that answer was going to satisfy me, he wasn't thinking clearly. The more I pressed, the more confident I was this wasn't what he wanted. Was it a family thing? The Hollen family didn't have a reputation for being human purists, but that could be a public persona.

"What things and better for who?"

He watched me closely but after a few seconds he dropped his head. "You won't believe me."

Strike disapproving family from the list. "Try me."

"Why?" He locked his gaze on mine. "Can't you just accept it won't work?"

His tacit acknowledgment of our connection confirmed he hadn't left because he didn't like me. "No. Not when we both don't like how it ended." I held up my hand to stop him from responding. "I didn't tell you this before, but I'm partially empathic. Your control is phenomenal, but I picked up enough to know you didn't plan to sneak out when you said you'd stay."

Bart's chin dipped and he stared at the top of his desk, occasionally sneaking a glance up to see if I was watching him. He didn't clamp down on his emotions like I expected, but he didn't open himself to me either. Whatever he was holding back, he struggled with what to do next.

Seeing him so conflicted, I realized I'd been a jerk. I demanded answers because he'd hurt my feelings. I didn't give any thought to his mental state.

"If you don't want to tell me, I won't press you." I might have meant it on some level, but damn, I wanted to know so badly.

"You really *won't* believe me."

Regret tainted his words, but fear simmered just below. He left because our being together scared him. Ridiculous as it was, his revelation gave me a kernel of hope. I didn't know what made him afraid, but I optimistically expected once he gave voice to it, we could fix it and give us another try. Talk about thinking with my dick.

Still, I'd given him an out and he didn't take it. "Tell me anyway."

"I had a prophetic dream. If I didn't leave, you'd end up dead."

I opened my mouth to answer, but then my brain processed what he'd said. Snapping my lips closed, I blinked. Never saw that coming. It was an immutable tenet of magic that no one could see the future. Anyone who claimed to was delusional or a con artist.

"You dreamed I'd die if you didn't leave?" I didn't mean to

sound so incredulous, but I didn't try to keep it out of my voice. "Like a vision of the future?"

Nodding, he ran a finger over the spine of his book. "I saw us leave your hotel in the morning holding hands. We kissed and promised to make plans for Saturday night. I was about to tell you my full name, when I heard a scream and the dream shifted to a small grove of trees on campus. It was dark and I was fighting a demon. You and my brother Jan were dead, and I was probably next, but I woke before that happened."

Anger roiled inside me at his answer. Clairvoyance wasn't real. Sure, his last boyfriend left him gun shy, but he shouldn't treat me like a fool. I was about to light him up when he shocked me into silence by dropping his walls. He opened himself, and I could see he was telling the truth.

I *really* never saw that coming.

Steadying myself with a deep breath, I considered my next move. Did I accept his invitation and dig deeper, or was the offer proof enough? Given he'd practically broken my heart after one night, it should have been a simple choice. But this was Bartholomew Hollen, arguably the most powerful mage in a thousand years. He wouldn't open himself unless he wanted me to see he was telling the truth.

His confidence tore at the certainty of my beliefs. Seers didn't exist. Soothsayers, prophets, and oracles were carnies who belonged on a midway entertaining customers, not in the highest levels of academia.

I brushed the outer edges of Bart's emotions and froze. He hadn't just let me test the veracity of his words, he'd given me access to *all* his emotions. If I wanted, I could search for his feelings toward me. The trust he displayed left me lightheaded.

Rather than abuse Bart's faith in me, I limited my search to only what I needed. As expected, there wasn't a whiff of deception. The regret he exuded earlier was for leaving me. He didn't want to go. He left because he truly believed staying would cause my death.

Our eyes met and a weird hopeful twinge left my chest tight, as if a weight had been placed on me. Bart sighed and restored his shields.

"Bart." His name came out shakily. "No one can see the future. Whatever you think you saw, it wasn't—"

"Pembrook Arms Apartments. Overbrook Avenue and 63rd Street. Unit 4F."

"—real." My voice tailed off, but he'd heard me. He stared at me with a somber expression, as if those few words explained why he had to continue his tragic denial.

The anger I'd smothered returned, but I kept it banked. How had he gotten my address? I'd warded my apartment against scrying, and while a mage of his power could break the bindings, I'd be alerted to the attempt. The only other source was the school's database.

He'd used his family's influence to find where I lived, but to what end? And why was he telling me now? "Right. I know where I live."

"You told me in my dream."

His answer should've been my signal to leave and file a complaint with the administration, except I'd no doubt if I asked, he'd let me test him. I had trouble focusing. No one could see the future because it didn't exist until it happened. "That's . . . Did you bribe one of the staff this morning to give you my address?"

He shrugged, looking mildly disappointed. "I said you wouldn't believe me." Holding up his hand, he shook his head. "No, I didn't ask anyone to tell me where you lived. I didn't sneak into HR to dig through the records. Why *would* I do that? I figured you'd be happy to get a new mentor and I'd keep out of your way. The last thing I expected was you'd come asking why I left."

The explanation made sense. Unless he'd foreseen this conversation and wanted to give me a good reason for why he left. That, however, meant he really could see the future, and his vision was real. It all made my head spin. He wasn't making it up, but there had to be an explanation that didn't refute thousands of years of magical practice.

"Hold on." I said it softly, because the thought wasn't fully formed. "Is it possible you read my thoughts while we were sleeping? Not on purpose, but subconsciously maybe?"

I was grasping. Every mage learns to create shields that stay up when asleep or unconscious. He might be the greatest mage of our time, but I was no slouch. I'd have known if he'd been in my head.

Shaking his head, he kept his gaze down. "It's okay, Cael. No one believed me the other times. Go with the accepted wisdom that I made up a bullshit story because I'm embarrassed I snuck out in the middle of the night."

It would be easier to believe, but it didn't fit with everything I'd learned about Bart. He hadn't played me then, and he proved it today when he lowered his shields. True or not, he believed he'd seen . . . "Did you say other times?"

"Four before this. I stopped telling people after the second one." He shrugged. "It's easier to take action without telling anyone than to try to convince people of something they won't believe."

He had a point. Sneaking out was easier than waking me to say he had to go because he'd had a prophetic dream where I'd die if he didn't leave. That would have made my reaction in the conference room look welcoming.

Talk about catching a tiger by the tail.

"Where does that leave *us*? And don't tell me to get a new mentor. There isn't another professor under a hundred years old."

A thin smile softened his features. "If that's your sales pitch, it doesn't make me feel wanted."

I didn't read too much into the "feel wanted" bit, but he'd

made a joke rather than saying no. That counted as an improvement.

His vision, if we agreed it was one, accurately captured how I'd felt. I'd have gladly walked out holding his hand, kissed him before he left, and made clear my desire to see him again. It must be how he felt, or he wouldn't have felt compelled to leave. Which meant there was hope.

"Fine, I suck at compliments, but I don't want a different mentor."

Bart let out an exasperated sigh. "It's a bad idea, Cael. Please accept I can't and ask Gretchen for someone else."

A minute ago, he was going to tell her; now he wanted it to come from me. The key was convincing him our dating wouldn't end with someone dead.

"You changed the first part of your vision when you left. Doesn't that change the future?"

"I don't know. This vision is so different from the others. I've never been involved in the precipitating event."

Had he not opened himself to me, I'd have assumed this was an excuse to avoid saying he didn't like me. "You're going to need to help me understand that."

"The first vision I had was about my brother, Jannick. I was five and had a vivid dream of a woman and boy I didn't know. She tripped and fell down a stairwell. The image shifted and I saw the boy crying in front of the casket of a woman, who I realized was his mother. Two days later, my father brought Jannick to our house. He told everyone that he was Jannick's father, and his mother had died the day before. She'd slipped and tumbled down a flight of stairs at the hospital where she worked."

His words were raw and painful, as if by telling me what he saw, he relived the events again. The grief rolled off him for a second before he clamped down.

"When I was nine, I saw a classmate climb a rock to test out a flying spell he learned from an older sibling. The spell didn't work, and when he jumped, he broke his neck and died. The next day Henric died when he leapt off a rock."

He closed his eyes and fought back the tears.

My God. How traumatic had it been for him that it still affected him decades later? "That's . . . I'm sorry. I didn't know this would be so painful."

"It's not your fault. How could you know?" His Adam's apple hitched at the top of his throat. "Whenever I talk about Henric's death, I see the terror on his face when he realized he wasn't flying. It haunted me for months. My sister Avie is an inquisitor. I told her about Henric's brother giving him the useless spell. She confronted the brother, and he confessed. Then she asked how I knew this information. She reprimanded me so hard for lying, I swore I'd never tell anyone about my visions again."

Deputy Inquisitor General Avaline Hollen was one of the most formidable mages of our time. It wasn't hard to imagine how intimidating she'd be to her nine-year-old brother.

"Two years later," he continued before I could comment, "I dreamt Jan and I were riding our bikes into town. We'd been planning to get the latest X-Men comic when it hit the stores. On the way, Jan darted onto the highway and a truck slammed into him. It was a blue-and-yellow Kringle's Circus truck. The one with the elephants.

"The next day, I got up early and broke our bike chains, so we'd have to walk. Halfway to town, the Kringle's elephants truck roared past us."

That proved nothing, and everything at the same time. These events had too many details to be coincidence. It was also incredibly distressing for a preteen boy to see people he loved die, even if in his dreams.

"I understand now. Thank—"

"I saw Aunt Gretch die when I was fifteen. It was the night before my brother Otto's graduation party. She was talking to my mother and eating those stupid little food bites." He swallowed hard and licked his lips. "Aunt Gretch choked to death because no one knew how to do the Heimlich maneuver or had a spell handy.

"I spent the hours before the party learning both methods. When she started to gasp for air, I used magic to clear her throat. No one questioned why I knew that spell. They were just glad I had it at the ready."

The office was eerily quiet. I hadn't come prepared for Bart to bare his soul. This wasn't an explanation, it was an apology for hurting me when he'd meant to save me. He shared secrets he never told anyone else because he wanted me to accept what he'd done was necessary and move on.

Unfortunately, it had the opposite effect. "Bart . . ." My voice failed and I paused with my mouth open.

"It's fine, Cael. I don't expect you to believe me."

Except it wasn't fine. He really wanted me to accept he was telling the truth, which confused me even more. Surely he knew if I believed him, I'd forgive him. The opposite of what he wanted.

"You stopped your brother and aunt from dying by changing the vision you saw. We didn't leave together. That changes the future you saw for us."

He smiled and shook his head. "I don't think so. My actions didn't create the underlying danger for Jan and Aunt Gretch. Jan shot onto it without looking, and Gretch swallowed too quickly so she could answer a question. My dating you is what causes your death."

Logically, his conclusion made sense, but it wasn't the only outcome. He ruled out all other possible causation. There had to be other explanations for what led to the fight with the demon.

"You don't know that. In your vision, we left together and made plans to see each other later that day. That never happened, so the outcome should be different."

Bart's lips quirked up. It softened his features. He was beautiful, in a simple way. A strong jaw, high cheekbones, and perfect nose. His short hair, styled off his face, framed his features for maximum effect. And his amazing eyes.

This was the first time the light was good enough to see his stunning bluish-gray eyes. They were bluer now, and they watched me intently.

"You're right. It's impossible to prove something that hasn't happened yet will still occur. Without the context of Jan and I going to get the new X-men comic, or Gretchen attending Otto's party, I don't know when my dream takes place. The only objective fact I have is it was cold. This event is weeks in the future."

I stopped to consider my next words. Bart wouldn't act on his desire because of his dream. The accepted teachings overwhelmingly rejected he'd seen the future, and thus his fears were unfounded. On the other hand, Bart truly believed he'd had a premonition. Knowing my address was a good reason to believe he had.

"We had . . . *have* a connection. Don't kick that aside."

Bart sat straighter and looked me in the eyes. "I don't want to cast it away either, but—we can't be together. Ever."

I was flailing. Everything I wanted was in front of me, but out of reach. He needed evidence his vision wouldn't come true, and I didn't have that proof.

My need for him surprised me, but I didn't rein it in. I wanted Bart, and not just for sex. He had depth you needed to peel back, like an onion. He'd shown me some of it, but there was more to learn.

"Then don't," I said softly. "Even you don't know what your dream means."

"Cael, I know you don't believe me, not truly, but something bad *will* happen."

He was wrong, I did believe him. He was too serious to make it up, and too nice to lie just to push me away.

"I know you saw something, and I'm sure now that it was real. But how can you be sure the second part will come true when you made sure the first part didn't? Why are you so sure the demon will kill Jan and me because we start dating? Even if we don't date, that doesn't mean I won't be there if a demon attacks."

"It's not that simple, Cael."

Nothing was simple about us. Before I arrived on campus, I was certain prophetic dreams were a hoax, and there was no way I'd want Barry to be my mentor. The only simple thing was how we felt about each other.

"Tell me you don't want me as much as I want you and I'll leave." I held up my hands in mock defeat. "I'll tell Gretchen to assign me someone else, and I won't bother you again."

Bart shook his head and whispered. "You know I can't say that."

I did, just as I knew nothing bad would come of our seeing each other. I didn't have a lick of proof, but I knew the demon would appear regardless. The harder part would be to convince him I was right.

"Then don't push me away again."

"I can't give you what you want." There was no hesitation in his tone.

I wanted to yell that, yes, he could if he didn't let fear paralyze him. Instead, I pulled back. He was genuinely concerned for me and Jannick. Bart was selfless. I wasn't.

I didn't think of myself as self-centered or selfish, but I had to fight the system for what I wanted. You don't give up when you know you're right.

"Fine. I won't ask you for what I really want, but you're still my mentor."

"Cael . . ." He slumped in his chair.

"Hold on. Nothing in your vision said we can't be friends. I'm not asking because we had great sex." His cheeks turned an adorable shade of pink because we *did* have great sex. "I'm asking because you're the best mage in the world. I came to Utrecht to teach the top young mages. I need to be the best I can be. I also need a friend. We already know we're compatible."

He frowned, stood, and then walked to his window. Bathed in the fading sunlight, he looked so hot. I fought the insane urge to mold myself to his back and hold him until he felt safe again. Every second that passed chipped away at my resolve to give him the space he needed.

"I agree." He turned slowly. "But we're colleagues and friends. Nothing more."

My goofy smile was so wide it hurt. It wasn't everything I wanted, but it was a damn good start.

"Agreed."

Chapter Nine

CAELINUS

The walk to Bart's office had started to feel familiar. Most of my reasons to drop in and chat were legit. Mostly. None required I ask him in person. Emails and phone calls, however, didn't allow me to see him, which was what I really wanted.

Bart smiled every time I opened his door. Not the fake, "Oh, I'm supposed to pretend I'm happy you're here" kind, but the type that sucked me in and made me want to stay all afternoon. I always checked but never detected a whiff of discomfort when I visited. If anything, he found reasons to keep talking.

Our conversations shifted effortlessly from one topic to the next. Rarely were they related to what I'd come to discuss. Bart loved intellectual conversations on a wide range of subject matters, and he pushed me to broaden my thinking. My favorite topic, however, was magic.

Bart had an intuitive grasp of magic that went beyond what we were taught in books or class. I was two weeks older than him, but when we talked mage craft, I felt like a student speaking to an older scholar. My favorite part was his joy whenever I made the leap from textbook to practical application. It wasn't fake effusive praise but a shared love of something we discovered together.

Often, I wanted to reach across the desk and kiss him, but he hadn't signaled he'd changed his position. We were just colleagues, maybe friends, but not more. It was frustrating, but I had to let him move at his own pace.

I didn't, however, stop finding reasons to visit. The question for this trip—could he recommend a good place to get lunch—was tricky. I'd asked for restaurant recommendations several times and twice Bart asked me the next day if I'd gone where he suggested. I hadn't and explained I didn't know anyone in town well enough to ask, and I didn't like to eat alone. Sadly, he ignored my not-so-subtle hints.

No more waiting for Bart to make the first move. This time, I'd ask him to go with me. Bart usually brought his lunch, but I had that covered, too. It was a beautiful day. We could eat outside after I got my food because I had a work question. It was flimsy, and he'd see through it, but it'd be hard for him to say no.

I stopped when I saw the door to my classroom was open. Normally I locked it after my last class. Curious, I stepped into the doorway. Bart had his back to the door and his mage stone in his right hand. The tourmaline gem was as stunning and unique as its owner. I'd seen purple mage stones before, but none had the clarity and deep hue of Bart's.

He moved his hand slowly, tracing a pattern only he could see on the window in front of him.

"I can see your reflection in the glass, Cael," Bart said. He continued whatever he was doing without missing a beat. "You can come in. You won't disturb me."

Good vibes zipped through my body. I should have been annoyed he invited me into my own classroom—a room he hadn't received permission to enter—but seeing him standing there made me too happy to complain. He finished his work and snapped the stone back.

"What are you doing?" I asked.

He pivoted on his right foot and his smile made my knees weak. "Come see for yourself."

The invitation suggested so much more than just a look at his latest work. I wanted to scream to the great earth spirit for giving him the dream that kept this distance between us. It wouldn't change anything, but it might help to vent a little. Instead, I took a deep breath and marched to his side.

Bart took another step back to give me access. Faint, almost invisible violet lines were etched into the pane of glass. I'd never seen this pattern before, but I wasn't an expert on glyphs. "What does it do?"

His shoulders sagged. "You can't tell?"

I wanted to bluster my way through and say, "Of course, I see it," because I didn't like his deflated tone. Since I really couldn't tell, however, I knew he'd be more disappointed if I lied. "No. I mean I see the symbols, but I don't know what they're for."

"Interesting." Bart moved closer to the window, raised his hand, but didn't touch the glass. He looked at me with a fond smile. "You inspired this spell."

My mood improved immediately. I inspired him? To a non-mage it might seem corny or pointless, but I was floating. I was his muse for some new bit of magic. "I did?"

"Yes. You did."

He touched the smooth surface, and fresh air enveloped me. It smelled like damp earth and new growth. I closed my eyes, breathed deeply, and held the air in my lungs. I imagined visiting the elven homelands deep in the western forests. The soil under my feet, the leaves dripping dew, and the clean air. The sensation sank deep into me and roused my elf side.

My eyes flew open, and I locked gazes with Bart. "What did you do?"

Color drained from his face. He snapped his left hand at the window and the inflow of air ceased. He looked scared as he stepped closer. "Are you okay? Did I hurt you?"

The urge to shift faded as quickly as it happened. "No, I'm fine. But how did you do that?"

"I'm not sure what I did now. It was supposed to be a fresh air spell that tapped into earth magic." He shrugged. "I thought you'd appreciate clean forest air in your classroom. Our discussions of earth magic gave me the idea."

I staggered under the enormity of what he'd said. Making my classroom smell like home was incredibly thoughtful and kind. I wanted to stay in that moment and bask in Bart's gift, but his explanation of how he did it went against everything I'd been taught. I waved at the glass. "That's not possible. Earth magic doesn't work with glyphs. There needs to be a direct connection."

"Sometimes what everyone *knows* isn't accurate," he said in a soft voice.

His dampened enthusiasm hit me like a gut punch. He'd tried to do something unbelievably nice, and I ruined his gift. Taking a step back, I let the magnitude of the gesture fill me. Bart used his extraordinary talent to give me something money couldn't buy. It might be the most romantic thing anyone ever did for me, and we weren't even dating.

I swallowed the lump in my throat and waved at the window. "Can you activate it again?"

Bart shook his head and refused to look at me. "I can, but I won't. I'm embarrassed I didn't think this through, and it hurt you. I'll remove it immediately."

His concern left me ashamed of all the nasty thoughts I'd had about Dickwad Barry, the selfish asshole. By the end of my first day at Utrecht I knew that wasn't true. This was more proof he was worth my interest.

I grabbed his arm before he could undo his work. "I'm not hurt, Bart. It caught me off guard, that's all. This is amazing. Thank you."

He turned with a hopeful expression, his eyes searching mine. The heat of his gaze rekindled my desire. Bart shivered and the distance between us seemed less. He parted his lips and drew a breath.

We both jumped back when footsteps echoed in the hallway. Bart's face turned red, and he stepped closer to the window. He raised his fingers until they nearly touched the glass.

"Professor Reinhold—" Bart's cousin, Professor Dylan Jurgenson, pulled up in the doorway. The startled expression disappeared a moment later. "Oh, hey Bart. Are you two working on something?"

"Hey, Dylan." Bart twisted to face his cousin. "I'm working on a new glyph. Want to check it out?"

Dylan looked at me. "Sorry if I'm interrupting, but I had a question for Professor Reinhold."

I didn't know Dylan that well. He taught on the high school side of Utrecht, but I knew he and Bart were tight. He would've found a reason to leave if he realized what he'd interrupted. It was frustrating, but I let it go.

"Please call me Cael." I snuck a glance at Bart. "You're not interrupting. Bart already finished the spell. It's pretty amazing."

"Translation: Bart's showing off again," Dylan said.

Shooting his cousin a nasty look, Bart said, "Remind me why I like you?"

Dylan laughed. "Because you couldn't live without me. Anyway, show me your proud new creation."

Bart let out an exaggerated sigh. "Some days I wish that weren't true." With a wink, he waved Dylan closer.

A jolt of resentment rippled through me at their display of familial affection. It was stupid. They were first cousins who acted like brothers. It wasn't sexual, but it spoke to a closeness I didn't have with Bart. It didn't matter that intellectually I understood the difference, watching them left me on edge.

"Wait a minute. This is Cael's classroom," Dylan said, pulling me from my thoughts. He shifted his gaze between me and Bart. "You did this for him?"

Bart's cheeks flushed immediately. Talk about no poker face. Recognition flashed across Dylan's face but before he could say anything, Bart said, "I thought it would be a nice welcome to the faculty gift."

"A gift? Oh right, a welcome gift." Dylan so didn't buy Bart's answer. "I forget. What did you get me when I started?"

"Nothing, doofus. We started the same day." He stuffed his mage stone in his pocket and turned to me. "I should go. I have a one o'clock appointment with Aunt Gretch."

He was three steps away before I processed what happened. "Bart. Wait." He stopped and I caught up to him. "You didn't tell me how to activate the spell."

"Sorry. Just touch it with your earth magic and it'll work. See ya, Dyl." He said the last bit over his shoulder without looking back.

I watched the door for several seconds after Bart's ass disappeared. Dylan moved behind me, and I remembered he was in the room.

"Sorry. I didn't mean to interrupt like that," Dylan said. "I didn't know you two were . . . dating?"

My irritation bubbled up, and I had to swallow a snarky response about cock blocking. He hadn't and honestly, I don't know what if anything just happened with me and Bart. His running out didn't bode well. "You didn't, and we're not."

"Right, because Bart blushes like that whenever I see him do magic." He closed his eyes and bowed his head. "And that was totally inappropriate and none of my business. I'm sorry."

Dylan's sincere apology blunted my frustration. None of this was his fault. Bart and I left things vague and what just happened felt very specific. At least until Bart snatched it away and we were back to ambiguous. And the gods know I hate not having a clear understanding of something.

"You're fine. Bart and me . . . it's complicated. But you'll need to ask him for an explanation." Especially since I didn't have one. "So. What can I help you with?"

※

I waited in my classroom until I saw Dylan walking across the courtyard. His untimely visit had put the brakes on what I hoped would have ended in a kiss. Not just a kiss, but the restart of something we both wanted.

Certain Dylan hadn't gone to see his cousin, I headed for Bart's office. Dylan didn't know Gretchen had a meeting off campus all afternoon, but I did. Bart was holed up in his office to avoid me and what nearly happened.

I paused outside his door. Bart had been hesitant to be my mentor, but there was nothing reluctant in his "welcome" gift. It had to have taken hours to create and perfect the spell. Then there was that look when I thanked him. Any hotter and I'd have burst into flames. None of which said stay away.

I drew a breath to steady myself and knocked.

"Come in."

A sense of déjà vu hit me as I opened the door. Bart sat behind his desk, but the computer was off, there were no papers in front of him, and he didn't have any books within reach.

"Hey, Cael," Bart said as if he'd been expecting me. "Have a seat?"

The large oak desk separated us by more than just two feet. It was a sign we'd stepped back from where we'd been minutes ago. I didn't want to move backward anymore. We needed to move forward.

"Thank you again for the glyph. It's amazing. I really appreciate it."

Bart nodded but avoided looking at me. "You're welcome."

As I expected, Bart's shields were back. In the classroom, his emotions had been in control, and now they were locked up tight. I needed to gently nudge him back to that moment and his gift was the key.

"How did you know you could use a glyph to tap into earth power?"

Some of the tension slipped from his body. "I didn't until I tried, but I assumed it would work. We use glyphs to lock different types of magic into a specific place, so I tried it with earth magic."

I wanted to say how much I loved his gift, but he'd shut me off if we started talking about feelings. I needed my mother to coach me on what to say next, but she wasn't around. "I've never seen earth magic bound to a glyph."

"I hadn't, either." Bart leaned back in his chair and crossed his right leg over his left knee. "I assume elves don't like working with runes?"

The more casual position was a start, but I needed him emotionally closer. For that, I needed to share things I usually kept private.

"It's not that simple. My relationship with earth magic is personal and more intimate than my connection with regular magic. We don't use glyphs because it turns that bond into something artificial."

"If this is too personal, please tell me, but is that why you stay in your human side? Most beings keep to the human side to move about easily in our world. Elves are close enough physically that they can interact with our buildings in a way a griffin or dragon could not."

Bart tried to be sensitive to shifter prejudice, but his "close enough physically" description was an insult to elves. We could have that discussion another day.

"Apart from it's harder to blend in as an elf, I prefer to stay in my human form so I can use human magic. In my human form I'm a mage and can use a power stone; I can't as an elf. The converse is also true. I can't use earth magic in human form like I can as an elf.

"But the biggest reason is my elf side is nurtured by earth magic. Most elves travel barefoot because our skin on the earth gives us the best connection. If I take my elf form in a city, I start to feel hollow and empty. There's no physical harm, but it's always there. I get irritable and my mood changes. That doesn't happen when I'm in human form."

"And my using earth magic to change the air upset your inner balance." He bowed his head. "I'm so sorry. I should have known better."

I rounded his desk and knelt in front of him. He closed his eyes to avoid me, but I took his hands in mine and wouldn't let go until he looked at me.

"You didn't upset my balance or hurt me in any way. Just the opposite. Your spell didn't just bring in clean air, it brought the earth magic to me. It called to me, and my elf side sang out in joy at the reunion. It's how I feel every time I go to the elven homeland after a long time away."

"But I saw how you were when it happened. You thought I'd done something nefarious."

The idea that he'd injured me distressed him so much I could feel it through his shields. "That's my fault. I had no idea what you'd done, so I thought the spell was meant to force my shift."

"No." He snatched his hands from my grip and slid the chair back. "I would never violate you like that. You have my word."

I missed his warm skin touching mine but let him have his distance. Baby steps. I couldn't force him to let go of his fears all at once. "I know you wouldn't. Your gift is the most beautiful thing you could have given me. It's not the same as standing on damp earth, but it's better than any substitute I've ever found. It's truly wonderful."

He studied me warily. I couldn't push him anymore. If I tried to bring us closer, he'd suspect I was trying to manipulate him. On some level I probably was, but I didn't want to turn his gift into something evil.

I smiled and returned to my chair. Bart watched me the whole time and finally wheeled himself back to his desk. "I wish I could say I knew that would happen, but it was just an air spell. I'm glad it's more and that you enjoy it."

My heart wanted me to lean over the desk and draw him closer for a kiss. Better, I wanted to entice him to kiss me. But it wasn't time. Not yet.

"I was coming to see you earlier to ask if you'd go with me to get food. I want your opinion on some changes to my lesson plan, and honestly, I'm tired of eating alone."

Bart wouldn't agree, not after the near kiss, but I needed to ask. I wanted him to get comfortable with me asking him for platonic lunch dates.

"Okay, but I need to be back by two for office hours."

"That's okay . . ." I was about to say "Maybe another time," when I realized he'd said yes. "Two p.m. isn't a problem."

Now I needed to be on my best behavior so he'd agree the next time I asked.

Chapter Ten

BARTHOLOMEW

"Thanks for seeing me early, Professor H." Harlan pushed his glasses up his nose. "I wanted to make the game."

I wasn't aware any of Utrecht's teams were playing. "Oh? What game is that?"

"Creative kickball." He shoved his book in his backpack. "Professor Reinhold is going to teach us how to play."

I managed to hide my surprise. Harlan no more fit the jock mold than me. The fact Cael persuaded him to play was impressive. "I never heard of creative kickball."

"Professor Reinhold said he played all the time in Chicago. You should come. It sounds like fun."

Harlan's enthusiasm tempted me, but seeing Cael kitted out for an athletic event wasn't the best idea. After our near kiss last week, I needed to work on my control around him.

"Thank you, but I'll pass," I said. "I'm stupendously *not* athletic. Go enjoy yourself."

Harlan rolled his eyes and swiped his free hand down his

skinny frame. "Does this look like the body of an athlete? You use magic to move the ball."

Cael teaching them a "game" that required magic piqued my curiosity. Quite the clever trick to get them to apply his lessons. If I wasn't already totally smitten, he'd have gone up another notch or two. "That sounds interesting."

Slinging his backpack over his shoulder, Harlan laughed. "It's a scam to get us to practice what he's teaching, but who cares so long as it's fun."

I pointed my finger at him and nodded. "Glad you caught that. Have fun."

"Thanks," he said as he left.

Returning to my seat, I unfroze my computer screen. The article my older brother, Otto, sent me on Viking seax stared back at me. It was an incredible find he'd received from a retired history professor in Denmark. It should have commanded my unwavering attention, but it didn't.

My mind refused to let go of the image of Cael on the field with his class. I wanted to watch him in action. Hell, I wanted to see him period, but we'd come way too close to crossing a line we shouldn't.

Correction, *I* almost crossed the line. Cael had kept his promise not to push things between us. He'd even made sure our working lunch had a real school question, not the pretextual one he'd used the first week.

Cael and I fit so well together. Sitting on the bench with our lunch, talking about teaching, was an ideal date for me. Yes, I was boring—something Declan had told me more than once—but much like my office furnishings, I liked people with character. Style and appearance were important, too, but they were secondary. Cael ticked all my buttons.

Unfortunately, the most likely interpretation of my dream was if I dated Cael, he would die. Cael believed the absence of new visions meant I'd changed the outcome. My counterargument was the event was too far off and the lack of a new dream proved nothing.

My screensaver kicked in, blocking the article I wasn't reading. "Fuck!"

Rather than unlock my monitor, I admitted defeat. My head was on the field with Cael.

※

Utrecht had several public areas that could work for the game; I picked the biggest one closest to our building and got lucky. Cael still wore his work clothes, minus his tie. It was disappointing he hadn't changed but better this way. He had his back to me, so I sat on a bench and watched him count players.

I was far enough away that I wouldn't be a distraction—this was about his students, not me. He greeted each coed with a fist bump and a smile. The easy way Cael kept their attention showcased his talent as a teacher. He connected with his students.

Everyone gathered around him and after a few seconds, Harlan pointed in my direction. Cael turned and with a big grin, motioned for me to join them. I waved him down because no, I wasn't playing, but rather than let me decline, Cael jogged over and stopped a few feet away.

"Hey. We need another player, preferably someone who's a fully trained, alpha class mage."

I rolled my eyes. "That's a very specific need. Why do I believe the game doesn't require such a player?"

"Because you're the smartest person I know." He crossed his arms and settled in for an argument. "Here's the thing. We need eighteen players. We have sixteen plus me. If I play, my team will have a decided advantage. Hence the need for another alpha class mage."

I didn't like his solution. There were other ways to solve the problem that didn't require I make a fool of myself. "Two flaws in your logic. First, I've never heard of this game before so I'm not a counter to you, and second, I didn't come to play."

"Yet here you are," he said with a smirk.

I'd come to see him teach his students, and I intended to stay on my bench. Far from the game. "Yes, but only to observe."

Cael's cocky grin disappeared, and the pleading look that replaced it battered my resolve before he even asked. "Please come play. I know that sounds totally loaded, but you're perfect. Players use creative magic to move the ball. The most important asset is how well you can control your talent. You'll be the ringer, not me."

My reluctance was flimsy at best. I couldn't tell him I'd come to watch him, not the game, so I played my ace. "I'm still going to pass. My lack of athletic skills is legendary."

"C'mon, Bart," he said softly. "I've seen you work out and I know you're totally ripped. Yeah, I went there, but it's true. You may not be a soccer or baseball talent, but you're athletic enough to play."

So much for my best excuse. The part of me that screamed "bad idea," couldn't combat my desire to make him happy. Ignoring my logical side, I stood.

"Do I need to summon sneakers to replace my shoes?"

Cael smiled and suddenly, I couldn't remember why this was a bad idea.

"Only if you'll feel more comfortable in them."

Loosening my tie, I retrieved my power stone. "Give me a minute and I'll join you."

It took me almost three minutes to change into sneakers, send my tie and shoes back to my office, and make my way across the field. I could have made it in half the time if I hadn't watched Cael's ass as he walked back to the group.

The playing field was marked like a baseball diamond; players stood by the bases. There were three outfielders and a pitcher.

The game was exactly like kickball only without the kicking. Magic was the only way to move or stop the ball.

My team "kicked" first, and the teacher in me started to coach the players. Cael did the same with his team in the field. By the third inning, the students had improved considerably, and the game got lively.

Cael's first time kicking, he used his skills to keep the ball moving once it touched the ground. He kept it from the fielders until he'd rounded the bases. Once I knew that was legal, I did the same when it was my turn to kick. By agreement, Cael and I didn't field the ball, so the students got more practice. We stuck to that rule, until my team pushed ahead in our half of the last inning.

Harlan proved particularly adept at keeping control of the ball and running. He'd pushed the ball to the edge of the field and was running home, when Cael wrestled control of the ball and tagged him out inches from home plate.

Fate, however, is a fickle beast. When it was Cael's turn to kick, he was the tying run. As he rounded second base, I ripped the ball from his magical grasp.

Cael's head whipped in my direction, and I smirked at his shocked expression. It was on. Trying to keep the ball away from everyone while running was hard. Much harder than standing still and aiming it at the runner.

As he and I struggled to establish control, he slowed from a run, to a jog, to barely a walk. Twice he tried to trick me by releasing his hold and then running, but I used those openings to bring the ball closer. The next time he tried it, I was ready.

He'd rounded third and made a dash for home. I surrounded the ball in a bubble that would repel any attempt to latch on and summoned it toward me. He stopped halfway down the line and tried to lock onto the ball, presumably to use the ensuing struggle to eke his way home.

I let him attempt his gambit, and when his spell slid off, I quickly drew the ball into the space between us. My team cheered in the field, encouraging me to hit him with the ball and end the game.

"Nice move, Bart, but you still need to touch me with the ball," Cael said.

Early in my training, I'd learned not to engage my opponent during a contest. This might be a friendly match, but it had become a test of wills between me and Cael. He couldn't go around me or leave the base path or he'd be out. Flying over me was also against the rules. The only way to score was to gain control of the ball, and I didn't plan to let that happen.

I anchored the ball so he couldn't swat it away and waited.

Cael raised an eyebrow. "No answer?"

I shook my head. Everything was about control, and mine was tight. He pushed at the ball with his magic and inched toward me. The ball didn't budge. Cael's eyes scanned the area, and I could almost hear his mind working.

There was a two-minute limit between kickers. Cael either had to return to third and risk being tagged out as he retreated, or score before time expired.

"Time, Harlan?" I asked, hoping to spur a mistake.

Cael glanced left.

"Twenty seconds, Professor H." The exuberant lilt in Harlan's voice oozed payback.

Everyone was quiet and all eyes were on us. It wasn't every day two Utrecht professors squared off in a semi-personal magic fight. Blows weren't being traded, but this was a test of magical ability.

I wasn't hyper-competitive by nature, but I wasn't giving in without a fight. Cael hadn't been entirely truthful when he said creative talent mattered most. My control helped, but Cael's experience allowed him to run circles around me. Having gained a tactical advantage, I intended to use it to help my team win.

Cael took a step back, as if he were retreating to third base. That was the safe move, but it was also a ruse. With his greater experience, Cael had played aggressively the entire match. He wasn't changing strategy now. I steadied myself as I waited for his real move.

A second later, Cael shifted his weight and lunged forward. Force pressed against the ball as Cael attempted to magically push off and vault over me. This was obviously a move he'd used back home.

This time, however, the magic I wrapped around the ball repelled his. The lift he'd expected didn't happen, and he flailed his arms trying to regain his balance. I released the ball from its anchor, and it shot up.

The ball struck Cael in his midsection, but it still knocked the wind from him. Off balance and gasping for air, he lost his tenuous hold on his balance and pitched forward. Instinctively, I caught him, but his momentum took us both down.

Slamming into the ground, I saw stars. Cael landed on top of me, and the breath whooshed from my lungs. I opened my eyes and Cael's face was inches away. My dick didn't need our lips to touch to let me—and Cael—know it enjoyed the contact.

Breathing deeply, I smiled up at him. "Tag. You're out."

Cael laughed. "You're right. I am."

He stayed still; I felt how much he liked being on top. Unfortunately, we had an audience. Even if we didn't, I wouldn't have let it go on much longer. I couldn't cross this line, even if my perfidious cock had other ideas.

"Ah . . . are you okay?" I side-eyed the field.

"Oh, yeah." He heaved in another breath and got to his feet. "Nothing broken or otherwise damaged, other than my pride."

He extended his hand to help me up. The skin-to-skin contact sent a tingle racing through me, fanning the fire that burned for more. I raised my eyes to meet his, and the heat in his gaze weakened my resistance.

Before either of us moved, my teammates pulled us apart and

surrounded me. I smiled as I was tugged into a group scrum and thought Cael winked before the others blocked my view.

My teammates patted my back and jumped around like we'd won something important, and I went along with their enthusiasm, sneaking glances at Cael as he spoke to his team. Half a minute later, I corralled the players to go shake hands with our opponents.

Cael and I played it cool, like two colleagues who'd played a game with their students. Inside, however, an inferno raged that I needed to smother. I didn't have the slightest clue how, but I'd find a way, at least until I was certain being more than friends wouldn't kill him and Jan.

Chapter Eleven

❧

CAELINUS

Tossing my keys on top, I skirted the desk and continued to the office's window. Still raining. I loved the rain, but I hadn't packed a lunch. My choices were don't eat until much later or teach my afternoon classes in damp shoes. Either way I'd be grouchy, so I needed to pick the least bad option.

I knew I should bring lunch on crappy days, but I never checked the forecast. And because doubling down on stupidity was an Olympic sport for me, I didn't look to see if the rain would stop by noon. Had I done *that*, I could have ordered delivery and eaten before my next class.

The problem was, I'd gotten into the routine of asking Bart to get lunch with me so we could talk. In the fantasy realm where I lived, he looked forward to it as much as I did. He certainly smiled enough. I even stopped making up work questions and just asked him if he wanted to go with me. Settling into that rut left me with hangry or wet and grouchy as my options on this rainy day.

My class deserved better.

Someone knocked and I turned from the window. "Come in."

The door opened slowly, and Bart poked his head in. "Is this a bad time?"

The clouds circling me parted and my mood improved instantly. It was never a bad time for Bart to come see me.

"Not at all." I waved to my serviceable but boring university issued office chairs. "Have a seat."

He shouldered the door open and walked in carrying a stack of plastic containers, a paper grocery bag dangling below the tubs. He flicked the door shut with his heel, and his smile told me he was up to something.

Ever since he'd charmed my window, he'd found little things that made me happy. He learned I liked rooibos tea with vanilla. Now he offered me some when I came to visit. I'd commented on how much I liked ice cream, and two days ago our lunch walk brought us to a small parlor that had the richest, creamiest ice cream I'd ever tasted. Each time he did something special, he wore the grin he was flashing me now.

"I noticed the one hundred percent chance of rain all day, so I made us lunch. We can eat here or if you'd like, we can use the faculty dining hall."

He brought us lunch. Because yes, Bart *had* checked the weather. How did he find the time to do so much? I struggled to get to work on time, while he did an entire day's work before he arrived.

"That's really nice of you, Bart. Thank you."

Bart's smile wavered and he set the food on my desk. "You never bring lunch, so I figured this would be a good idea."

Typical Bart. I wanted to use the moment to pull him closer, but he turned bashful whenever I acknowledged his kindness. Frustrating, but at least he wasn't running away.

"It's like you read my mind. I was debating whether to be hungry Cael or wet Cael. Neither is conducive to being a good teacher."

Two paper plates appeared from the bottom of the stack and Bart assembled our lunches. First, he pulled out two subs—hoagies as they called them in Philly—and then scooped fruit salad from a different tub. The watermelon looked red and juicy, the blueberries were plump, and the strawberries were a deep red. My mouth watered and then my stomach let it be known it was ready to eat. From the paper bag he pulled a large bag of potato chips and two reusable water bottles. He'd even brought napkins and metal forks.

"I know you're not a big meat eater, so I made eggplant parmesan. I hope that's okay," he said as he handed me my plate.

Okay? He noticed I didn't like meat, so he brought me an elaborate hoagie that looked like it came from the deli we frequented. The fruit had been cut perfectly, and he found my favorite brand of chips. I accepted my lunch and wasn't sure if I should eat it or admire it. It was way more than "okay."

"This is amazing. Thank you."

Bart's body released the tension I hadn't noticed building in him. A tiny whiff of relief rolled from his body and he finally gave me a real smile. "I wasn't sure. It's not for everyone."

I took a bite, and I didn't keep in the moan. Crusty bread that was soft inside, sauce with bite, eggplant that wasn't too greasy or mushy, and lots of mozzarella cheese. It was easily the best sandwich I'd had since I moved to Philly, and there were a ton of awesome delis in the area.

"Bart this is fantastic. You made this yourself?" I took another bite before my brain registered I'd totally insulted him. Chewing quickly, I nearly choked trying to swallow so I could apologize. He spoke before I could.

"Yes, but not this morning." He waved his hand as if dispelling me of that notion. "It's one of my favorite dishes, so I make a big batch and freeze some for later."

As if that made our lunch less wonderful. A smart elf would have let it go, but I was too curious for my own good. This was

Bartholomew Hollen, son of the richest family on earth. Why didn't the staff cook for him?

"Do you cook for your whole family?"

My question caught him with his sandwich at his mouth. He gave me a confused look before recognition washed over his features. Setting his lunch down, he shook his head. "I don't live at Hollen Hall. My house is a ten-minute walk from campus."

That shattered another image of the pampered prince, sitting down to dinner in a formal dining room along with the rest of his family. It was a ridiculous idea born of my own prejudices.

"Sorry." I hadn't insulted him, but I felt like I owed him an apology for my less-than-flattering thoughts. "I thought you lived in the huge mansion surrounded by family and servants. It's a lingering effect from the chip on my shoulder."

Bart cocked his head and smirked. "Chip on your shoulder, huh? You?"

I couldn't decide if I wanted to flick marinara sauce on his white oxford or kiss the grin off his face. Definitely the latter, but I'd be safer staining his shirt. "It comes with living in Chicago."

"If you say so." He grabbed a chip and crunched noisily. "Hollen Hall is . . . Jan and I moved out the week after we graduated."

Teasing information from Bart wasn't easy. He never refused to answer but he almost always made me ask. "So, you live with your brother?"

"No. He lives a few miles away in Havertown. After sharing a room for nearly twenty years, we needed our own places."

Maybe I was reading too much into it, but it sounded like Jan needed his own place, not Bart. "You two shared a room when you lived at home?"

Normally I wasn't this nosy, but he mentioned it and I really wanted to know more about Bart. He exhaled and pushed his lunch away from the edge. My meal lost some of its appeal now that I'd ruined Bart's. "I'm sorry. I shouldn't have asked."

"No. It's fine. I brought it up." He looked up and met my gaze. "I told you that Jan's my half-brother. As you can imagine, he was in a bad way when he showed up at Hollen Hall. His mom had just died, he'd only met our father a day prior, the place was huge, and there were a few vocal assholes in the family who didn't want a bastard living under their roof."

Anger laced his words, as if this had happened two weeks ago, not two decades. I'd opened a wound that probably never fully healed. Before I could tell him I didn't need to hear any more, he continued.

"The first few years, we stayed together because he didn't want to be alone. By the time we started at Utrecht, we were inseparable, so it made sense we'd room together. During the school years, there wasn't any reason to move into a new room at home, we were only there for short periods of time.

"Getting back to your original question, I don't cook for my family, but Jan comes over often." Bart picked up his sandwich. "He's hopeless in the kitchen."

I wondered if he really was hopeless or pretended so he had an excuse to spend time with his brother. "Where did you learn to cook?"

"When I was seventeen, I spent the summer in Tuscany at a culinary college. Now I record cooking shows for tips and recipes."

Which brought me back to how did the man find time? We ate in relative silence, something we'd started after talking too much the first week and not finishing our food. I had thirds on the fruit salad, and we polished off the entire bag of chips. I'd need to add miles to my daily run to burn all this off.

"Thank you again, Bart. That was amazing."

"Happy to do my part to shield the students from hangry or wet Cael." He took a quick drink and when he lowered the bottle, he asked, "How much do you know about ancient elven swords?"

My witty response to his "doing his part" quip evaporated in the face of his question. Elven swords? He didn't seem the type to be interested in weapons of any kind, certainly not something as specific as this.

"Not much? I got some training during summer visits to the elven homeland, but I'm not a weapons master if that's what you're asking."

I felt apprehension leaking through his shields. He wasn't making conversation or even telling me about something interesting he'd learned. Bart was looking for something specific, but the way it came out—do you like eggplant, would you like some fruit salad, tell me what you know about ancient elfish blades—didn't give me much to work with. So, I waited for him to expound.

The silence lingered, but before it got too weird, Bart swallowed. "No. Not how to use them, just . . . Let me start over. About two years ago, I bought an authentic Viking short sword in an antiquity shop in Oslo, Norway. It predated the Great Ward, and it had a name."

Thousand-year-old Viking swords with names? Lunch got a whole lot weirder and more interesting. "A name? Like a pet or a familiar?"

Bart smiled, but he didn't relax. "At first, I thought it was just a name, like Excalibur. Then I studied it, and learned it was forged to kill demons. When I used it during the fight last spring, it felt sentient, so I dug deeper."

He took out his mage stone. It pulsed a muted purple, and I felt his magic seal the room.

"Trouble?" My hand instinctively found my own gem.

"No." He shook his head and pocketed his stone. "But it pays to be safe."

And just like that, our semi-romantic lunch was gone. It didn't diminish how sweet Bart had been, but I wondered if he'd been waiting for a rainy day to raise this topic.

"That's cryptic, even for you, Bart."

"Sorry." He shifted a strap over his shoulder that I'd swear hadn't been there when he arrived and pulled a sword from its scabbard. "This is the Orme Seax, which means wolf sword. When I first saw it, I thought I was just a finely made, Viking short sword. Once I noticed the faint traces of magic, it took me almost a year to figure out its true purpose.

"When Declan raised the demon, I summoned the blade from my office. During the fight, the sword communicated how and where to strike the creature."

"It spoke to you?"

"Not with words, but I *knew* it wanted me to hurl it at the demon's back. Eventually, I did what it wanted, and it killed the demon."

The blade was pretty enough, but I'd seen nicer. A demon-killing blade, however, shouldn't be something sold in an antique shop. "That's incredible."

"Yes." His eyes were unfocused, as if he saw something only he could visualize. "The magic needed to help kill a demon is considerable. Giving the weapon even rudimentary consciousness shouldn't be possible."

Yet someone had done just that. "Why do you think it's elfish?"

"I think an elf imbued his life energy into the blade."

My body slowly flopped back against my chair. That would be . . . it would be counter to what it meant to be an elf. "Are you sure?"

"No, but there's enormous power in the blade." He slid the weapon back into its sheath. "Whoever wrought this needed a deep connection with the metals and gems used to create it."

A bond with the elements was the foundation of earth magic, and elves had the strongest earth magic of all the beings. Logically it made sense but bonding your soul to an inanimate object went against the core of our kind. "Have you spoken to anyone at the Conclave?"

"No, and I don't plan to. If I showed them this, they'd try to take it from me. Given what the future holds, I'm going to need this more than they do."

It hit me like a punch to the gut when I realized what he meant. Bart hadn't moved an inch from his position. The progress I thought we'd made was all in my head.

"Bart. We changed that future." I sounded hurt. I *was* hurt. All the time we spent together, the thoughtful things he'd done for me, it made me believe we were getting closer, that he'd agreed the future he saw wouldn't come true. Except he hadn't.

I was stupid for reading more into what passed between us. He'd been clear he didn't plan to change his mind, but I'd been determined he'd see I was right. I let myself grow attached to him as more than a colleague or a friend, because I thought he was inching toward getting closer. I was such a fool.

"Yes and no," Bart said. If he picked up on my disappointment, it didn't show. "I have to believe we changed some of it. I mean we didn't walk out together, right?"

His explanation added to my confusion. It sounded like he was hinting we could proceed, but he'd also said no. Bart needed to clarify this without my interference. "I'd say that's right."

"The problem is, we don't know how much has changed. Not all of it, that's for certain."

My brain still hadn't fully processed the stagnant state of our nonexistent relationship. If he expected me to follow along, he was going to be disappointed. "I don't understand. How can you know that?"

"In the dreams where Jan and Aunt Gretchen die, most of the things I saw happened. The Kringle's Circus truck with the elephants, Aunt Gretch choking while talking to my mother. The only thing that changed was I prevented their deaths.

"Someone is going to raise a demon on campus this fall. Who's going to summon it and when, I can't say, but it's going to happen.

The demon I saw is much bigger than the one Declan raised, so I'm going to need the Orme Seax."

Hope tapped at the walls I tried to smother it with. This was the first time Bart had agreed that we'd changed his vision. The problem was, in this new version, he still planned to fight the demon, and I was noticeably absent.

"Assuming you're right about the demon, why do you have to fight this? Campus security has enough high-level mages to deal with it."

"Do they? The only mage to fight a demon in the last twelve hundred years is me. I'm not sure Brador and his staff can stop what's coming."

I wanted to tell him this wasn't his fight, but it was. He was the most powerful mage of our time. If the rumors were true, he'd be the first archmage since Katarina Hollen. The world saw how well that title worked for her. She and her mate, a phoenix shifter, sacrificed their lives to save the world.

"Fine, then we help them. You don't need to do this alone."

"That also isn't accurate. The number one rule when dealing with demons is don't get eaten. If whatever comes through feeds on a mage's soul, it'll take a lot more firepower to defeat it than what security can bring to the fight. I won't risk an inexperienced security mage failing to ward themselves and getting eaten."

Why did he feel like he needed to defend the entire world alone? Even he had limits. Didn't he realize how many people would suffer if he died?

That might be me projecting my feelings, but the world would suffer if the demon killed him. "Then train them before this happens. Better yet, tell your sister and have a response team on standby."

"Train them to fight what?" He sounded frustrated. "No one believes I can see the future. Even you're not sure if it's real."

The defeat in his voice stung like I'd been slapped. Bart might not be an arrogant ass, but he was always confident. Even when we met, he was nervous but still self-assured. My disbelief hurt him in a way I hadn't realized. He kept his distance because he thought I didn't believe him.

I didn't think he was lying—he was certain he'd seen the future—but that didn't mean what he'd seen had to happen. We could change that future, but we needed help.

"Then *we* make them believe you, Bart."

Chapter Twelve

BARTHOLOMEW

Sweat rolled down my torso as I pulled my chin over the bar. My arms felt like rubber, but I had five more to go. Working out harder was supposed to take my mind off Cael, but it didn't. In the solitary quiet, all I thought about was him.

Then we make them believe you.

The image of Cael, looking me in the eyes and vowing to fight with me, nearly broke my resolve. I practically ran out of the room after my last class to get to the gym before Cael could catch up with me to continue that conversation.

We make them.

Grunting, I ground out another rep. The gym was empty so I could be that loud obnoxious guy who let everyone know how hard he was working.

This wasn't going to solve the problem. I needed someone who wouldn't roll their eyes when I told them about my vision. Someone to help me figure out if anything had really changed. Unfortunately, the only person who knew was hardly objective. He wanted me to ignore it so we could be together.

I strained and completed my last rep. Dropping to the mat, I snatched my towel and wiped sweat from my face and torso. Normally I wouldn't work out without a shirt, but I'd forgotten workout clothes. Rather than wear a sweaty T-shirt to our 4:30 meeting, I opted to go shirtless. Luckily, I had an extra pair of shorts in my office.

With every rep, my brain replayed our last conversation. My already shaky resolve was crumbling. Was I being stupid? I had no way of knowing what would trigger the demon or cause the three of us to be there.

I assumed it was dating Cael because that's what I saw first. But was it? The dream didn't come with a cipher to interpret the details.

How fucked up would it be if I kept him away and everything still happened?

I needed time away from him to sort things out. Clarity wouldn't come when my heart skipped beats every time I saw him. I'd tell myself I'd say no when he asked me to do something, and yes came out.

Or like today. I knew he wouldn't bring lunch, and he wouldn't know about the rain. I could have . . . should have called to remind him. Instead, I got up early and made us both lunch. Cael's expression told me it hit all the feels. It was something you didn't spontaneously do if you were just friends. I knew the signal it would send, and even though I shouldn't have done it, I did it anyway.

I covered my face with the towel. "Fuck. I'm so screwed."

Pulling the cotton square down slowly, I resolved to sort this out before I confused Cael more than I had already. Tomorrow was my research day, and I'd planned to do that from home. That meant a three-day weekend with no Cael. No more straddling the line. All in or not at all.

The door opened and Cael entered. His white dress shirt hugged his body and the green Utrecht tie settled perfectly on his chest. A long brown strand had escaped his hair tie and floated down his right cheek. He was so beautiful, my breath caught in my throat.

When I saw his tight lips and the anxious way he scanned the room, my stomach clenched. Something had happened since we'd eaten, and it wasn't good. I swallowed the fear and waited for him to tell me.

Taking another step into the gym, he eyed me up and down. His lips twitched, and he exhaled, but his body remained tense. "I'm sorry to interrupt, but I need your help."

The way he studied me, I knew exactly what he wanted—because my cock decided it didn't care if it was wrong. But this wasn't a booty call. "What's wrong?"

My voice snapped him back to the present. He groaned and scrubbed his face with his right hand. "This sucks minotaur balls. I really want to stay and look at you."

His choice of species killed my mood—fast. "My cousin, Dylan, is mated to a minotaur. I'm sure Xavier could help with that fetish."

Cael snorted. "Oh no. The only being I want is in front of me."

So much for derailing the flirting. Heat flushed my cheeks, and I avoided his gaze. I didn't trust myself not to kiss him. With a supreme effort, I pushed us back to why he was here.

"Doubtful that's what had you rushing down to the gym to find me." I arched an eyebrow and red painted Cael's cheeks.

"Right." He rubbed his nape. "Sorry. A glyph appeared on the floor of my classroom that I know wasn't there this morning."

Dread squeezed my guts so hard, I almost vomited. This wasn't a coincidence. I should have pushed back harder when the university refused to let me help cleanse the classroom. Avie's people missed something important.

"A glyph?"

"Well, a partial glyph. It's not fully formed. I tried to dissolve it, but I can't. Gretchen said to tell you immediately."

I swallowed the rebuke on the tip of my tongue. Cael was a powerful, well-trained mage, but he hadn't studied glyphs and demon summoning near enough to deal with this problem. Partial glyphs were at best unstable. He should never have tried to remove it.

Done was done, and we could discuss the stupidity of his actions later. The first step was to neutralize the danger. "Let me clean up and I'll meet you outside your classroom. Whatever you do, don't go back inside."

"Um . . ." He looked genuinely conflicted. "Your aunt said not to leave you alone."

Another drawback to having your favorite aunt head your department. She knew way too much about me. She and Avie decided I'd been traumatized and needed watching over.

"Of course she did."

Cael snorted. "She said you'd be salty, but she's just making sure you're safe."

Damn right I was irritated. Neither of them had killed that demon—neither of them *could* have killed it alone. I didn't need babysitting, even if they sent Cael to watch over me. "Aunt Gretch has been worried since the first attack that Declan might have left other traps for me. I don't need protection. I can take care of myself."

"She's worried. I never saw her scared, but I'd imagine that's what it looks like."

Siphoning off my anger, I wasn't sure which bothered me more . . . Aunt Gretch going all mama bear on me—again—or that she'd shared her concern with Cael. Probably the latter. "I need to shower, and you don't need to join me to comply with my auntie's instruction."

"Not trying to be pervy, but can you talk and shower? She

wanted you there yesterday and she wants me to fill you in before you get to my classroom."

I immediately envisioned he and I showering together. He hadn't suggested that, but it's where my mind took me. Unfortunately, what he said wasn't much better. Like him being in the locker room while I showered wouldn't arouse either of us.

I didn't need this. But I couldn't say no to him, even if the flame singed my wings. "Fine."

I grabbed my water bottle and headed toward the locker room. To keep focused, I steered us back to why he'd come to the gym. "Inquisitors swept the classroom several times after they removed the glyph. It's troubling they missed this. Can you describe it for me?"

"I'm not expert on glyphs, but this is peculiar. Part of the symbol's visible, but the rest is hidden in the floor."

I knew glyphs as well as anyone, and I'd never seen anything like that. It shouldn't be possible. His classroom had been scrutinized with such care that something like this shouldn't have been missed. Unless whoever helped Declan was an inquisitor or on the Mage Council.

Sitting on the bench, I removed my sneakers "How did you discover it?"

"I didn't. A student sitting close to it said she felt weird, but it passed when she got to my desk. At first, I thought she was . . . you know, flirting. But when I walked to the back of the classroom, I saw it."

A flash of jealousy raced through me, and I lost my train of thought. I was too close to the situation. I'd look at it because Aunt Gretch asked, then I'd have Avie bring in her team.

First, I needed to get cleaned up. I stood and swallowed the weirdness of being naked around Cael given the state of our relationship. Pushing my shorts over my hips, I wrapped the towel around my waist.

"If it had been there last spring, the inquisitors should have detected it. Which begs the question, did they leave it there on purpose, or is it new? Give me five minutes to shower."

I didn't want to go in that room again if it had an active glyph. Almost being served to a demon for dinner would deter any sane person. I wouldn't do it, except my aunt was a powerful mage and this spooked her enough she didn't want to wait for Avie to handle it. She'd also sent Cael to guard me.

What Cael described shouldn't be possible. Adjusting the temperature, I stepped under the spray and washed off the sweat. Granny Pederson once told me if something happened, it was possible. The problem was our lack of knowledge.

Placing my palms against the wall, I let the water roll off my head. I needed to suck it up and face my fears. If Declan left dark magic in that room, it needed to be removed. After another minute, I shut the taps and dried off.

"You weren't kidding when you said five minutes," Cael said when I reached my locker. "This is probably wildly wrong, but you've got a smoking hot body."

I preened inside at the compliment, but outwardly my face burned so hot, my hair would be dry before I got dressed. Cael hadn't been shy about his interest, and while I never expressed my similar desire for him, I was certain he knew.

I dropped my towel and stepped into my boxers. "You've seen it before."

"Not in the light," he said with a playful smirk.

The regret I'd worked so hard to bury surfaced with a vengeance. Had I stayed, this wouldn't be the first time he'd seen me naked in the light.

"Sorry." Cael walked to the far end of the bench. "I wasn't trying to go there; I really meant it as a compliment."

His apology carried the same remorse I felt. Not that he'd insulted me, but it mirrored my disappointment we weren't more. I couldn't tell him how I felt, not until I sorted everything out.

The last thing I wanted was to give him hope, only to snatch it away.

"Please stop apologizing. You're fine." I shrugged into my shirt. "Let me finish and we can go check out what you found."

<hr />

After I killed the demon, Avie suggested I had PTSD and should see someone. I brushed her off; I felt fine. Now, I realized she was right. It took more effort than I wanted to admit to enter the classroom.

I'd consider therapy later.

Cael and I weren't holding hands when we arrived, but we were close enough that we could have. Standing outside the classroom with Brador, Gretchen raised an eyebrow, which was so wrong. She'd sent Cael to "guard" me. What did she expect? She and I were going to talk later.

"What took so long?" Brador asked.

Prior to the demon attack, Brador and I had barely spoken. He had "no use for pampered privileged mages" and considered me one of the worst. I didn't like people who judged me without knowing me first. We'd agreed to ignore each other.

Then Declan released a demon in Haeger Hall. We weren't friends, and he still saw me as privileged, but we'd been cordial after that day.

"I needed to clean up first."

Brador glared at me; I ignored him.

Too bad if he disagreed. Magic required focus and every mage had their own way of achieving optimal efficiency. A demon glyph was complex magic, and I planned to be comfortable before I tackled the task.

I stepped around him with Cael on my heels. The magic I'd placed on his window called out to me. Had I unwittingly activated this glyph when I enchanted the glass? I'd check that later.

An area near the back wall had been cleared of desks and chairs. I picked my way through the remaining furniture and stopped just inside the open space. The glyph was nothing like the original one. It was smaller and more compact. The summoning Declan had created had been complex, but this one made his look like a child's drawing.

"Can you raise the wards around this room?" I asked Cael. My calm tone masked my fear. Turning, I met his gaze. "Set them to implode inward if I'm killed."

"Are you crazy?" Brador asked.

I ignored him. Cael looked stunned and had a healthy amount of fear, but I didn't see panic. Excellent, because given what we were about to do, he couldn't freak out. I shifted my attention to the others in the room.

"Mr. Brador, please take my aunt and wait outside the door."

I didn't have the authority to order him to leave, but Aunt Gretch did. She and I locked eyes and she understood. Brador, however, didn't like being told what to do, especially by me.

"I'm the head of security, Hollen," he said, his voice a deep growl. "I don't take orders from you."

"Which Hollen were you addressing?" Aunt Gretch said in her scary-as-fuck voice. "We *are* going to step outside."

"Hold on." He held up his hands and moved away from the door. "I'm not leaving without understanding more."

I had to give Brador his props. He wasn't afraid to do his job his way. "Cael? Can you raise them now please?"

Cael pulled out his stone. Before Brador could object, the stone pulsed once, and he nodded. "Done. Why did I do that?"

The trust Cael showed me might get us both killed, but it's what I needed at that moment. This was far more dangerous than the one Declan created months ago. One wrong move and we might unleash something that would kill scores of people before it was subdued.

Brador opened his mouth, but I spoke first. "Hold that

thought, Mr. Brador. I want to bring Avie into the conversation before I explain."

When cell phones were developed, communicating through power stones had gone out of practice within the mage community, but not within my family. Phones could be hacked, and people could hear your side of the conversation. Stones also let you share more than just your voice or image.

I formed Avie's image in my mind and pushed out. A second later, she joined me.

"Bartholomew? What's wrong?"

Of course she knew this wasn't a social call. *"Hey Avie, give me a second to bring the others into our conversation."*

"Others?" she asked tersely. *"Who?"*

"Hang on." I knew she didn't like it, but I didn't have time to explain everything two or three times. I pushed invitations to Cael, Aunt Gretchen, and Brador. *"Avie? Aunt Gretch, Anton Brador, head of security, and Caelinus Reinhold, the new creative magic professor are with us. We're in Declan's old classroom. There was a second glyph."*

That silenced any objection to my adding people to the conversation without her approval. My sister was the most competent mage I knew—not the most powerful, but easily one of the deadliest.

"Impossible." She wasn't skeptical—she knew me too well for that—but she was angry. *"I put my best team on this. They scrubbed every erg of magic from that spot. Someone must have created a new one."*

"There have been no dark magic events on campus since Professor Hollen stopped the demon," Brador said.

"We didn't miss anything," Avie said. *"I personally checked their work. The spot was barren."*

"And yet," he said. "One is reforming in the same room as the original."

I should have seen this coming. If Brador didn't like me, he liked Avie less. In his mind, she was the epitome of the nepotism that created the two-class mage society. He was partly right.

Nepotism was a cancer needing to be corrected, but Avie was the most qualified person to lead the inquisitors. She was powerful, stayed calm, processed the facts, and made the right decision better than anyone I knew.

"Can everyone pull back their horns and let me speak?" I let my annoyance flow through the link. *"I want to examine the spot, but first I need to know what methods your team employed. I don't want to trigger a kill switch."*

"The team utilized the standard procedure for removing black magic symbols," Avie said. *"After dissolving the magic, they scrubbed the area of any residual energy. They left nothing behind."*

Avie and her team leaving behind even a minute speck of dark magic seemed unlikely. They knew the dangers of being careless, especially in a classroom full of mage students. Either someone put a new symbol on the stone—an equally dubious proposition—or there was something unique about this.

"Wards up, everyone. I'm going to probe the area." I didn't give anyone the chance to stop me. Connected as we were, Avie could see everything I observed. *"No sudden or loud interruptions, please."*

"I know how to do my job, little brother." She only called me that when I'd gotten under her skin.

"If I felt otherwise, I wouldn't have invited you to join me." My response was for the others. Avie knew I trusted her implicitly.

I knelt at the edge of the visible symbols. They were tightly drawn and held more magic than was typical for their size. The power was also incredibly restrained. Given how close the lines were to each other, they couldn't leak power or the entire casting would fail.

"I've never seen anything like this before. Do you see how it's only partially formed? It's like . . ."

"Like what, Bartholomew?"

I ignored her and narrowed my probe. The silence lingered until I saw something that helped me understand the sigil in front of me. "Whoever created this crammed the same magic the larger glyph used into smaller lines."

"But how did it get here?" Brador's bravado was gone. He understood this wasn't a childish prank.

"I'm not sure, but whoever did this, it was here when Declan raised the demon."

Avie sighed and I braced myself for her rebuke. "Bart. We've been over this. No one controlled Declan. No one else was working with him. You need to let go of this idea he isn't to blame."

"And you need to stop thinking like I'm a love-struck tween and start looking at this objectively." I felt the others gasp, but I'd lost patience with everyone sticking their head in the sand. "There is no way Declan did this. He wasn't capable of this kind of magic. And don't give me that crap about I'm too close. I was never in love with him, and my judgment isn't clouded. I'm telling you, there's someone else involved. Someone way more dangerous than Declan. And because you can't get past whatever mental block you have, they're free to plan their next attempt to breach the Great Ward."

The silence that met my outburst lingered. Avie wasn't bleeding into the link, but she was angry. No one challenged her like I had. Too bad. I didn't work for her, and she wasn't Chancellor of the Mage Council—yet.

"Before you write off my opinion again, let me show you what I found."

"Fine," she said tersely.

Avie was going to chew my ass off for yelling at her in public, but after I proved I was right, she'd better be prepared to get the same from me. First, however, I needed to deal with this threat.

"Look at the edges. It's like soil eroding, exposing a fossil below." I tried to point to the areas without touching them. "The stone isn't even, but the difference is so small that you'd need to get down to the microscopic level to see it. There's no power source, at least not yet, and it's not fully charged."

"If there's no power source how did it activate?" Gretchen asked.

"I'll need to dig deeper for that answer, but clearly it had some power. The glyph started to eat its way through but ran out of steam before it reached its goal."

"Is it possible to lay one glyph on top of another one?" Cael asked.

I felt Brador scoff, but Cael believed me. Hopefully, the others didn't feel the warm glow that spread through me.

"Not that I'm aware, but that's not what we have exactly. Somehow, they drew this one, buried it under stone, and then etched the second one over the first. It's like a layer cake."

Avie snorted. "Leave it to you to bring in baking, but the analogy helps. How did you suss that out?"

She didn't want me telling her how to investigate a case, but this was my area of expertise, and she respected my opinions. This was so advanced maybe four people in the world could draw it. Declan wasn't one of them.

"This spell was inactive until today, so it can't be the one that summoned the demon. And it's not fully revealed. My guess is when your inquisitors scrubbed away the glyph we could see, they rubbed away some 'icing' separating the two layers."

"Assume you're correct," Aunt Gretchen said. "Why is it showing up only now?"

"I don't know for sure, but I suspect it's been slowly building up energy since last spring." I paused but no one jumped in. "Cael said one of his students felt weird. It probably reached a tipping point today and started pulling energy from her. Once it made the connection, it started to pull in more until she moved."

"That's . . ." Brador stared at me with an expression I couldn't read. "Can you prove it?"

Surprisingly, it wasn't a challenge, but he wasn't sure, either. It didn't faze me. My whole life, people who couldn't do something I could had doubted my skill. This, at least, was respectful.

"Probably, but I'd rather not. If I feed it energy and it tries to draw more, then I'm right. It also might bring it to life, and we'll have to face the demon it summons."

"Bartholomew, you are not to try that," Avie said. "Can you remove it, or do you need me to send someone to help you?"

No one on her staff could handle this. Her "offer" was payback. She let everyone know who was in charge. "I can, but I'll need help."

I turned to face Cael. He seemed surprised, but he nodded quickly.

"What can I do?"

"Whoa," Brador said. "Stand down. This isn't something you rush into."

"On the contrary, Mr. Brador," Avie said. "If there's an active or potentially active portal in the school, its removal is an extreme priority."

"Fine. I'll put together a team and we'll take it down."

The man wouldn't cede an inch. There was no one on *his* team, either, who was qualified to remove a partial active sigil, but he'd be damned if he let the Hollens tell him what to do.

"Bartholomew is the most qualified person to do this. More than you or me or any of my inquisitors," Avie said. "I thought you'd learned that by now."

"He might be an expert on this, but he isn't a trained inquisitor," Brador said. "And Professor Reinhold has been here less than a month. We have no idea if he can handle this."

Brador looked at Aunt Gretchen who gave me a hard look. "Are you sure about this?"

And this is where shit got real. I was sure I needed to do it, but that wasn't what she wanted to know. Brador was right about Cael being green, but experience wasn't what I needed.

"I need someone I trust . . . who I'm close enough to that we can work together seamlessly right away." I snuck a glance at Cael. His expression was neutral. "And who's strong enough to maintain his defenses if this goes sideways."

Cael's brow furrowed. "What does that mean?"

"He means if it blows up in his face," Brador answered for me. "He'll be dead, but he wants to be sure you're able to defend yourself."

Cael's gaze bore into me. He wanted me to rebut what he'd heard, but I couldn't. This could go wrong so many ways I couldn't dwell on them. But the odds were in my favor. *"I'm the most qualified person to do this. So long as you maintain your wards at full strength, you'll survive."*

"But you won't."

My body tingled at his concern. It chipped away another layer around my heart. His feelings also made him the best person for the job, inexperienced or not. I swept my defenses aside and let him see all of me.

"I need to be able to connect to the spell. I can't do that if I don't let my defenses down. I wouldn't ask you to do this if I didn't think you could do it. We have a connection, which will make it easier to work as one."

Gretchen could explain to Avie and Brador if they hadn't figured it out already. I locked eyes with Cael and let him see the strength of my conviction. When he finally blinked, he nodded.

"Tell me what to do."

Chapter Thirteen

❦

CAELINUS

My heart thumped from more than fear. Bart had let his walls down and I saw clearly what I'd only caught glimpses of before. He admitted his feelings for me in front of the others, and then let me see the depth of them.

I also knew he would attempt to remove the glyph with or without me. He should pick Gretchen to help him, but he'd ask Brador. The tension between them, however, would weaken their collaboration, putting Bart's life at risk.

"I need to siphon off the energy to dissolve the spell. As I free it, you contain it so we can destroy the black magic. I'll create the vessel, but you need to make sure it all goes inside. There can't be any spillage."

What he described wasn't complex, but it required focus and strength. Keeping my gaze fixed on him, I confronted the elephant in the room. *"What could go wrong?"*

He watched me with his beautiful blue eyes. When I first met him, they sparkled with life. Since that day, they've been guarded and wary. As we stared at each other, I saw his conflict. He didn't want to lie, but he didn't want to burden me with the truth.

"You trust me to have your back. Trust me enough to tell me what I'm facing."

Bart's smile unlocked his spirit. It didn't free him from doubt, but he'd resolved some inner conflict. *"You're right. Whoever set this probably anticipated it might be discovered and they'll have built in a failsafe. If it were me, I'd include an element that would activate the spell if anyone tried to remove it. I can compensate for that possibility and others, but only to a point. There's no way I can anticipate every conceivable threat. In theory, my precautions should protect me, but it's not a guarantee.*

"There is also going to be feedback when the spell unravels, which can happen at any time. Again, I can take steps to protect myself, but I can't predict every outcome."

A rush of giddy energy joined the adrenaline that whooshed through me. It was a mix of pride, admiration, and concern. This was Bart at his core. He placed everyone ahead of himself. But this time, he was the right person to take the lead.

"Thank you for trusting me."

He sobered. *"There's more. I'm not sure if it's possible, but if the glyph goes live, we're going to have an angry visitor. The room's wards need to implode inward. If we can't make it out, neither can the demon. The Great Ward is still working, and we compensated for the last breach, so it probably won't work, but it's still dangerous. If it can't open a portal the energy needs to go somewhere."*

The bucket of ice water doused my euphoria. Brador was right. I preened like a fourteen-year-old who learned their crush liked them back when I might be dead in a minute.

"Understood."

The shrewd, probing eyes were back. His tongue appeared between his lips, and he nodded once.

"Avie, I need to clear the link. Connect with Aunt Gretch."

"Be careful, Bart. You're my favorite brother by a lot. I can't replace you."

After the tense exchange a minute ago, her admission spoke to how close they were. In a lot of ways they were similar, but Bart lacked her hard edge. She needed it, but he didn't.

"I love you, too, Avie. I promise I'll take every precaution I can."

The link went silent, and I missed the closeness with Bart. He squeezed my shoulder as he walked past me and stopped in front of Brador. "You and Aunt Gretch need to leave. One way or the other, we'll neutralize this threat."

Brador's aggressive posture had softened. He was still alert, but he didn't project the hostility to Bart he'd had when they first spoke. "Are you sure we shouldn't wait?"

"Yes. This is like malware that hides in a computer hard drive until it's triggered. Once that happens, you need to take aggressive action to contain it fast. I promise to take every precaution. I don't have a death wish, and I don't want any harm to come to Professor Reinhold."

Stupid as it was, a warmth spread through me. Gretchen leaned in and hugged Bart.

"Be very careful, dear. You're special to me and a lot of people. We want you alive." She kissed Bart's cheek, motioned to Brador, and exited the room.

"Is there anything I can do to help?" Brador asked.

"Pray I don't trigger the spell?"

"Do you really think that will happen?"

Bart breathed in deeply and I anxiously awaited the answer.

"It's possible, but highly unlikely. The Great Ward should prevent it from working, and I couldn't find a power source. If I wall off my work from the passive collection part of the spell, it won't be able to feed. The biggest risk is it explodes."

"That's . . . incredible. I can't fathom creating such a spell."

"Even before the Great Ward, raising a demon with the requisite containment was extremely difficult. These spells are unbelievably complex. Whoever did this is brilliant."

Brador raised an eyebrow and I wished I could see Bart's face. "Then I'm glad we have the even more brilliant Bartholomew

Hollen on our side." He held out his hand and they shook before Brador turned and joined Gretchen.

When the door shut and it was just us, the seriousness of what I'd gotten into hit me. Any slip-up and Bart could trigger the spell. He hadn't said it, but if that happened Bart didn't expect to survive. That left me to face whatever appeared. Nothing like a live action test of your theoretic skills.

Bart turned and smiled assuredly. If he lacked confidence, it didn't show. "Ready to clean your classroom?"

We were about to risk death to destroy a half-functioning glyph, but all my brain focused on was the man staring at me. He cared for everyone else but didn't let anyone tend to his needs. I wanted to be that person.

To do that, I needed us both to leave this room alive.

"Can you explain exactly what we're going to do?"

Squatting, he pointed to the exposed edge of the symbol. "I'm going to enter here and erase the symbol. Before I do that, I'm going to check again for any hidden booby traps in the part we can see. I didn't find anything in my first exam, but I believe there is something."

Bart's handsome face drew me to him at first, but it was his brilliant mind that made my knees weak. Our lunch conversations revealed a thirst for learning, and a dedication to teaching. He saw things few others did when it came to magic. Avie had been right. No one else could handle this.

"What if what you saw is all there is? If they didn't expect us to find this until it was too late, they wouldn't bother with tricks. Too many layers would make it harder to conceal the whole thing."

His eyes lost their focus. A second later he nodded. "You're right. In which case I risk setting it off because it ends up pulling energy from me."

It pleased me more than it should have that he considered my advice. I hadn't figured out what it was, or how to remove it, but he still thought my opinion had value. Before I could respond, Bart stood and put his hand on my chest.

"That brings up something we need to discuss. If I tell you to leave, you go. No questions or debate."

"No."

"Cael, I'm serious." His fingers pressed against me. "If it comes to that, I've screwed up and I'm dead already. I'll contain things long enough for you to leave, but you have to go."

It gave me chills how easily he talked about dying trying to save everyone. He saw his death as a serious possibility but didn't shy away from trying. Instead, he made plans so the rest of us made it out alive.

I shook my head. "I'm not agreeing to that. I won't leave you to die without trying to help."

"You won't be able to help me. I give you my word, I won't tell you to flee unless I'm certain it's too late. Which means you have to get out fast." He laid his hand on my face. "Please. I strongly believe it won't come to that, but if it does, you have to listen to me."

I couldn't believe he expected me to run away like a frightened rabbit. Despite what Brador said, I wasn't a first-year novice mage in training. I had power and talent and could protect Bart.

"How about you focus on getting out alive and we stop talking about when and why I might have to leave you to die."

Bart's shoulders sagged and he exhaled. "Obviously I can't make you, but if I'd known you weren't going to listen, I'd have taken my chances with Brador instead of you."

"Hold on." I pointed an angry finger at him. "This isn't about me or you. It's bigger than that. We're the right pair for this job. Either we're a team to the end or we leave and let someone else handle this."

Bart's lips were pressed so tight they were thin slits of red. His eyes had the glassy look of someone thinking. Finally, he drew a deep breath. "All in or not in at all."

That applied to a lot of things with us. "Exactly. So, which is it?"

His loopy grin returned. "Let's do this."

※

We went over the details for a few minutes, and I had an even deeper admiration for Bart. He'd not only dissected the problem and devised a solution in minutes, but he also broke it down for me into small bites—what he expected to find, how he'd handle it, where he needed help, and how I could best support him. It made sense the Deputy Inquisitor General assigned this to her brother. He was beyond brilliant.

Not that I wasn't biased. In the crazy, screwed-up world only I lived in, I thought of us as a thing. He'd publicly announced he trusted me, that we have a connection. Why do that if he didn't see us as a good match?

I wasn't blind to his inner conflict. Mom would know exactly what he felt, but I was a living mood ring. I could sense basic emotions, but nothing more detailed. To understand Bart, I required Mom's skills.

Bart grinned when I suggested we use the trash can to create the containment vessel. I picked it because I didn't care if it was destroyed in the process. He wove the cleansing spell into the pail, and I reinforced it so nothing could spill out.

Bart knelt and settled back on his heels. His tourmaline stone pulsed purple, and he wrapped his fingers around it. My gem glowed a deeper shade of blue, confirming we were linked. I didn't like that I sat behind full shields, and he had none.

Non-mages couldn't see our defenses and didn't understand how vulnerable we felt without them. Tackling this unshielded was like attacking a grizzly bear with a toothpick and a water gun.

A slim shaft of light dropped from his palm to the ground. The ebony lines sizzled at the touch of the purple beam and disappeared. Energy flowed into the containment vessel, where it was cleansed and released.

The process took more time than I expected, but Bart worked methodically. I got it. He didn't want to leave any trace behind, and these lines were crammed with power.

Bart paused after he cleared the south-east quadrant and our link turned anxious. The stream of light remained fixed in the same place and his jaw tightened. He frowned and took shallow, quick breaths.

From the moment a mage gets their first lesson, it's drummed into our heads: Never interrupt someone performing complex magic. The work Bart was doing could kill us both if I didn't follow that rule, but the desire to help him threatened my willpower. The seconds dragged on and beads of sweat dotted his forehead. Whatever happened, Bart hadn't panicked, but he pushed himself to do . . . something.

The light intensified and a second later a jolt coursed through my stone. Bart grunted, followed by a burst of light and a popping sound that knocked him back on his ass. I forgot the admonishment to stay behind my shield and lunged forward.

"Are you okay?"

Bart puffed out air and lowered his stone. "Fuck, I'm tired."

A giddy laugh burst from my lips, and I dropped next to him. "Is everything . . .?"

"It's gone." He breathed deeply and exhaled again. "Let the others in. I'll call Avie and brief everyone at once."

※

"*So it was a trap?*" Brador asked.

I'd liked Brador from the first day, but if he asked every question four times, I was going to Kirk out. He had to see how drained the procedure left Bart.

"*No.*" Bart rubbed his temples. "*A trap requires you lure an unsus-*

pecting person into something nefarious so you can do whatever you plan. The spell itself was nefarious."

Brador crossed his arms and sat back. *"You're being pedantic."*

"I'm not. The distinction is important." Closing his eyes, Bart pinched the bridge of his nose. *"I don't believe we were supposed to find it, and certainly not the way we did. The inquisitors ended up unbalancing the spell. When it found its victim, parts of the glyph were uncovered before others. That disrupted things.*

"I couldn't determine everything it was supposed to do or how, but I saw enough. Like I suspected, it was designed to find a victim, hold that person in place until it was fully powered, and then activate."

"Great Guardians," Gretchen said, touching her heart.

"Exactly." Bart opened his eyes. *"Had it worked, it would have immobilized the victim for the demon to consume. The creature would be fully powered before anyone could mount a credible defense. Fortunately, it wouldn't have pierced the Ward even if it was activated. Not now anyway."*

"Why do you say that?" Avie's question reminded me she was with us.

"This glyph wasn't created to breach the Ward. It was meant to work in tandem with the one Declan used to open a portal. If I had to guess, this needed to be used while the portal Declan created was open. This glyph would immobilize the demon Declan summoned—or Declan if he'd bested the demon—and use their energy to open another portal. Possibly a permanent anchor to our world."

We all kept quiet trying to digest what Bart had just told us. It was insidious, yet brilliant. I'd been incredibly lucky. But for a botched removal, the spell would have exploded in my classroom. Even if I survived, I couldn't have saved the students closest to the glyph. I shoved those thoughts aside to ask what I still wanted to know.

"Before it disintegrated, you were struggling," I said. *"If there were no traps, what happened?"*

He smiled at me, and it went straight to my balls. *"We were both partially right. They didn't expect us to find the spell, but once the spell degraded beyond a certain point, it had instructions to implode. Kind of like demolishing a building. Blow up the right supports and the building collapses.*

"*I almost didn't notice the cascading effect until it was too late. As it was, I barely managed to siphon off enough energy through our gems to reduce it to the pop and flash you saw.*"

He yawned long and loud, and then grabbed his drink.

"*I think that's enough,*" I said. I didn't care if I hovered like a protective mother. We didn't need to be lovers for me to care. "*Bart's exhausted. Instead of peppering him with more questions, we should let him get some rest.*"

"*I'm fine.*" Bart lazily waved his hand.

"*No, you're not,*" Gretchen said. "*You're going home to rest.*"

"*I don't—*"

She cut him off with a flick of her hand. "*Did that sound like a suggestion? You're already approved to be off tomorrow, so I don't want you back in the building until Monday.*"

"*But—*"

"*Professor Reinhold,*"—she turned her back on Bart—"*could I impose on you to drive my nephew home? He only lives ten minutes away.*"

"*Uh . . .*" I didn't want to sound too eager, but this was a gift I never expected. "*Sure.*"

"*Aunt Gretch, that's silly.*" Bart's protest lacked conviction. He sounded exhausted.

"*No, it's serious. And don't think you can sneak back into your office and hide there until Monday. Once you leave, Mr. Brador is going to reprogram your badge to alert him and me if you set foot on campus. I'll not have a repeat of you living in your office for thirty-six hours to avoid being detected, not eating properly, and nearly passing out in class.*"

Bart huffed and I couldn't hold back a snicker. "*I did that once to finish important research.*"

"*Once was too many times. Your sister threatened to have me investigated for abuse of professors.*"

"This time I'll charge him with violating university rules." Avie said it way too eagerly, if you asked me.

"You can't charge me with that." Bart rolled his eyes, not that his sister could see it.

"Do you want to bet?"

"Why are you fighting me?" Gretchen asked. *"You requested tomorrow off. Would you prefer I asked Mr. Brador to escort you home? Is that what this is about?"*

Brador swallowed a snort but didn't hide his amusement. I, however, didn't laugh. Was that the real reason Bart was fighting her? Was he opposed to me taking him home?

"No, it's not and you know it. I . . ." He snuck a glance at me, and his mood changed. *"Fine. Cael can drive me home, and you won't see me until Monday."*

"Excellent. I'm glad you didn't make me call your grandmother to talk sense into you."

"Whatever." He sounded like a petulant teenager.

Avie laughed first, followed by Gretchen and soon we were all snickering except Bart. My laugh had nothing to do with his antics. I got to take Bart home. That made the whole ordeal worth the scare.

Bart glared at me, but I tilted my head and raised my hands. A thin smile broke through the sour expression and finally he laughed, too.

"Good." Gretchen stood and looked at me. *"If he gives you any trouble, call me. I'll set him straight."*

"I'm so not straight, Auntie."

She rolled her eyes. *"So I'm told. As for you, Professor Reinhold, I don't want you back until Monday either. Your classroom is once again a crime scene. My niece is going to send a small army of inquisitors to rip the entire room apart before they let students back in here."*

She left before I could answer. Gretchen wasn't even trying to be subtle. The question I had was, why?

The link went dead, and Bart pocketed his stone. Brador

looked at me and Bart, smirked and shook his head. I thought he'd follow Gretchen, but he walked over to Bart.

"I owe you about a hundred apologies, Professor Hollen. Not just for today, either. I judged you based on the arrogant, self-important stuffed shirts who'd come through the school. Not one of them would have risked their lives to save everyone else."

Bart looked exhausted, but he managed a thin smile before he extended his hand. "Thank you. I'm glad I finally earned your respect. It means a lot to me."

Brador shook hands, nodded to me, and left.

Chapter Fourteen

❧

BARTHOLOMEW

Stuffing my laptop into my bag, I double-checked my office for things I'd need on my impromptu three-day exile. Aunt Gretchen banning me was unexpected but not completely unreasonable. Avie *was* going to flood the campus with inquisitors searching for any other time bombs left behind. If I was around, I'd end up elbows deep in the pursuit. This way, if Avie needed me, I was a ten-minute walk away.

Aunt Gretch playing matchmaker, however, scrambled my brain. So much for being discreet. Even Brador scoffed when Gretchen suggested he walk me home instead of Cael.

Not that I was ashamed if people thought I liked Cael. He was the most perfect being I'd ever met. If this went tits up, however—and it certainly could—we had to work together, for fuck's sake. I could've taken the out Aunt Gretch gave me and let Brador escort me home, but I wanted it to be Cael.

"Ready?"

I turned and my insides went to mush. Cael leaned against the doorframe. *That* was why I didn't want Brador. It sent chills down my back, across my arms, and up my neck. My brain screamed this was a mistake.

I ignored my brain. "Yep. All set. Since you live close to campus, I assume you don't own a car."

"Nope, but I have a license." He shrugged off the wall. "I can drive."

My first thought was I knew how well he *drove*, and I wouldn't mind doing *that* again. Of all the people Utrecht could hire, it had to be him? My relationship with Declan nearly unleashed a demon onto campus and now I lusted after his replacement. If my wards weren't working, I'd worry someone had hexed me to fall for the creative magic professor.

The depth of my feelings for the two were worlds apart. I'd liked Declan, and we'd had good times, in and out of bed, but he didn't consume my thoughts like Cael. When it ended, I was mildly disappointed, but I moved on quickly.

Cael, on the other hand, occupied too much of my free time. That fresh air glyph alone had taken hours of research and several tests over most of a week to get right. I memorized every stray comment he made to find ways to incorporate things he liked into our routine. Knowing I did something to make him happy had become almost addictive.

I realized Cael watched me, waiting for an answer. My cheeks flushed, and I was glad he couldn't read my thoughts.

"I took a Lyft today." I slipped the bag over my shoulder. "I didn't want to park in the lot and carry all the food. I'll hire us a ride."

"I can do that." He pulled out his phone, but I put my hand over it and pushed it down gently.

"No, you're not spending your money because my aunt has lost her mind and thinks I'll die on the way home." I tugged my phone from my pocket. "I'll take care of it."

"In fairness to your aunt, you looked pretty spent when we

were talking." He winked and my hands shook so much, I couldn't open the app.

I looked into his hazel eyes and wanted to shut my door, press him against it, and kiss him until we both came. Blinking those thoughts away, I focused on my screen.

"That's because I was tired." I punched in the details and waited longer than necessary to confirm it went through. "We should wait out front."

※

I thanked the driver and hooked my messenger bag over my shoulder. Cael stood beside the stone columns on either side of the driveway and peered across the lawn at the house.

"This is really nice."

Wealth didn't impress Cael. Old wealth, like my family's, impressed him even less. I might be biased, but my house was the perfect balance of nice, but not ostentatious. I'd loved it immediately.

"Thank you." I gestured toward my house. "Would you like to stay for dinner?"

"I don't want to impose."

Cael had been clear what he wanted since his first day at Utrecht. I wasn't stupid. Inept maybe, but not clueless. If he didn't want to stay, he'd have said no and made up a reason why he couldn't.

"Since it's not a bother, that's a yes to dinner. I need to see what I have ready to cook."

"Hold on." He grabbed my arm. "Gretchen said you needed to relax. If I'm staying, I'm ordering takeout."

The warmth from his hand seeped through my shirt. His touch sent waves of pleasure through me, and it was hard to focus. It was silly. We'd been naked and intimate—*very* intimate. Why did this tiny contact have such an outsized effect?

I blinked to collect my thoughts.

"Over my dead body," I said with a laugh. "First, Aunt Gretch doesn't run my life. I'm an adult, I'm not on campus, and I'm off the clock. I'm free to do what I like. Second, and more to the point, I won't overexert myself. I just need to put something in the oven."

His face was calling bullshit, but he let go and followed me up the path. "You should probably let me order something. If you run out of steam midway through cooking, I'll burn it, overcook it, or find a way to make it inedible."

I peered over my left shoulder and smirked. As arguments went, his sucked, but the self-deprecating humor was cute. On him at least. I'd probably find most anything he did cute, but I ignored that thought. "Let's live dangerously and risk it."

Unlocking the door, I toed out of my shoes, put my bag on the antique hall tree, and hung my keys on a hook. Cael followed my example and slipped off his shoes before I asked. I pointed to the dark brown wooden bench and he deposited his backpack next to my bag.

Cael slowly swept his gaze around the foyer. He ran a finger over an ornate newel post and stared as if looking below the surface. A second later, he turned toward me, smiling.

"Most of the details are original," he said approvingly.

I grinned like he'd said my child was beautiful. He saw things most people missed. Nodding, I pointed toward the kitchen. "Yes. The previous owners preserved as much as possible. Some things, like the kitchen and central air, needed to be changed out, but just about everything is original. Anything I needed to replace, I got from an architectural antique salvage store to keep things as close to original as possible."

The ultra-modern kitchen with rich, golden granite and commercial grade appliances was my one real indulgence. I'd hired Marta Duvall, one of Philadelphia's best architects, to design the room. My instructions were to create a dream kitchen but preserve the old house décor. The results surpassed my expectations.

"Holy shit!" Cael obviously appreciated it, too. "This is fantastic."

Marta had found the original plans, researched period flooring and cabinetry, and then hired old world artisans to custom design everything. Even the top-of-the-line appliances looked original. It had been a vanity project, costing five times more than a typical high-end remodel.

"Thanks." I pulled open the double doors of my freezer and pointed. "We had the eggplant parm for lunch, so lemon chicken, sole almondine, crab cakes, meatloaf, or pasta. I have veggies in the fridge that are cleaned, cut, and ready to cook, but okay, you got me, I'll need to make pasta or rice."

Cael peered into my mostly full freezer. "How in the world do you do all this?"

Baking had already been my stress release, but too many sweets made me jittery. Rather than risk a permanent twitch, I used my free time on the weekends to prepare meals for the week. Judging by how full my freezer was, I might have overdone it.

"I do it on weekends, so I don't have to bother during the week. If I'm craving something specific, I'll cook after work, but that's rare."

"This is incredible. I've always found it hard to cook for just me. Making bigger lots and freezing them is smart." He ran his fingers over the shelf holding the meals. "Of course, I'd need a bigger freezer if I tried your approach."

His admiration was misplaced. I didn't try to cook small. Instead, I made triple and quadruple what I needed and stored the rest in the bigger walk-in freezer in the basement. Friday afternoon, the local homeless shelter came and collected my excess.

"It's still a work in progress." To change the topic, I channeled my inner TV game show presenter and waved my hand into the cool air. "Anything in particular you fancy? If nothing appeals, we can get takeout."

He licked his lips. "I loved the sauce on the eggplant. How about pasta?"

"We have a winner." I pulled the marinara from the shelf and shut the doors. From the fridge, I took arugula and fixings for a salad.

"Can I help?" Cael asked. "I'm not you, but I'm not hopeless."

"Normally, I'd say no and make you sit, but truth? I'm exhausted." I removed the pots from a cabinet. It wasn't an exaggeration, either. If Cael hadn't come over, I'd have made a sandwich and gone to bed. "Would you like a drink? I have some excellent white wine, there's beer, water, I think some lemonade, and a couple of the wretched diet sodas Aunt Gretch drinks."

He put his fingers to his chin. "The way you talk up those diet sodas is tempting, but I'll go with the wine."

Images of us sitting quietly together, sipping our drinks, flooded my brain. We weren't going to do that tonight, but it was still a compelling idea.

"An excellent choice." Smiling like a fool, I pulled down a long-stemmed white wine glass, set it on the granite counter, and shut the cabinet door.

"Aren't you having any?" he asked.

I couldn't tell what he was feeling. My heart wanted it to be disappointment that I wasn't going to join him. The truth was probably a lot closer to self-consciousness about drinking alone in my house.

"Do you want to test your cooking skills when I pass out?" I stifled a yawn.

Retrieving the bottle from the chiller, I poured him a generous glass. I handed him his drink, and then retrieved a second glass. The tiny amount I poured myself was barely a swallow, but I could say I didn't make my guest drink alone.

Cael eyed my hand and laughed. "Is that even worth it?"

It wasn't really, but I wanted to be polite. "It's enough to toast you with. I'll have some with dinner. If I fall asleep after we eat, it won't be quite as rude."

"What are we toasting?" He raised an eyebrow suggestively.

I wanted to say us, but there wasn't an us. There might never be if I correctly interpreted my dream. I shouldn't encourage him any more than I already had, but I didn't want him to leave. I liked the sound of his voice, the failed attempts at not flirting, and the way he watched me as I worked. It was like rubbernecking a car wreck on the Schuylkill Expressway; I shouldn't do it, but I couldn't help myself.

I raised my glass, and he did the same. "To you, for all the help you gave me today."

"To us and a job well done." He lifted his glass a tiny bit higher. "We make a great team."

Cael went for the "us" I'd avoided. It was my fault. I'd given him hope for more, and he wasn't giving it back.

I pressed the glass to my lips to cover my conflicting thoughts. Savoring my one swallow, I watched him take a tentative sip. His eyebrows went up and he returned for a real taste.

"It's good, isn't it?"

"The best I can remember having." He punctuated that with another drink.

I held up a finger and disappeared around the corner. Taking another bottle of the same vintage from my wine rack, I paused. With anyone else, I wouldn't have thought twice, and I hated that I had to scrutinize every action I took with Cael. Squeezing the bottle tighter, I brushed aside my doubt. It's what I'd have done if we were just friends.

Cael watched me over the rim of his glass. I set the bottle on the counter close to him. "Take this one home with you. Consider it a belated housewarming gift."

"You don't need to do that." He twisted the bottle so he could read the label.

"I want to. You can enjoy it one night and remember how we saved the school and probably thousands of lives today."

"Thank you, Bart. This is very kind of you."

It wasn't thoughtful at all. If anything, grabbing a bottle from my wine rack and calling it a gift bordered on insulting. Cael, however, appreciated the gesture so years of etiquette lessons kicked in before I said the wrong thing. "You're welcome. I hope you enjoy it."

"I'm sure we will." He winked, set the bottle down, and retrieved his glass.

The naked desire in the way he watched me made me fidgety. He'd never hidden it. I'd explained why I couldn't give him what he—and I—wanted, but that didn't stop me from wanting him.

"Can I show you the rest of the house?"

"I'd like that."

CAELINUS

A buzzer went off, and Bart excused himself to check on dinner. I continued to snoop, as I had the entire tour. Bart didn't seem to mind; he usually commented on things I touched. He liked sturdy, old furniture and favored dark woods and soothing earth tones and realist art.

Bart collected ancient weapons, diecast cars, old books, and my favorite—comic books. I could have sat in his library sifting through his collection to find a couple hundred to read. We were two weeks apart in age, and the man had furnished an entire house with things that weren't easy to buy. The comics and cars he might have started as a child, but the art and the weapons were things he'd spent his adult years buying.

I could never invite him to my apartment. We'd have to sit at the table I ordered online, eat using plates and utensils I bought at Target, and relax on furniture I found at IKEA.

Putting a comic book back in its plastic sleeve, I stood still for a moment. I projected my insecurities onto him. He wouldn't care one bit that my stuff wasn't as old or expensive as his. In fact, he'd find a way to compliment me and mean what he said.

Smiling, I left the study and wandered into a music room. In the center of the back wall was a black Steingraeber & Söhne upright grand piano. I'd never heard of the maker, but it was magnificent. To the left was an upright bass. A violin and guitar were on the right.

I stopped in front of one of the dozen or so pictures on the wall. Five young men, dressed in black and white, held their instruments and smiled for the camera. Bart was on the left, holding the tall bass.

"Connor, the one holding the banjo, had us try out for a talent show," Bart said. "We did well enough that they asked us to play other shows."

I returned my gaze to the pictures. Bart smiled like he owned the world. I tried to imagine a slightly younger Bart playing blue grass and folk music in front of a crowd, and surprisingly, I saw it clearly.

"Do you still play together?" Because if he did, I wanted to come see him.

"No. Connor moved to New York after we graduated. He was the glue that kept this alive. Without him, we lost our heart and withered away."

The sense of loss thrummed from his choice of words. This had been important to him. From what I'd seen so far, Bart didn't like fleeting things. He made close friends, established roots, and committed to things long term. His friend leaving had stabbed him in the heart.

"Did you collect everyone's instruments and store them for a reunion tour?"

He smiled fondly and shook his head. "No reunion tours, but I keep them in case we ever get together and want to play again. How about you? Do you play anything?"

"Violin, but before you ask me to play, the answer is no. I haven't played in four years. I'm not playing for anyone until I get more practice." I definitely wasn't playing for Bart on the fly. "You have an upright bass in almost every picture. Was that your favorite?"

"Not really. I like piano best, but no one else wanted to learn the upright. A band needs a bass player, so I took it up. Once I learned, I found I liked it." He aimed his thumb over his shoulder. "I need to finish getting dinner ready. Feel free to keep snooping."

He smiled, and it was the most relaxed he'd been around me since . . . since we hooked up. This was the real Bart, and I wanted to see this side every day.

"I most definitely do not snoop. That would entail a lack of invitation. This is called admiring your furnishings."

He laughed, but it sounded tired. "I'm glad you cleared that up for me. Carry on admiring."

Much as I wanted to learn more about him, he needed to take it easy. "Nah, I'll come help you. It's no fun snooping alone."

❧

Dinner lived up to my expectations. Bart cooked better than he baked. The marinara was so thick, I could scoop it with my fork. It clung to the spaghetti and flavor exploded in my mouth with every bite. I'd grown up with sauce from a jar, and there was no comparison.

When dinner ended, Bart was dragging. I ignored his protests and helped him clear the table. His objections to my washing the pots had less strength, and he didn't say anything when I helped him put everything away.

We took our wine into the living room, and Bart put on some

soft jazz. He surprised me by sitting on the couch only a few inches away. His hand touched mine, and I expected him to pull it back like it was on fire, but he left it there. Soon his thumb moved slowly over my pinky.

I should have moved my hand. Bart hadn't resolved his conflict; this was playing with matches standing in a puddle of gasoline. Nothing good could come of this. But I stayed still.

Unlike anyone else I'd ever fallen for, Bart and I had started with sex. Great sex. The hour or so we spent talking was different, too, but I was still thinking hookup when we left the diner. Somewhere between there and orgasm, we both decided we wanted more. With each new bit of information Bart gave me, I plunged deeper into my desire to be with him.

I'd been good, despite wanting Bart with a need I hardly recognized. I pretended all our lunch dates weren't dates. That his incredibly kind fresh air glyph was just a welcome gift and hadn't taken days to create. I even ignored the instant boner he got when I fell on top of him at creative kickball. All because he asked that we not cross a line.

With every swipe of his thumb, however, he erased part of the divide between us. I spread my fingers and my heart pounded harder when he slipped his between them. Squeezing them together, I pulled his hand up and pressed the back to my lips. I wanted to blow a hole in that line too big to ever be closed.

Bart had his attention fixed on our hands. He bit his lower lip and glanced at me from the corner of his eye. I winked and he gave me a lazy smile before resting his head on my shoulder.

I freed my hand and put my arm around him. Bart snuggled in and sighed as I adjusted my position to make it more comfortable. With my free hand, I stroked his hair. He purred under me and cuddled closer. It was easily the most intimate moment I'd experienced in my dating life. Tender, warm, and simple. There was no urgency. It felt so natural.

"This feels amazing," he said in a soft, dreamy voice. "I'm going to fall asleep if you keep doing that."

This moment eviscerated the boundaries between us with a totality sex couldn't. We'd connected on a deeper level than carnal need could delve. I felt him in my bones and at my core.

I kissed the top of his head, settled back, and closed my eyes. "Thank you again for dinner."

He shifted and his lips touched mine for a brief kiss that tasted like sweet wine. It sent frizzles racing through me. "Thank you for being here."

He kissed me again, and I wiggled onto my back. Bart shifted to the inside and wedged his body between me and the cushions. He rested his head on my chest and flung his free hand over my torso, molding himself to my side. I could feel his hard-on pressed snugly against my leg.

My dick twitched and I resisted the urge to drag him on top of me and assault his mouth with my tongue. Bart had to take the lead. With my free hand, I massaged his neck. He sighed and hugged me tighter.

We lay still and I soon realized he'd fallen asleep. I ignored the voices screaming stop. They warned me I'd get burned. The smart thing would be to wake him gently, make sure he got to bed, and call a ride to take me home. Instead, I threw jet fuel on the fire and kissed his hair.

He moaned contently and I yawned as the music washed over me. I closed my eyes, allowing my senses to drink in everything about this moment.

Bart was still sleeping on my chest when I woke an hour later. It was one of the most perfect moments of my life. Sweet, sensual, and romantic enough that I never wanted it to end.

I watched him for several minutes before I decided to wake

him. As wonderful as this was for me, it would be more restful for Bart if he were in his bed.

"Bart?" I rubbed him gently. "Wake up."

He stirred and his eyes fluttered. "What . . .?"

"We fell asleep on the couch. You should go to bed."

Blinking, he slowly pushed himself up and rolled on top of me. He nuzzled my neck and slipped his hands under my back.

"Stay with me?" he whispered. "Please?"

Those four words, spoken softly and with a desperate need, tilted the world on its axis. My emotional center careened out of control as I labored to decipher the meaning. Did he ask because he was tired and needed someone, or did he want *me*?

It was a bad idea—we needed to define us before we lurched into something that would hurt one or both of us—but that was my brain talking. My heart didn't care. Not trusting my voice, I nodded my agreement.

Bart pressed his lips to my neck and gave it a soft kiss. Sliding off me, he grabbed my hand and helped me to my feet. His eyes stayed focused on my face, and he cocked his head to the right.

"Are you sure you're okay with this?" he asked.

My face must have shown my indecision. I'd been pressing him for weeks; I should have been all wide grins and high fives now.

Instead, I was tentative and apprehensive. Some of that was concern for him. He'd spent a considerable amount of energy undoing a very complicated bit of magic. But that wasn't my real issue because even if all we did was sleep in the same bed, it still altered everything.

Bart's invitation changed what "us" looked like for me, but I didn't know what "us" he envisioned. "I think the better question is, are you?"

I expected him to take a moment to consider the question, but his gaze never left mine. There was a calm intensity in his blue eyes, and they twinkled in the soft light.

"I'm sure." His lips grazed mine. "Tonight was everything I knew it would be if I gave us a chance. This may sound arrogant and privileged, but I don't need money or things. The most precious gift you could give me is your time. I want to spend it with you, hold you, and feel your heartbeat against mine. I want to do the simple things, like make dinner, listen to music, and talk about whatever comes up. I did those things, and they were amazing.

"Waking up in your arms felt too perfect to be dangerous. I'm probably being an idiot, but I don't want to fight what my heart wants any longer." He kissed his fingers and pressed them to my lips. "So, yes Cael, I'm sure."

Of all the things I thought of to change his mind, this never occurred to me. It made total sense. This was the moment I'd been chasing. I was on such a high, I thought I'd float off.

Until something he'd said latched onto me like a lead anchor.

Bart's vision seared him with a heart-numbing fear. He wasn't letting that stop him, but he hadn't forgotten. I had my reservations about premonitions, but the closer Bart and I became, the more I believed what he'd seen was real. For all my bravado that our actions had nullified that future, if I was wrong . . .

Nope. I wasn't going there. Bart chose us over fear. It was everything I wanted. Nothing was going to spoil that.

"I'd love to stay tonight."

Chapter Fifteen

※

BARTHOLOMEW

Nearly every night since I left Cael in his hotel room, I'd remember what it felt like. Warm, solid, comforting. When I woke up just before dawn, I had that same feeling. This time, instead of memories, I had soft breath washing against my neck and an arm across my chest, holding me protectively.

I'd been so tired, we barely got ready for bed, kissed a few times before I fell asleep. I'd worry about how Cael would take it, but he'd been the one pressing me to get some rest.

"There'll be time for more in the morning."

That might have been the one time he didn't give me a boner with a suggestive look. I mean, maybe I got one, but I'd passed out before it could register.

Nestling back, I embraced the serenity and bathed in the peace it brought. This was the most complete I'd ever felt. I breathed deeply and held it so I could capture the moment.

Then I inched his arm off me and slipped away from the lie.

Like the last time we'd slept together, I had a dream. It shattered the illusion of happiness I surrounded myself in for one night. It had been foolish to ignore the truth. Worse, I'd given Cael false hope, only to yank it away when he woke up.

At least this time I'd explain it to him instead of slinking off in the dead of night.

I left my bedroom and used the guest bathroom to wash up. The face staring back at me looked haggard and pale. Seeing people you loved die, in vivid detail, did that to a person.

I'd never had two dreams in a year before, let alone two about the same incident. Everyone could tell me they weren't real, but they were. This was going to happen whether or not anyone else believed it was true. And getting close to Cael triggered his and Jan's deaths. I knew that to the depth of my being.

Making my way to the kitchen, I switched on the coffee pot and turned on the oven. Cael probably wouldn't eat once I told him we couldn't see each other again, but it gave me something to do while I waited for him to wake up. And it prevented me from giving in to my instinct to run away again.

The biscuits cooled on the tray, and I was having a second cup of coffee when I heard Cael leave my bedroom. My nerves frayed as I waited for him to come down the stairs. I felt a twinge of guilt that I'd snuck away again, but this time I hadn't gone far. If he followed his nose, he'd think I woke up early to make him breakfast.

His unruly hair made him look younger as he shuffled into my kitchen in his T-shirt and boxers. Even with bedhead he was gorgeous. I avoided a small gasp by a whisker. A wave of sadness flushed my body as I realized what I couldn't have.

He'd entered the room with a wary scowl, and my guilt returned tenfold. After how sweet and caring he'd been, the last thing I wanted to do was make him unhappy. He spied the food and then he found me at the table. His frown faded and I forced myself to smile.

"Did you sleep well?" I asked.

"I did until I woke up alone. I had a horrible sense of déjà vu.

Then I remembered I was at your house, and you couldn't have run off." He smirked. Little did he know how close he'd come to the truth. "What time did you get up?"

Guilt twisted my stomach. Last night he'd enveloped me in more than just his arms. The closeness soothed a deep ache I'd carried for a long time. Despite wanting more than a cuddle, he'd been tender because that's what I needed. He'd been the being of my dreams.

And I left him alone again. Didn't matter that I'd only gone downstairs. I could have woken him and given him the choice and I didn't.

"About five." I pushed my chair back and gestured toward the place setting across from me. "Sit. I'll get you some tea."

He blocked my way to the counter. "What's wrong?"

My gaze met his and I flinched. It added to the pile of shame I'd need to dig out from when he went home. I shook my head. "Nothing."

Cael refused to let me pass. "Calling bullshit. I feel your anxiety."

I turned away but didn't block my emotions. It was too late for lies. Rubbing my face with my right hand, I retrieved my cup. "Everything."

Cael reached for me, but I held up my hand to stop him. I was hurting him again, but what choice did I have? He hadn't seen what I had or felt the pain.

"Please, Bart," he said softly. "Tell me what's wrong."

I wanted to tell him, but he didn't want the truth. Cael wouldn't accept any words that didn't allow us to be together, and I didn't have those to share.

"I had another vision—the same one again. I was fighting the demon on campus." I sucked in a breath to steady myself. "You and Jan were dead." *Again.*

"Bart, it was just a dream."

I stared at him, disappointed he'd brushed aside my warning. Only, this time, he couldn't.

"Your parents are coming to visit next Saturday. Their flight gets in around eleven a.m. You're going to ask me if I wanted to meet them."

Cael's shoulders sagged. "This is crazy. Prophetic visions aren't possible."

They were, and I knew he believed me, but Cael didn't want this one to be true. His dismissal shored up my shaky determination not to get close. I leaned against the counter and crossed my arms. "You know they are. And you know this one is real."

He kept his eyes on the floor for a few seconds. When he looked up, he'd swapped defeat for determination. "Tell me the details."

I stepped around him and turned on the kettle. "Would you like a biscuit while I make your tea?"

"Not right now." He pulled back the chair and sat. "What did you see?"

His voice was soft and tentative. He didn't really want to hear the truth, but he couldn't avoid it anymore. I sat across from him and took a sip to bolster my flagging courage. Reliving those dreams hurt. They rubbed my emotions raw.

"I was in the kitchen, making us breakfast. You came in, phone in hand, and told me about your parents. You kissed me, called me babe, and invited me to have dinner with you three." I wanted that future so bad it hurt to tell him. "Before I could answer you, I was back on campus. It was dark and cold enough to see my breath."

"What was I doing?"

Dying. Something I would prevent if it killed me.

"You were on the ground to my right. I heard you moan and saw you move your hand. Jan was face down, and his stone was cold. I don't know how you were both taken down, but the demon pounded on my wards with both hands. I saw it gathering for another strike and I woke up before it landed the blow. Just like the first dream."

"Was there any link between us and the fight with the demon?"

Rubbing my temples, I frowned. He moved from disbelief to finding an interpretation that fit his desire. I couldn't give in to such foolishness. "I know what you're getting at, but I know they're related. I can feel it."

Cael shook his head, the frown easing. "There's no proof of that. What if you're wrong?"

That wasn't the right question. If I was wrong, we'd all survive and figure it out. Being wrong meant death for Jan, Cael, and I didn't know how many others. "You're trying to give us false hope."

"No! I'm trying to get you to see that without more, you could be wrong." The strength in his voice almost made me believe him. "Bart, listen to me. I know you like me as much I like you. Don't convince yourself we can't be together based on a vague dream."

He still saw what he wanted and ignored the truth. This wasn't a vague dream. The details were so vivid, there was no difference between them and real memories. But he wasn't wrong about my feelings. I desperately wanted to be with him, and he was wearing me down. I couldn't, however, let that happen.

"It's not ambiguous, Cael. The details are graphically real. Every time I try to get close with you, I see an image of the near future, followed by your death. The universe is trying to get me to see something only I can prevent."

"I agree that you're seeing something you can prevent, but it's the way you do that I disagree with."

I took another sip. This was something I'd spent the last three hours considering. All evidence pointed to a different outcome than Cael promoted. "Except the second part was the same this time as in my first dream. Not walking out of the hotel together didn't prevent your deaths."

"Or maybe that wasn't the event that needs to be changed. Think about it. In all your other visions, the thing that caused the death was a very specific action: slipping on a set of stairs; jumping off a rock using a spell that didn't work; riding your bikes onto the highway; getting food stuck in your throat. Each of those presented a clearly defined action that, if prevented, would change the outcome. That isn't the case here. Whether you push me away or not, I'm still going to like you the same. You're still going to like me. If that hasn't changed, how will it alter the outcome?"

A kernel of hope warmed inside me, and I struggled to stop it from blooming. He *might* be right, but if he was wrong the consequences were beyond tragic. I considered I hadn't found the defining event, but it was tied to me and Cael. It had to be, because I didn't start to see this vision until I'd met him. Whatever caused my premonitions was warning me not to follow my heart.

"Obviously I don't know for certain, but my gut tells me our being together creates the outcome. Unfortunately, you're the only person who believes my visions are real, and you're not objective. You want the solution that keeps us together. I want the one that keeps you alive."

He reached for my hand and placed his over mine. "You act like they have to be mutually exclusive."

I didn't pull away. Cael calmed me. Last night, wrapped in his arms, I'd slept better than any night since we'd met. Pushing him away made my stomach queasy, but it was the only option if I didn't want to see him dead. "I don't see any other answers."

"Maybe you haven't seen it yet," he said with a desperate pleading.

I knew I could be interpreting the dreams wrong but going down this path was dangerous. The closer we got, the harder it would be to walk away. I could barely do this now. If we spent weeks together, I'd never be able to push him away. Not even to save him.

"What if our being together is the solution to saving us?" He held up a hand when I tried to answer. "Wait. Hear me out first. Yesterday you said you were keeping the Orme Seax because no matter what we do, someone is going to raise a demon on campus. If you believe that, then our being together has no bearing on that part of your vision. The part you need to change is how we fight the creature."

I ignored the "we" he had slipped into his conclusion. Even if he wasn't the catalyst for the demon's summoning, I wasn't letting him anywhere near that fight when it happened. He did, however, make a good point. The demon would be summoned. Stopping it without Jan and Cael dying was the key.

"I need to think about that before I can answer you."

"Our connection is strong. We're a great team. We stand a better chance of defeating this demon together."

My soul was weary of my brain fighting my heart, and I didn't see the answer clear enough to choose. Every reason Cael gave for us being together was just as likely to be right as any counter I might offer. Faced with this impasse, I looked into Cael's eyes and saw the same need for me I felt for him. I remembered how right it had felt, molded to his body.

And the decision seemed so obvious.

Cael pushed back, came over to me, and held out his hand. "Let's go back to bed. You didn't rest enough."

His groin was inches from me, and sleep was the last thing on my mind. I grasped his hand and stood. "If we go back to bed, are we really going to sleep?"

He smirked. "Eventually."

Contrary to my flirty banter, Cael had been right. I was exhausted. And it wasn't all from unraveling the glyph. I hadn't slept well in weeks. The struggle over what to do gnawed at me, kept me awake late into the night. Having Cael in my bed cured my fitful sleep, at least at first.

None of my other premonitions had left me as drained as the last one. When I'd woken from the dream, my heart burned in my chest. The calm, centered feeling was shattered, and the angst of the previous weeks returned tenfold.

Until Cael led me back.

I wasn't convinced his assessment of my dreams was correct, but it was as plausible as mine. More than a little of my willingness to accept his version had to do with how much I wanted him. It might be a recipe for disaster, but I'd worry about that later.

When we reached the bed, Cael lifted the sheets and allowed me to snuggle into him. A deep sense of peace washed over me. He'd known what my body required and pushed his desires to the side. It was something I'd never experienced. I didn't let others watch over me, I took care of them. My brain might have protested, but I needed this to recharge my energy and calm my weary soul.

I pulled his hand to my lips and wished for a dreamless sleep.

※

I woke pressed to Cael's body, his arm around me, his thumb gently rubbing my hand. I was tired of being afraid, of pushing him away. He gave me the closeness I'd ached for, and it was an ointment for my battered soul.

Nothing had changed, so why was I letting go of my fears? I'd had no new premonitions, and no epiphanies. Cael's analysis of my dream lacked my insight. It wasn't hubris, it was just fact. And yet, I'd accepted his explanation anyway. Why?

Lips pressed against the back of my neck. "Good morning. Again."

That was why. I wanted to wake up every morning next to Cael. "Is it still morning?"

He pulled me tighter. "It's 10:24. Squarely in the morning part of our day off."

Rolling over, I kissed his cheek. "I need a shower. Will you join me?"

He blinked and stared blankly for a couple of seconds before a dirty smirk stretched his lips. "That's the most direct you've ever been about what you want from me."

Since the first day of the semester, I'd walked a knife's edge, balancing my desire against my fears. I knew I risked pushing him away, but the image of him clawing at the dirt, trying to get up was always there. I still saw that haunting picture, but he'd convinced me to find a different ending.

"I don't want my fear of something that may never happen to stop me from being with you."

I kissed his cheek again and rolled out of bed. Either he'd join me, or he wouldn't, but I'd made my interest clear.

I grabbed the mouthwash and swished some around while I adjusted the water temperature. I spit the minty liquid into the sink and slid the glass doors back, wondering what Cael would decide.

I'd tried to keep the house true to its original design, but that didn't apply to my bathroom. My shower was oversized, with three overhead jets and two on the wall. If there were such a thing as a decadent shower, this was it. The frosted glass doors weren't see-through, but I could see shapes. Not that anyone could make it to my bathroom without my knowing they were in the house.

The water raining down was warm and soothing. I slicked back my hair and picked up the soap. The comforting aroma of chamomile and sage centered me. I hoped Cael liked it, too.

I was washing my groin when Cael's shadow covered the opaque glass. My dick twitched at the memory of him naked.

Cael's cock was at full attention as he slid the door open and stepped up to me. Reaching out, he took the soap and spun it in his hands. He worked up some suds and skimmed the bar over my chest and abs. Moving lower, he washed my cock and gently massaged my aching balls.

"Turn around," he whispered in a voice thick with lust.

Cael traced his fingers down my spine and eased them between my cheeks. Running his fingers up and down, he lightly nudged a digit inside.

With a moan, I arched my back to give him better access. Energy sizzled through me as he moved in and out. After a pause, he directed water across and down my ass.

I spread my cheeks, ready for Cael to press into me. Instead, he knelt, put his hands over mine, and buried his face in the soft skin.

The first swipe of his tongue made my knees weak. I steadied myself against the tiles and moaned when he did it again. "Oh God, that feels amazing."

"Yeah," he breathed against my skin. "Want more?"

More? I wanted everything. "Fuck, yes!" I pushed my ass back toward him.

He swirled his tongue around and darted it in and out, his stubble tickling the sensitive skin as he pressed his face harder against me. Pulling back for air, Cael pushed a finger into me.

"Hmm," I purred. "You feel so good."

Cael slipped out and stood. He gently nudged me around until I was pressed against the slippery wall. I kissed him and our tongues danced around each other, fueling my craving for him. We paused to catch our breath and Cael leaned back. His eyes raked over me and he flashed a wicked, filthy grin that made me shiver.

Instead of taking control again, Cael held out the soap. "Wash me?"

Despite the unexpected switch, I gladly did as he asked. I ran the soap over the tight muscles of his torso and used the time to explore every inch of skin. I ran my slick fingers over his nipples and pinched the little nubs. Cael's body convulsed and he let out a moan.

"Like that?" I did it again.

Cael tossed his head back. "Gods and goddesses, yes."

I lingered another few seconds, but I wanted to touch and taste Cael's cock. Suds trailed my hands as I washed the coarse hairs of his groin. Cupping his sack, I gently massaged his balls with my soapy fingers. Before I could lean in and capture my prize between my lips, Cael turned to face the wall.

I took the hint. Starting at his shoulders, I kneaded the tight muscles and worked my way down. My right hand continued lower, and I slid my index finger into the cleft of Cael's butt.

Squirming, he sucked in a breath when I ran my finger over his opening. Every reaction I teased out, I filed away for future use. Sliding up and down, I let the tip of my finger curl up. Cael clenched his muscles around my digit as I inched it forward.

He reached around, grabbed my cock and guided me lower. "Fuck me?"

From the time I followed him out of the Trade Den, I'd wanted to fuck his perfect ass. I almost asked if he was sure, but he lined me up to his entrance and pushed back. You didn't get much surer than that.

"Please, Bart. I want you inside me."

Cael's need mirrored mine. It was a nuclear dose of oxytocin, fanning an all-consuming need to be closer than close. To feel so connected, we were one being.

Without saying a word, I leaned forward and eased into him. Cael hissed and clenched when I pushed through his ring. I stopped but didn't pull out. It was better to keep going, but I didn't know if that's what he wanted.

"Don't stop." He pushed back a bit and froze.

Cael might have told me to continue, but his reaction didn't match his words. I gave him a few extra seconds to adjust. Flipping my hair off my face, I grabbed his hips and gently edged forward. Cael pushed back at the same time, and I ended up balls deep inside him.

"Oh, fuck!" Cael ground his ass against me. "That feels amazing, Bart."

A giddy rush filled me, and I wanted to shout out my love. I couldn't think of anything beyond how amazing it felt being connected this way. "You feel so good, Cael."

Closing my eyes, I molded my body to his. I feathered kisses up his neck and nipped at his ear lobe as I waited for a sign he was ready for more.

"Fuck me, Bart," Cael panted. "Please. I want you to fuck me hard."

The carnal need ignited a new fire inside me, one that wanted to give him every pleasure he demanded. I eased back and shoved hard, my body smacking against his. Cael's grunt had a guttural edge to it, and he squeezed his muscles around my cock.

Grasping his shoulders, I started with quick hard thrusts. Each time I pulled out a bit more until I was barely inside before I slammed back. "Fuck, you feel so good."

"Yeah," Cael moaned. "More. C'mon Bart, give it to me."

This wild, needy, demanding side was unexpected, but totally hot. His body shuddered every time I slid into him, spurring me to let go, to fuck harder.

"Yes, more," Cael panted.

Between the stream of filthy comments and how tight and warm it was inside him, my body raced toward release. I couldn't hold it back and didn't try. "Oh fuck, I'm coming, Cael."

"Give it to me." Cael squeezed his muscle tighter around my cock. "Shoot it in me!"

I let my walls down and Cael's energy barreled into me. It fueled my lascivious appetite. I fucked him with short, hard movements that created exquisite friction. "Yeah? You want this?"

"Yes!"

Sliding my hands under Cael's arms, I pulled him onto to me

as the first spasm tore through me and pumped into him until I collapsed against his back.

"That was fucking amazing." My words came out in a breathless whisper.

Cael laid his hands over mine, squeezed once, and released them. His body quivered and his muscles clenched around my cock. It took me a second to realize what he was doing. "Let me take care of you."

"Next time," he said, not missing a stroke. "I love feeling you inside me. I want to come this way."

Ignoring how hypersensitive I was, I pushed up, making sure to hit his prostate. His breathing got shorter and louder, and he twitched every time I drove into him.

"Oh, fuck!" he shouted. "Oh, fuck!"

His ass clamped around my cock like a vise with every spurt. Cael gulped for air, his body pulsing. I held on, keeping us connected until he relaxed.

"Fuck, I love how you feel inside me."

"As one who totally loves a cock inside him, I know what you mean."

Cael laughed and his body tightened and released around my cock. "Holy shit, Cael. Stop. I'm too sensitive."

"What? Can't go two in a row?" I thrust up, causing Cael to exhale quickly. "Okay, point taken."

I kissed the back of his neck, and he twisted his head until our lips met. It was short but packed all the feels. That made it more urgent I find an answer to my vision—I'd fallen so completely I couldn't survive without him.

"Let's clean up for real now," I whispered against his ear.

Chapter Sixteen

❦

CAELINUS

Tugging the end of the bow tie, I undid my pathetic attempt at a passable knot. I should've paid more attention when my father tried to teach me. Another life choice I regretted.

Normally I avoided formal events. Exceptions, however, were required when the guy you were dating surprised you with tickets to a private concert by the Philadelphia Symphony. *Dating*. As in me and Bart. I'd worn a constant smile in the week since Gretchen asked me to take Bart home. That deserved any number of exceptions.

Not that I'd been unhappy before we met. I had great parents and awesome brothers, plenty of friends growing up, and professionally, I was living the dream. Hell, I'd even come out in tenth grade and gone to the junior prom with a guy. Greg and I didn't work out, but we'd had a good time that night.

My relationship with Bart blew all of that away. We'd spent every night together the past week. Bart had been vision-free and more relaxed with each passing day. It brought out the romantic streak I knew he had. Each day it was something new. Walks along the river, a visit to the Rodin Museum, watching a movie in the park, and of course romantic dinners for two. When I mentioned I felt guilty he did all the cooking, he gave me lessons so I could take a turn some night. Just not soon.

Bart picked things for us to do that were free; only the museum had an admission fee. When he gave me the tickets for the symphony, however, he was bleeding anxiety.

At first, I thought it was the cost, but then he pulled a tuxedo from his closet that miraculously fit me perfectly. Hanging next to it was one of the new suits I'd bought before I started at Utrecht. I'd been too verklempt at how much effort he put into the surprise to be upset. His "punishment" was he had to let me take him to dinner before the concert.

Closing my eyes, I focused on tying a perfect knot. Knowing my date, he'd be impeccable from head to toe. I didn't want to embarrass him.

It took me two more attempts, but finally the ends were perfectly aligned, the knot centered against my throat. My eyes landed on the small package on my dresser. Bart wasn't the only one with a romantic streak. I picked up my gift and moved it to the living room.

The buzzer went off as I poured a glass of water. I smiled as I pressed the intercom. "Hello?"

"Hey," Bart said. "It's me."

Three words and I was swooning. "Come on up." I pressed the button to let him in, cracked the door, and went to my bedroom for my coat.

Double-checking my bow tie, I smoothed a stubborn lock of hair and went to meet my date. Bart was waiting by the couch, his blond hair combed back, his coat over his shoulder. He looked like he'd come from the runway at a fashion show.

I eyed him up and down, but it wasn't enough. He was so

confident. It was sexy. Most people said he was arrogant and stuck up—they saw his name, his family's wealth, and his talent. They were wrong. *I* was wrong until I got to know him.

Bart didn't care what others thought of him, because he measured himself against things he controlled. On those metrics, he had every reason to ignore their opinions.

"Wow." I fanned my face with my hands. "You look so amazing, I'm tempted to forget the show and admire my smoking hot date for an hour."

"Thank you." The creeping color in his cheeks was cute. "I might have been admiring the view in front of me as well."

Now his blush made sense. Bart like to give the compliments, not get them. At a minimum, he wanted to be first. Personally, his words didn't matter that much. He beamed and I did that. We made each other happy.

"Funny thing." I stepped closer to kiss him. "This tux fits *absolutely* perfect. It's as if someone knew my exact measurements."

"I'm sorry. I know it was wrong, but I wanted to—"

My lips smothered the rest of his pointless apology. I wanted to push my tongue into his mouth, because making out with Bartholomew Hollen was one of my favorite things to do, but he'd put too much effort into this date to miss the show.

"Yes, babe, you should've done everything you did. It's hands down the most romantic thing anyone's ever done for me." I still got chills thinking about it.

"Most romantic ever?" he asked softly.

Two things I'd learned about Bart: He didn't do anything halfway, and he liked to make people happy. I didn't know where he found the time to plan everything for our date, but he'd made it happen. The best part was his smile when he'd seen my reaction. You'd have thought I'd surprised him.

There was, however, room for two hopeless romantics on this journey.

"Hands down." I nicked a last kiss and picked up his gift. "This is for you."

Bart liked giving gifts, but he got embarrassed when anyone gave him something. Which wasn't all bad, because what did I give someone from the richest family on the planet? Fortunately, it wasn't about money. The thought put into something mattered most. Kind of like surprising me with a tux and tickets for the night out. It had taken work, but I thought this was perfect for him.

At least I'd thought it was when I bought it. Now that it was in his hands, I worried it was lame. Why would he like anything I could afford? I wiped my sweaty palms on my pants as he eyed his gift.

"You shouldn't buy me anything, Cael."

Under the frown, I sensed his excitement as he unwrapped the paper. My heart pounded harder as he freed the picture frame. It was upside down and confusion wrinkled his face. The moment he turned it over, his eyes widened, and his smile brightened my apartment.

He pinched the wooden sides with his fingers and lifted his gaze. "Where did you get this?"

I shrugged, trying to act like it hadn't taken a few days to find the perfect image. "I did some research and found some old photos of the neighborhood."

Setting it down gently, he hugged me tight. "It's . . . this is amazing."

If you didn't know Bart, you'd think he was being polite and the gift would end up in the trash. To someone who owned priceless art, a simple black-and-white photo would be a trifle. But I'd been inside his house. The things he valued the most were personal.

"You like it?"

"I love it. I can't believe you found a picture of my house from more than a hundred years ago." He kissed me a few more times before stepping back. "This is the best gift I've gotten since I was fifteen. Thank you."

That made it worth all the work. "You're welcome."

"Now before you distract me again, can I say I didn't think you could get more handsome, but dressed up? My wards may not be strong enough to keep the men and women away."

I rolled my eyes. If anything, I was the ugly half of this couple. "No worries, I'll make sure mine keep you safe."

"My knight in shimmering wards." He glanced at his gift. "Can I leave it here?"

Funny how a week could change everything. We'd spent every night together for the past week. We *were* spending the night together; it was just a question of where. "Are we staying here tonight?"

"I'm not sure. I've been trying to get this guy I really like to ask me to spend the night, but I kinda fucked up the first time we tried, and I think he's afraid to ask. I figured if I leave this here, I have to come inside and maybe he'll forgive me by then and ask me to stay again."

He said it in a light voice, but Bart still felt guilty about leaving me without saying goodbye. No matter he'd done it with good intentions, or that we'd moved past that night. I could still see him flinching at my angry outburst when Gretchen left us alone in the conference room my first day at Utrecht. No doubt he saw it as a sign I hadn't totally forgiven him.

"Bart, you didn't fuck up, not even close. I've never asked you to stay because I wasn't sure you'd be comfortable here. My place is so small compared to yours."

"Before I become a walking cliché and say I'd stay anywhere if you're there, I love this place. It has such character. It makes me wonder about the other tenants who've lived here and how it's changed over the decades." He swept his gaze around the room. "Wouldn't it be crazy if we could sit quietly on the couch, and see people move in and out? Or get a snapshot of what it looked like at the start of each year?"

I loved the quirky, complex facets of his personality. Unless you spent time with him away from school or other official functions, you'd miss this side of him. Others talked about his generosity—how steady and reliable he was, and his calm, measured demeanor. The face he presented to the world.

Bart showed me the rest. He trusted me enough to share himself without fear of being judged. Chills ran up my body, like a cool wind on a warm muggy day, leaving my skin tingling. It was ridiculous how much I liked him already. Every time I tried to rein in my emotions, he did something simple and sweet, and I couldn't hold back the flood of feelings that engulfed me in their beauty.

"I can't say I wondered those things, but I knew this was the place once they showed me a unit." I took the picture from his hand, set it on the table and pulled him into a hug. "Spend the night with me here? Please?"

The peck on the lips turned into a full-blown kiss—I was so full of feels for him, I couldn't help it. I pulled back before clothes came off and we spent the entire symphony in bed.

"Damn," he whispered.

That didn't begin to capture what his kisses did to me. "We can pick up from there when we get home, but we need to go or we'll be late."

He held out my coat. "You'll need this to get into the theater."

I debated tossing it out the window, but this was too romantic a moment to let my dick think for me. I shrugged into the coat and helped him into his.

We took the stairs and when we emerged in the lobby, he slid his hand into mine. I floated out the door, fearful I might burst from all the perfectness of the night.

A vintage white car was parked in front of my building when

we walked out. Bursting apart was becoming more likely by the second.

Bart swung in front of me but kept a grasp on my hand. "Before you ask, it's not mine. I borrowed it for the night from the family motor pool."

Qualifying it that way didn't make it less of a reminder of the disparity in our backgrounds, but it came from a good place. Bart did everything he could to maintain the illusion we were both just university professors.

"It's . . . wow. What kind of car is that?"

"A 1960 Bentley S1. As you know, I prefer old classics. It doesn't get much use because it isn't big or ostentatious enough. Plus, it only seats three comfortably."

A description that fit Bart perfectly; simple yet classy. "Sounds perfect for two."

"It is," Bart said.

A large man, who looked around our age only with white hair and who exuded Ursidae, walked around the car and beat us to the door. "Isaac, this is my date, Caelinus. Cael and I work together at Utrecht."

"Nice to meet you, Caelinus." He winked at me. "You two are going to turn a lot of heads tonight."

Bart laughed. "You're just saying that because you want me to request you drive me this weekend to avoid Matilda and that worm she married."

He gave the least apologetic shrug I'd ever seen. "I don't see why it's wrong to enjoy being appreciated."

Shaking his head, Bart put his hand on the man's arm. "Find me a car like this, and I'll take you on full time."

Isaac nodded. "I'll bring you some options next week."

"Perfect." Bart let me get in first. "As for this weekend, Cael's parents are going to be here, and we could use a driver. I'll put in the request on the way to the symphony."

"Thank you." He sounded almost relieved. Bart slid next to me, and Isaac shut the door.

"We?" I smirked. "Did I miss something."

Bart tensed and I immediately wanted to take back the quip. I been waiting for the perfect time to ask him to spend time with me and my parents, but it hadn't presented itself. Meeting the parents was one of those relationship milestones, and I wasn't sure we were there yet. Going all snarky on him didn't help my cause.

Isaac got in and Bart leaned forward. "Can you put up the privacy screen, please?"

"Of course." There was just enough innuendo that Bart's cheeks turned pink.

"That's not why I want privacy." Bart's frown was too much to be serious. "At least not on the ride *to* the symphony. On the way back, absolutely."

The screen sliding up cut off Isaac's laughter.

"He's completely trustworthy, but what he doesn't know he won't have to hide. This goes to why I generally stay away from my extended family." Bart heaved in a breath and thrust his shoulders back. "There's a pecking order in my family. My grandparents are first, followed by my dad and his siblings in order of birth. After that it gets complicated. Suffice to say, if Isaac picks me up first, what he does after that isn't questioned. He can drop me off outside your building and I'll walk home."

And just like that, the perfect time arrived. Meeting his gaze, I shook my head. "That won't work. He'll need to pick us both up, because I plan to be with you in the morning."

"I like that thinking," he said with a smile.

My heart clanged against my sternum. Christ almighty. It was one smile, and I turned into a pile of putty. "As for walking home, I'd rather you join us for the day."

"I don't want to intrude on your time."

More like he wanted to kick that can down the road. I would

if I were him. His attempt to beg off didn't, however, have the same level of mortification mine would have if our roles were reversed. Sensing an opening, I pushed a bit further.

"I'll take that as a yes, and let my parents know you'll be joining us." I kissed his cheek. "I've wanted to ask a dozen times but worried it was too soon to meet the parents."

"Of course it's too soon. My 'I don't want to intrude' was a polite way of saying, 'Are you fucking kidding me?' Meet the parents? I require at least a dozen overnight dates before I risk that."

I might have believed him if he'd had the frightened look of a hunted being. He might not be eager to meet my parents, but the idea didn't scare him witless.

I tapped my chin with my fingers. "A dozen, eh? Can I give you an IOU for the ones I'm short?"

"How good is your credit?"

His tacit agreement sent nervous butterflies flapping furiously in my stomach. This wasn't merely meeting my parents. Bart was signaling he was letting go of his fears and ready to commit to an us.

"Impeccable."

He stared at me, and I worried I'd read too much into his response. A few seconds later he blinked. He must have found what he'd wanted because he smiled widely.

"Okay, then. I'd love to spend time with you and your family. Anything to stop talking about us as a business transaction."

A pattern started to emerge. Bart acted like he was agreeing to keep the peace, rather than appear too eager. It mostly made sense. His brain and heart waged war with each other. Right now the heart was winning, but his brain wouldn't quit the fight.

I squeezed his hand. "Babe, you're so not business. You're a sweet, wonderful man, who just made me very happy."

He pressed his head to mine, and I closed my eyes to soak in the moment. "I'm good with making you happy. I know you've been looking forward to this weekend. We can spend as much or as little time together as you want while your family is here."

I shifted until my lips met his and put my hand behind his head. Normally I'd be more reserved knowing Isaac was up front, privacy screen or no, but I couldn't contain how much I wanted Bart.

"Thank you," I said when I pulled back for air. I pulled us together until our foreheads touched. "You're the best."

Chapter Seventeen

※

BARTHOLOMEW

"Honey, are you ready?" Making sure I had everything, I zipped up my backpack. "Isaac'll be here in a minute."

I'd never liked pet names, but when Cael called me "babe," it felt right. I broke a lot of my rules for him. Which proved how stupid those were because I'd never been this happy dating anyone. Jan said he didn't recognize me and checked to make sure I wasn't under an enchantment. I threatened him with three eyes and a green witch's nose with a large hairy wart if he didn't shut up.

He wasn't totally wrong. Since I bought my house four years ago, I'd stayed home unless Jan managed to drag me out or I was dating someone. Even then I preferred to do things at home. Now? I spent a lot of time thinking of places to go and things to do together.

"Hey, babe," Cael said from the kitchen doorway. "Where'd you go?"

"Thinking about how happy you make me." I kissed him as I walked past.

"Not that I want to interrupt such important thoughts, but you said Isaac will be here soon."

My phone vibrated and I saw the limo in the driveway. "And he's here."

Hands snaked around my waist. Cael pulled me against his long, hard body. "Thank you again for doing this and for coming with me. Meeting someone's parents is never fun."

I almost said, "Anything for you," but it was premature to profess my undying love, even if I felt that way. We didn't know for sure what my dreams meant. Just because we pretended his wistful interpretation was correct, didn't make it so. My explanation might be right, or maybe the answer was something neither of us had considered. I followed my heart for the moment, but I wouldn't toss caution aside.

Covering his arms with mine, I leaned back. "It should be interesting. Your mom sounds like a hoot, and I'm a stodgy old man."

"There are too many things wrong with that to get into right now." He spun me around and kissed me.

The effect was immediate. I adjusted myself and growled at him. "Thank you for making me totally hard as we're about to go out."

"Hey, holding you gave me a boner. I didn't want to be the only one." He grabbed his bag. "C'mon, we don't want to be late. Mom will totally blame you."

Cael was joking, but it twisted my stomach into a knot. His family was important to him, that was part of what made him so attractive. His mother, however, was *the* most important to him. She'd been his teacher, confidante, and fail-safe for when he couldn't control his empathy.

She also freaked me out. I could hide my doubts from Cael because of all the joyous energy we generated together, but Cael's mother's powers were exponentially stronger than his. She was also detached from our relationship. Locking down my emotions, however, was itself a red flag. The "I always wall myself off, especially around empaths" explanation would only go so far.

"Super. Just the first impression I want to make."

⁂

We were early and the flight was late. Extra time for me to fret about what Cael's parents would think of me. His father would be easy to deal with. He was a high school spell casting teacher and told Cael he was anxious to talk magic with me. Cael's mother, however, was going to be more difficult than I first thought.

In addition to being empathic, she was also a mage psychologist. I'd be an open book. If she told Cael what she sensed, it would cause a rift between him and me or him and her. Both options sucked.

"You're worrying again." Cael kneaded my trapezius muscles. "They're going to love you, but if you don't stop leaking, you're going to give Mom a headache."

I strengthened my shields, but it was hopeless. I couldn't keep them up every minute of his parents' visit.

He squeezed my tight shoulders harder. "Whatever you did made it worse. You're locked down so tight I can feel your effort. She'll think you're hiding something."

She'd be right. Cael understood my fears for the future because he believed my visions were real. His mother didn't; she'd misinterpret my apprehension. I should've thought this through and agreed it was too soon to meet his parents.

"You're not helping," I said. "What if they hate me? I don't want to come between you and them."

"And that's why they're going to love you." He spun to face me. "You have the best heart. They'll see that."

My chest was so tight I didn't know if my heart was still there.

Over Cael's shoulder I saw a couple who could only be his parents. Cael looked like his father.

"They're here." I nodded behind him. "Go say hi, while I throw up in the fake potted plant over there."

He grabbed my hand and pulled me with him. I caught up, because as nervous as I was, I didn't want his parents to think I didn't want to meet them.

"Hey!" Cael said, waving his free hand as if they hadn't seen him.

Their eyes twinkled and they smiled so wide, I expected their faces to split in two. Cael let go of me, practically ran the last few feet, and swept his arms around them for a group hug right there in the airport terminal, forcing people—some smiling, others grumbling—to walk around them. He kissed his mom's cheek and his dad grabbed his shoulder in one of those "dad" moves and shook gently. After another quick hug, he spun around.

"Mom, Dad, this is Bart. Bart, these are my parents, Fiona and Jake."

Like the stiff I knew I was, I held out my hand to his mom. "Dr. and Mr. Reinhold, really nice to meet you."

His mom looked at my hand and moved in for a hug. The only adult who wasn't my family who hugged me was Grandma Pederson and in every way that mattered, she was family. I tried not to stiffen more and returned her hug. When she pulled back, she stared at me and I knew she'd read me to the core. Only Cael's presence kept me from walking off. Reaching deep, I shook hands with his father.

To my surprise, his mom hooked her arm around mine as we walked.

"Bart, relax." She brought her other hand around and squeezed my arm. "We're not here to judge you. If we drive you away, Caelinus might never invite us to visit again."

"I'm sorry, ma'am. I don't mean to hit you with my emotions.

It's just . . ." I'd never been this unnerved meeting anyone, and I'd met some of the most powerful beings in the world.

"You really like our son, and don't want us to hate? Too late." She rubbed my arm. "We already like you. Cael sounds and looks happy. You passed. I promised Cael I'd curtail my powers while I was here. You're safe."

The rush of relief robbed me of my words. Maybe Jan was right. This wasn't normal for me or anyone. "Thank you. I—"

"But if you call me ma'am or Dr. Reinhold again, I'll rethink that decision."

A wave of calm washed over me, and I couldn't tell if she'd done something. When my anxiety abated and I relaxed, I knew something had happened, just not what.

I managed a smile that didn't fool her. "Deal."

Fiona released my hand and joined Cael and Jake on the walk to the baggage carousel. They chatted happily, but I didn't pay attention. My imbalance was abnormal. I shouldn't have been so anxious to meet them or so relieved when they said I passed. It wasn't a hex, my wards would have alerted me. Could destroying the demon glyph have altered something?

I needed to speak to Avie, but there was no way to get away for at least a few hours.

"Is something wrong, babe?" Cael asked softly. "You feel off-kilter."

"I'm better." It wasn't a lie, but I wasn't myself either. "Let's find your parents' luggage and get them settled."

Then I'd sort out what had happened with me.

※

Isaac stopped in the no-parking zone in front of Cael's building and got out. I exited the front passenger seat and opened Cael's door. He'd watched me all through lunch, and he searched my face when our eyes met.

"I'm fine." He didn't believe me, but he didn't call bullshit.

Although I'd kept my shields in place, several times during lunch my anxiety spiked, and he'd turn as if I'd elbowed him. He shouldn't have felt that, but he did. Not Fiona, just him.

"Bart," Fiona said as she followed Cael out of the car. "You were right, the food and the view were spectacular. Thank you for taking us."

Points to Avie for suggesting it. "Confession? I haven't eaten there since high school. I remembered the view, but my sister vouched for the food."

"Our thanks to your sister, then," Jake said, patting his stomach. "Although she did my waistline no favors."

"We can go for a run if you like, Dad." Cael shot his mom an amused look. "The route Bart and I take has a couple of cardio-intensive hills."

He held up his hands. "That's okay, I'll just take the stairs instead of the elevator while I'm here."

Between Isaac, Cael, and myself, we got the luggage up to Cael's apartment. Cael set them up in his room; he was using the smaller one. My balls might think otherwise, but we'd agreed to wait a couple of days before he suggested he stay with me.

After depositing the suitcases he'd carried, Isaac glanced at me. I nodded and he slipped out of the apartment.

"If you'll excuse me," I said. "I need to take care of a few things before dinner. Are you sure you don't need Isaac to drive you anywhere?"

"No dear." Fiona patted my cheek. "You've been more than generous with your time and Isaac's, and I don't plan to go out before dinner. It'll give us time to chat with Cael and plan what we're going to do when you boys are working."

"Terrorize the neighbors, no doubt." Cael avoided his mother's swat. He allowed his momentum to bring him to me.

I envied their playful interactions a little. My family had so many eyes watching us, we rarely let our guard down, even in private. Smiling, I said, "Isaac and I will be by around seven."

They nodded, and Cael and I waited as they retreated to the bedroom. I didn't want to leave, but Cael needed alone time with his parents, and I really did need to sort out some things.

His arms snaked around my waist, and I draped mine over his shoulders. "I'll see you in a few hours," he said.

The way he said it, he was concerned. I got that. I leaned closer, and mindful of his parents' proximity we kept our kiss chaste. "I'll call you when we're on the way."

"Bye." He nicked another kiss before he let me go.

Stepping out, I waved before Cael shut the door. Isaac had waited for me in the hallway. I dug my phone from my pocket as we walked.

"Did she answer your text?" he asked as he opened the car door.

"Yes." The back seat smelled like Cael. Closing my eyes, I breathed in, and it felt like he was next to me. His scent soothed my jittery nerves. That thrilled and scared me at the same time.

I pushed the thought aside and opened my eyes. Isaac was staring at me in the rearview mirror. "She's in Wyncote right now, but she'll meet us in Plymouth Meeting at the mall."

He checked his phone and nodded. "Plenty of time."

"Let's do it." Hopefully, I'd find my answers.

CAELINUS

Collecting two sets of towels, I turned and nearly tossed them across the hall.

"Jesus Christ, Mom. Why do you still sneak up on me like that?"

"Old habits?"

Mom's serious expression tipped me off. "What's wrong?"

"I'm not sure anything is wrong, but we need to talk. I put the kettle on, and your father is checking through your tea."

This was worse than needing to talk. Something unsettled her, and I was the cause of her distress.

"You snuck up on me, enlisted Dad to make tea, and you want to talk. Something's definitely wrong."

She pursed her lips and nodded several times. "Come on dear, let's have tea. I promise you, it's nothing dire."

I collected the towels so I had time to think about what to say. "Let me set these in the bathroom, and I'll meet you in the kitchen."

My chore wouldn't take long enough to make sense of her behavior, so I didn't try. Putting the linens for my parents in the bathroom, I hoisted my big boy boxers and headed for the kitchen. Dad was at the counter and Mom was seated at my small table.

I tensed and stopped in the doorway. This had evolved into seriously wrong. "What's up?"

Mom sat straighter and folded her hands in front of her. "Tell me about Bart."

Bart had them all worked up? What had he done other than be wonderful? Annoyed, I chaffed under her maddeningly vague, probing questions. "What do you want to know?"

"Whatever you want to tell us," she said.

Dad avoided my gaze. So much for a discussion. Mom planned to interrogate me.

"Come on, Mom. Cut the psychoanalyzing crap. What are you really after?"

Mom's steely expression never changed. "Please humor me, Cael. You know I'm not doing this without a reason."

Just because she had a reason didn't make it right. I wasn't a client or a criminal. If she didn't want to discuss things like an adult, I wasn't obligated to participate. "I'm going for a run. Enjoy your tea."

"Did you notice how unsettled he was at the airport?"

Like always, she managed to turn me in the direction she wanted. It irritated the fuck out of me that I couldn't resist answering her. "He didn't want to cause tension between us. Why are you trying to create some now?"

"I'm not, dear. I'm pointing out he was extremely anxious to meet us. It seemed excessive. And then—" she snapped her fingers "—in an instant, it was gone."

A knot formed in my guts, and I started to shake, trying to hold in my anger. Bart's fears were coming true. They hated him and wanted to push us apart.

"What's going on? Why are you trying make something out of nothing?"

"Calm down, Caelinus," Dad said. "We're not trying to create a rift between you and Bart. We like him quite a lot."

"Good." I crossed my arms and leaned against the doorframe. "Because I like him too."

The kettle whistled, and Dad took it off the heat. He shot my mom a look and turned his attention to making the tea.

"How *much* do you like him, dear?" Her calm tone hid something beneath the words. She'd stopped being my mother and turned into my therapist. Only, I didn't want a shrink.

"Stop it! There's nothing wrong with me and Bart."

"Calm down, son." Dad came over and put his hand on my shoulder. "Of course there's nothing wrong with either of you, but you've known him less than six weeks."

Did they think I was fifteen and this was my first crush? "Newsflash, I'm twenty-eight and have had a few relationships in my lifetime."

"You've known each other for less than two months, and Bart was on the verge of a breakdown because he was afraid we wouldn't like him." Mom stood and joined Dad. "He's an otherwise well-adjusted man, a powerful mage, and someone who meets important people all the time. That's not normal.

"And now you're snapping at us because we're asking questions about your relationship. I've asked you far more personal and intimate questions, and you didn't react this way."

I raised a finger and opened my mouth to fire back at her, but her words sunk in before I could speak. Mom had grilled me a lot worse when I first started dating, and I hadn't gotten this irritated. Yes, I was an adult, but she hadn't asked anything remotely personal.

"I guess I like Bart more than I liked anyone before him."

"That's an understatement." Dad's comment earned him an elbow from Mom.

"It's quite clear you both have *extremely* strong feelings for each other," she said. "Feelings that evolved *extremely* quickly."

Annoyance bubbled inside me again. "You make it sound like it's a crime."

"No, dear. It's definitely not a crime," Mom said. "It's exactly how it should be."

How was this what she expected? Why wasn't she telling me to tap the brakes or take precautions? I shifted between anger, confusion, and relief. "What are you talking about?"

"This is what happens when mates find each other."

Silence followed as I processed her statement. Blood pounded in my head and my legs felt weak. Did she really say . . .

"Mates?"

Chapter Eighteen

BARTHOLOMEW

I checked my watch for the umpteenth time and paced. Again. Why had she said to meet in a mall parking lot? Thankfully it wasn't packed, or she wouldn't find us.

A big hand blocked my way. "Calm down," Isaac said. "She's here."

The big Buick coming our way was such a grandma car. It parked parallel to us and Sally Pederson, all five foot four inches of oversized personality, stepped out. She looked me up and down and frowned. "You look like shit, Bart."

I barked out a laugh. Granny P. always served hugs and kisses with a healthy dose of truth.

"Thanks, Grandma." I reached out and folded her into my arms. "You look wonderful, as always."

"I just came from the salon." She stepped back and tossed her head around. "Not bad for an old broad."

Jan and I also learned she shamelessly fished for compliments. It was mostly a joke, but I suspected some of it was real. Our grandmother was powerful enough to be on the Mage Council but had never been asked.

"You're not old. You're perfect for your age."

"And you're still a flatterer." She pinched my cheek like I was eight. Turning, she smiled warmly at Isaac. "Good afternoon, Isaac. Still blocking the sun, I see."

"It's genetic." He smirked. "My younger brother's bigger."

"Bears." She sighed. It didn't stop her from pulling him down for a hug. "How are your parents?"

"They're doing great. My sister had twins in March. Mom's a typical grandmother."

"Boring." She rolled her eyes. "Okay, let's go inside. I have a table for us."

I scowled. This is when her quirky persona drove me nuts. Did she even think for a moment that what I wanted to talk about might be personal? If anyone recognized me, my business would be all over social media.

"Hold on, Grandma." I reached out to stop her from walking off. "I can't talk about this in a mall. Let's use the limo."

"Why don't you trust your old gran isn't batshit crazy and knows what she's doing?" She fixed me a glare that erased any hint of spacey, carefree Sally Pederson. Freeing herself from my hand, she grabbed her bag from the car. Still looking annoyed, she pointed to a small building set away from the mall. "My cousin Irene owns that restaurant. There's a room in the back where we can talk."

The freestanding building didn't look like much, but the best place to hide something was in plain view. "Sorry."

She patted my cheek. "I understand. It's why we need to talk."

I followed her into the busy coffee shop. An older woman I'd never met came around the counter to hug my grandmother. She eyed me and Isaac.

"I'm not sure it will fit all three," she said.

Clearly my grandmother had called ahead.

"Isaac will wait for us out here," she said. "He wanted to stay with the car, but he'd miss your wonderful pecan cinnamon rolls if I'd let him have his way. Probably best to give him two. Can you bring two more for Bart and me? Oh, and two black coffees, and whatever else Isaac wants. My grandson will take care of the bill when we're finished."

Grandma wasn't shy about spending my money, but it gave us cover if anyone noticed. Sally Pederson wasn't a Hollen. No one would look twice at her grandson.

"Hi." I held out my hand. "Bart. Nice to meet you."

"Irene McCafferty. Nice to meet you."

Grandma led the way down a narrow, gray-walled hallway. Metal shelves lined the right side crammed with cups, plastic utensils, napkins, and other café-related things. The door we stopped in front of didn't look like anything special until I studied it closer. Powerful wards and charms protected it and the room beyond.

I tried to touch the door, but she slapped my hand away. "What?"

"You know better than to touch someone else's wards." She placed her palm on the door, and the gray wood shimmered. A portal opened and she shooed me inside.

I stood rooted in place. This was powerful magic. Why was it here?

"Bart, I need you to move," she said through gritted teeth.

Scurrying to comply, I entered a private dining area. There were three chairs around a small wooden table. It was as small as Irene had suggested. So why all the protection? "What is this place?"

"Wait until Irene brings us our order, and then I'll seal the room."

We didn't need that level of security for my problem. "Gram, this isn't Mage Council business. It's personal."

"We'll talk once the room is locked." She put her bag on a chair and pointed to the one opposite her. "Sit. It won't be long."

I did as she said. Filling my lungs, I held it until I was calm at my core. "You always said I ask too many questions."

Slipping her fingers around mine, she put her other hand on top and squeezed. "I might have said that in a moment of frustration, but what I remember most is the questions you didn't ask. You were the first person to welcome my Janny unconditionally. When I saw you two together, the way you put your arm around him and asked if he wanted to see your room, I knew he'd found his guardian.

"In twenty-three years, you've never proven me wrong. You're every bit as special to me as Janny." Her grip tightened before she let go. "Do you think I would give up the last five minutes of my spa time for anyone else?"

With those last two sentences, she reminded me why I cared about her so much. She loved fiercely and wasn't afraid to show people how she felt. "Probably not, but I'm grateful you came."

"Of course, dear."

The portal opened and Irene stepped inside. She and Granny P. shared a look as she set the tray down. Placing a mug and a plate in front of each of us, Irene flipped the tray under her arm and turned around.

"Enjoy," she said as she walked out the door.

The opening shrank in on itself, and it was just me and Granny Pederson.

"I'd suggest you eat first, but you've been patient enough," she said. "Tell me why we're here."

I'd chafed to speak to her, and now I didn't know where to begin. The concern in her eyes grew the longer I didn't speak. "The night I met Cael, I had a vision."

I recounted everything that happened since I'd met Cael, and Granny P. stayed oddly quiet. She'd never been a listener. Her keen mind always had questions, and she didn't wait until the end for answers. This time, she sipped her coffee, ate her pecan roll, and listened.

Every sentence I finished without her interrupting unnerved me more. I kept waiting for something, but she didn't even clear her throat. My stomach clenched so tight I had to struggle to keep my lunch down as I spoke.

When I finished, she tapped my mug with her spoon.

"I fear it's gotten cold, dear." She touched the lip, and I felt her magic warm my coffee.

Something *was* wrong with me. It must be worse than I suspected if that was all she had to say. I stared at my now steaming coffee. "What's wrong with me? Is it that bad?"

"No dear. There is nothing wrong with you at all. The revelation you're having visions took me by surprise. I'm deciding where to begin."

In my twenty years of knowing her, Granny P. had never been at a loss for words. I'd also told her about my first two dreams. "I told you about them before." *You didn't believe me.*

"The last time you told me was twenty years ago. It's odd not to have had any premonitions in so long and to have them again. And in such vivid detail. It's perplexing."

I opened my mouth to tell her I'd stopped telling people after the second when it hit me. "Wait. You believe I had real visions? What happened to divination is bullshit?"

She frowned. "You should eat and drink your coffee before it gets cold."

Now she was deflecting. She always plied us with food when she wanted to soften up something unpleasant. "What's going on? Why are we in this secret, warded room in the back of a café that's really a front for . . . something?"

"We're here because your love life is fodder for the tabloids, and this was the nearest safe place for us to talk." She pointed at my plate. "Eat and I'll explain."

Despite the churning in my stomach, I broke off a small piece of the pastry. The sweet, sugary coating was the perfect complement to firm, yet flaky cake. Irene's caramel had been cooked to the precise moment of maximum flavor and not a second more. Doing that for a small bunch was difficult, but for a bakery scale batch it was miraculous.

"These are amazing."

"You should invite Irene over and you two can spend hours making the rest of us fat," she said with a smile. It didn't last long. "Unlike every other magical discipline, divination is a completely random talent. The mage can't control what they see, the vision can't be verified before the event happens, and sometimes, the meaning isn't clear. Despite those limitations, the chance to know the future would be too great to ignore. Seers would be the most sought-after beings in the world. To protect those rare few with the gift, the Ocular Society taught that foresight didn't exist."

With every word, my fury burned hotter. I trusted her like she really was my grandmother. I thought she loved me. It was all a lie. "How . . .? You . . .? How could you lie to me like that?"

"I'm sorry, Bart." She didn't back away from my anger. "You were nine. Far too young to manifest such talent. If you'd had a vision after the onset of puberty, we'd have had this talk then."

"But I did."

She arched her brow. "There were others?"

I blinked as my brain processed everything. I hadn't told her. After Henri, I didn't tell anyone until Cael. "Two."

She frowned, but it wasn't directed at me. "Tell me."

I recounted the dreams involving Jan and Aunt Gretchen. When I finished, she sighed.

"I wish I was perfect, Bart, but sometimes I get it wrong. You were so young." She squeezed her eyelids tight. When she opened them, tears welled at the edges. "I'm so sorry. We should've ask —*I* should've asked you. The youngest verified seer was thirteen. For most, their talent revealed itself in their late teens. In hindsight, given your extraordinary ability, it would manifest itself earlier than we expected."

It hurt to see her so upset. Granny P. had been Jan's rock growing up, and I'd come to rely on her strength, too. She'd handled our problems with a stoic yet loving embrace. "It's not your fault. I never told you about the others."

She reached across and rested her small hand on mine. "Ever the loving child. Thank you, Bart, but the fault is mine. After Avie scolded you for lying, you weren't going to tell anyone if you had any more."

Thoughts zipped, colliding with each other and making me dizzy. I'd come here because my relationship with Cael was causing havoc with my emotions. This new revelation did nothing to help center me.

She exhaled, sat straighter, and fixed me a look that said my rock was back. "I have a whole speech about what we know, when we knew it, and why we hid it, but that can wait. First, we should talk about you and Cael."

Bringing me back to my original problem only made my mental whiplash worse. I wanted to discuss both at the same time, but I knew we'd have that talk soon. "The visions started when I met Cael. My emotions have been wonky since that night. I'm up, I'm down, I'm worried his parents won't like me. I know my foresight and Cael are connected, I just don't know how or how to fix it."

Granny P. looked at me with concern. She tilted her head, her eyes opened wide. "Oh, my." She put her hand on her chest.

Her reaction wasn't what I expected. Clearly it was worse than I thought. "What? What's wrong?"

She chuckled and waved me off before I got mad. "There's nothing wrong, dear. It's actually quite good."

I waited for her to explain, but she kept quiet. As much as I loved her, she could be maddening. She did things on her schedule or not at all. Clearly, she wanted me to ask, so I took the hint.

"Can you explain that, please." If I sounded exasperated, who could blame me? I'd come hoping for clarity, but Gran made it worse.

"Your foresight isn't causing your emotional turmoil over Cael. It doesn't work that way. Yes, it might cause you anxiety over his safety, but it wouldn't trigger the mood swings."

I was disconcerted by how amused she looked. If the problem wasn't from my visions, I didn't see how it was good. "Then what's causing me to be so unbalanced?"

"Normally, I'd try to walk you through things so you'd figure it out on your own, but you're too agitated for that to work. Do you remember when I told you that Declan wasn't the one for you?"

Declan? Why did everything come back to him lately? "How could I forget."

"I couldn't see more because your aura was cloudy, but now it's crystal clear. Cael's your mate. The anxiety you're feeling is normal when you perceive he's threatened."

I sat back in my chair so hard I almost teetered over. Gran thought this was *good*? Shaking my head violently, I stood up. "That's not good, it's terrible. He can't be my mate."

"Cael *is* your mate, Bart, but it's not bad. It's wonderful. A mate bond is one of the most beautiful forms of love two people can experience."

I struggled to breathe until I finally gasped for air. "Weren't you paying attention? He's going to die."

Chapter Nineteen

CAELINUS

A six-mile run hadn't brought any clarity. If Bart thought being with me put me in danger, he'd run away. I had to convince him we were stronger together. First, I needed to convince myself that was true.

I'd been skeptical of Bart's interpretation of his visions, but if we were mates, he'd been right. There was a connection between the two parts of his premonitions, but we didn't know what it meant.

The shower spray soothed my body but not my thoughts. We hadn't completed our mate bond. Hell, did he know we were mates? Talk about a cluster. Would completing the bond help?

Probably not. I doubted we'd have an epiphany just because we mated properly. The whole thing was annoying as fuck.

Mindful of my parents, I cut my shower shorter than I'd have liked. The perils of single living and one bathroom.

Bart and I needed to talk tonight. I had to convince him running away would make things worse and not better. Together we could face down whatever anyone threw at us.

Even a demon.

I styled my hair with my fingers, wrapped a towel around my waist, opened the door and . . . nearly ran over my mother.

"Jesus, Mom!" I yelled as I jumped back. She slapped a hand to her chest and held up the other. "Sorry."

We looked at each other and laughed. "Sorry, Caelinus. What're the odds I'd knock a second before you open the door?"

Standing in just a towel, I felt practically naked, which was irrational. A bathing suit showed way more skin and that never bothered me. "Evidently really high. I'm done. You and Dad can use it."

"That's not why I came to find you. Your father and I are staying in tonight. We're tired and we had a big, late lunch. I'll make us a salad or something light."

Them bailing on dinner shouldn't have thrilled me as much as it did. I tried not to sound too pleased. "Are you sure?"

"Apart from we're tired, you two need to talk. When he left, he was unsettled. I agreed not to read him, but I didn't need empathy to know he was troubled. And since you two are already sleeping together, you don't need to pretend for our sake."

Mom's totally open approach to sex and sexuality was refreshing at first. She'd been clear at an early age: she didn't care who my brothers and I were attracted to, she and Dad would always love us. Talking about the particulars of my sex life, however, wasn't necessary. I growled at her, but I was in a towel. It wasn't very menacing. "Woman, you are *so* evil."

"How is it that when parents don't pretend, they're evil? Would you rather I think of you as the cute six-year-old you used to be?"

Used to be? I was still fucking cute. "You went all the way back to six?"

"You stopped being sweet right around your seventh birthday." She shrugged. "I call it like I see it."

I should have called bullshit, but I had been a pill when I hit my tweens. Plus she'd purposefully moved away from what I did behind closed doors, so I owed her.

"Let me get dressed and check in with Bart, and I'll make sure you have everything you need." I took a step and stopped. "Since I won't be back until morning."

She snorted as she walked away. Kicking the door shut, I tracked down my phone. There was a message.

{**Bart:** Call me? I need to beg off dinner. Isaac will pick you up as planned.}

How did I respond? Was he running again, or was there a good reason? The phone vibrated.

{**Bart:** I know we said we'd wait a couple of days, but can you come over after you and your parents eat? I really want to see you.}

That should have appeased my worried heart, but something was off. Adding the last bit was out of character. It implied he needed something. Bart usually asked and if I said no, he'd say he understood. I tapped the call button and he answered on the first ring.

"That was fast." He sounded relieved.

Texting was a terrible medium when feelings were involved. Hearing his voice and the implied sigh made it the right choice.

"I just checked my phone. Is everything okay?"

"Not really, but nothing seeing you won't fix." He added a small laugh. "Do you think your parents will mind if you come over tonight?"

More pressure. Now that Mom had connected the dots for me, I could feel Bart's mood clearly. He needed to see and touch me. Until we saw each other, he wouldn't be content. "Funny you should ask. Mom and Dad are tired; they want to stay in and go to bed early."

"Oh?" His more hopeful tone eased my anxiety. "Did you want me to—"

"Nope. They're good. We ate late, so they're not hungry, and flying always makes Mom tired. Too many people, too close, leaking negative emotions. Evidently fear of flying is way more common than we know. It drains her, staying closed that long."

"Is she okay?"

I swallowed a blip of irritation. I wanted his focus on us, not my mother, who was fine, but I couldn't be mad at him for caring. "Yes. The pitfalls of being an empath. It's no worse than a headache after reading all day. Nothing a good sleep won't cure. Hold on. I need to put you on speaker so I can get dressed."

"Why? I like you without clothes."

I tapped the button and dropped my phone onto the bed. His playful tone did me good. Bart rarely put himself first. I needed him to see how vital it was for his health and ours. "Down tiger. There's a time for that."

"Yes, it's called 'all the time.' As in all the time is the right time for you to be naked."

Of course, my filthy mind returned to that awkward conversation we'd had with Gretchen when we told her we were dating. I laughed and stepped into my boxers. "Your aunt would disagree."

"I didn't say I wanted her to see you naked. Just me."

My silly grin might've made me look crazy, but I didn't care as I pulled on my shirt. "No worries, the only person I want to see me naked is you."

"Damn." He laughed softly. "I was kidding, but now I'm wondering why you're getting dressed. I'm just going to rip them off the moment you get here."

The banter barely masked the truth. Bart wasn't totally kidding, and I felt the same. If this is what being mated felt like, we'd be staying home a lot.

"Restrain yourself. The neighbors don't want a show."

"Not that they could see anything, but I have a bit more self-control. I'll drag you inside first."

Our silly conversation seemed to restore his balance. It gave me chills to know he was feeling better. "I'm glad you texted. I really want to see you tonight, too."

"I'll ask Isaac to come get you before I give him the night off," he said. "We still have the reservation, but I assume you want to stay in tonight?"

What I wanted was him. To touch and hold him, smell his scent, and feel his breath on my skin. "I do. We need to talk."

"We do. See you soon. I . . . can't wait to see you."

That wasn't what he was going to say, but I understood. "I feel the same."

※

Isaac pulled away and I stared at the house that had already started to feel like home. Butterflies exploded in my stomach as I hitched my bag and started walking. It was stupid. Bart nearly used the "L" word. But what if he didn't want a mate?

In theory, who wouldn't want to meet "the one" person they were fated to be with? No more dating for months only to learn you weren't compatible. Reality, however, didn't match up perfectly with theory.

Textbooks held numerous examples of fated mates who despised each other. Usually, it happened at the start, and they worked out their differences, but not always. Being drawn to someone you despised but couldn't bear to see with anyone else never ended well.

Bart and I didn't have that problem, but it didn't mean he'd be happy about this. Some people don't want to be told who they'd spend their lives with.

Bart had texted he was in the backyard, so I shifted my backpack and walked around the house.

The hum of the city clashed with the sounds of the suburbs as I rounded the corner. My heart stilled when I saw him in a chair gazing into his yard. On the table between him and an empty chair, he'd set two glasses and a bottle of wine in a chiller. It had the perfect feel of two people at peace.

He turned as I walked closer and stood. His smile calmed any lingering doubts. I could feel his tension washing away with every step. I did that. Without saying anything, he wrapped me in a fierce, needy hug.

It was the most perfect thing I'd ever felt. Warmth spread from where his head touched mine and his love swept through me. We hadn't fully bonded, yet it was so intense. It should have scared me, but it didn't.

Bart loved fiercely and completely. Nothing that beautiful could scare me.

I squeezed him back with the same passionate need. I had no more doubts. Bart was mine and I was his. Forever.

"Bart . . ." I buried my face in his neck and fought back tears.

"I know." He rubbed the back of my head. "Me too."

We clung to each other like lovers who'd been kept apart for years. In a way it was true; we'd been searching for each other our whole lives without knowing what we needed.

Bart heaved in a breath. "You smell so good."

My throat tightened and my body trembled. Knowing who we were to each other unlocked feelings I'd held back out of fear. Certain he wouldn't reject me, I let it out. "I love you."

Bart melted into my hold. "I've wanted to tell you that, but I thought it was too much too soon."

I could feel his heartbeat against my chest. His breath, warm and light, tickled my neck, leaving me completely content. We stayed pressed together until I felt him tense beneath my grip.

"The night I snuck out." His words were clipped and soft. "I'm sorry. I saw . . . Jan was dead and you . . . you were dying at my feet. I didn't know what else to do."

His tears rolled onto my neck and his pain crashed against me in waves.

"Shhh." Drops slid down my cheeks as his anguish enveloped me in its crushing embrace. I cupped his nape and pressed us tighter. "That won't happen. We'll figure out how to stop it, babe. I promise."

I had no idea how, but I'd find a way.

Chapter Twenty

❧

BARTHOLOMEW

Funny how few words we'd spoken since Cael arrived, but how much we'd said. I hadn't told him everything Granny P. said, but we'd talk later. We needed to enjoy the new us first.

The small table on my patio separated us, but Cael was close enough it might not be there. I wondered if distance mattered or if it was a state of mind. We wouldn't always be physically together. It would be problematic if that affected us negatively.

"When I was kid, Jan and I would sneak onto the roof and stargaze on the ledge," I said without looking over. "Once I dozed off and dreamed my consciousness left me to search the galaxy for other life."

"Are you sure it wasn't real?" He reached over and I laced our fingers. "I mean, you have such talent. It could've been real."

It'd felt too vivid to be a dream, and I'd woken panting from fear and excitement. "At the time I was convinced it actually happened, but it isn't likely. I've never done it since."

"That doesn't mean it isn't a thing, just that no one figured out how."

If seeing the possibility of something that hadn't happened was real, why not exploring the galaxy with your mind? "I told Gran about my visions. The Ocular Society has known foresight is real for thousands of years, but kept it secret to protect the seers."

His anger sizzled in the air between us as I recounted our conversation.

"That's ridiculous," he said when I finished. "It sounds very Machiavellian. How many mages had their lives ruined because no one believed they could see the future?"

His righteous anger on behalf of me and others gave me a warm, bubbly feeling. If my mate, the one I'd be forever drawn to, had been a pompous, self-absorbed twat, we might have ended up killing each other or ourselves. Thankfully fate sent me someone I could love and respect.

"I agree, but they acted centuries before I got a say in the matter."

"Was it bad?"

I smiled at his compassion for a boy he didn't know. "No. The last time I mentioned having a vision was after Henri died. There were so many people in and out of our house, no one remembered it the next day. In my heart, I knew what I saw was true and that was enough. I resolved if I ever had another premonition, I'd deal with it myself. And I did."

Cael reached over and squeezed my hand. He understood. I'd been a defiant breakwater, standing fast despite what others thought, but it still hurt.

"Grandma Pederson is coming tomorrow to talk to us," I said.

Cael rolled his head to look at me. "About?"

I'd asked her the same question, but she'd put me off. "She wouldn't tell me. I assume my visions, but we'll need to wait to find out."

"Delightful."

I released his hand and stood. "Let me make tea and coffee."

We took our drinks and dessert onto the patio and sat in peaceful silence. Cael and I still needed to talk about so much. Given my limited knowledge of mate bonds, I was pretty sure we hadn't completed ours, and I sensed his hesitation. Or maybe I was projecting my uncertainty onto him. I really didn't know.

When I thought about us sharing our lives, a deep pocket of contentment bubbled up from deep inside. It rushed out like an eruption, filling the tiniest bits of my body. I understood what made this so powerful. Cael was an unmovable anchor I could tether myself to and be grounded amid the chaos of the world. We were stronger than me.

The uncertainty of my vision, however, chipped away at that security. What we didn't know outnumbered what we knew. Did we alter the outcome I'd seen or serve to make it more certain? One thing I knew for sure, some version of my premonition would take place. Maybe not the way I saw it, but there would be a demon.

"You're pensive," Cael said. "What's wrong?"

No matter what I said, it would be the wrong thing. If I downplayed my fears, I'd have to lie. Telling him the truth, however, risked a full-blown argument. Cael was itching to convince me I was wrong, and he wasn't going to accept defeat.

"Us. Me. My visions. I don't know what to believe anymore. I thought I understood them and could use them for my benefit, but I don't. We don't know what it means, but I'm sure of one thing: you and Jan are in danger. I am, too, but I have to fight this demon. You two don't."

"Bullshit!" He waved his hands to cut me off. "Nope, I'm not listening to this. You no more *have to* fight this demon than Jan or I have to. It's called a choice."

This was his heart talking, not his mind. I understood he wanted to keep me safe, but this was different. Only I had the power to deal with this threat. The better question was, did I have enough to survive.

"You haven't seen what I did."

"I don't need to. I see and feel everything coming from you. It's bad. I get it. But if you can handle this alone, our being there can only help. If you can't, well don't expect me to step back and let you go off by yourself. That isn't how this is going to play out."

From the first night, I knew Cael would love fiercely. He didn't know how to do anything less. All in or not at all had been how he achieved his goals. Fighting a demon, especially one the size I saw, was different. You didn't kill it with determination.

"You asked why I was uneasy. I knew this would be your response."

Cael's face tightened, and his gaze never left mine. Exhaling, he lost some of his tension. "Do you think it'll be any easier for me to let you go alone than it is for me to be there? I get it, Bart. You want to protect everyone you love. News flash. We want to protect you, too. Your vision doesn't show you walking out alive, does it?"

The answer wasn't as simple as he tried to frame it. My position was precarious, but he knew I hadn't seen how the fight ended. "I never see the final blows, I only see you and Jan dead or dying."

"I know. You wake up before the killing blow lands," he said. "My point is, we—*we*, Bart, not you alone, we—need to find a better way."

It was a nice idea, but it began with a flawed premise. Neither Jan nor Cael had studied how to fight a demon.

I wasn't going to win this argument until I had more details. Since I didn't know how to coax that out of my visions, it was time to concede. "I agree. The outcome I've seen so far isn't one I want to experience. With or without you."

Cael opened his mouth and closed it as his lips morphed into a smile. "I thought you'd fight me harder. Thank you."

Guilt gnawed at the edges of my emotions. I shoved it down to hide it from Cael's powers. My agreement wasn't permanent. I might change my mind if the situation required. "You're welcome."

A yawn snuck up on me and I stretched instinctively. I was bone-tired. I wanted to curl up with Cael; he was good for my soul in a way I'd never experienced. "Sorry."

"That's my cue to say we need to go to bed." He grabbed the plates and stood. "These can wait until the morning."

The sentiment was sweet and appalling at the same time. I'd never be able to sleep with a sink full of dishes. I popped out of my chair and grabbed our cups.

"No, they can't. I guarantee Gran will be here before either of us is fully awake. I don't want her to think we were so anxious to get into bed we didn't bother doing the dishes."

"We *are* that eager." He slid the door open. "But I guess a few more minutes won't kill either of us."

He was right on both counts, but he wouldn't enjoy me tossing all night worrying about my less-than-clean kitchen. I nicked a kiss on the way in. "You'll thank me in the morning."

Cael wiggled his brow. "I'm not waiting that long to show my appreciation."

The filthy look he gave me set my insides on fire. He licked his lips, and my face was a mirror to his. I seriously considered dumping the dishes and promising myself I'd get up early to clean. My brain screamed I wouldn't keep that pledge, and that bucket of cold reality cooled my lust just enough that I stuck to the plan.

Granny P. didn't have a key to my door or a way past my wards, but if I kept her waiting on my doorstep—or worse, on the street—we'd be sorry.

"Then let me finish this quick and you can show me."

Cael stepped closer and turned on the faucet. "If I help, we'll get there in half the time."

I'd planned to do triage, just enough to get by, but working together we got it done in six minutes. Putting the last dish away, Cael hung the dish towel and pulled me in for a kiss.

His lips were soft and warm and sent ripples of happiness through me. I pushed my tongue into his mouth; my hands ran up his back and I dug my fingertips into the muscle. He cupped my head and crushed our mouths together.

My dick was painfully hard in just a few seconds. I moaned as his hard-on ground against mine, fueling my need for him. "Bedroom," I gasped during a break in our kiss.

"Yeah."

I took his hand and headed for the stairs. Smiling happily, I made it a quarter of the way up before light exploded behind my eyes. If Cael hadn't been clutching my hand, I'd have slammed face first into the wooden risers.

"Bart!" Cael's scream gave me something to grasp for as darkness tried to claim my consciousness.

Another flash of white filled my vision, and I caught a glimpse of a street. There were cars, spells flying, screams of pain. Three standard, government-issued, gray SUVs were surrounded by four high-end sports cars. Men and women stood behind doors pounding at each other. Three of the attackers went down, but the rest managed to take out everyone in the middle vehicle.

The back door of the defenseless SUV exploded high into the night and two men ran up and pulled someone from the back seat. The person had a bag over his head, meaning he was a mage of power.

"Bart!" I blinked up at Cael's panicked face. "What happened? You were yelling."

The stairway came into focus and I realized I was at home. "I had a vision."

"Have you ever had one when you were awake?"

I closed my eyes, as much to clear the receding pain as to commit as many images as possible to memory.

"Never."

Chapter Twenty-One

CAELINUS

Bart was so pale, I worried he'd pass out. He didn't act hurt, but through our link I felt his body was out of rhythm. When his vision hit, he seized like he'd been hit with a taser. It only lasted a few seconds, but his magic was depleted. I panicked and called for help.

An hour later, Mr. and Mrs. Pederson arrived. With barely a glance at Bart, they ordered us to his safe room. I didn't know he had one, but with seven independent wards on his house, I wasn't shocked.

I followed everyone to the basement, a place I'd not been yet. Bart's house was big, and we hadn't been dating long enough for me to explore every room. It was definitely not because we spent so much time in the bedroom. That was the story I was going with if the Pedersons asked.

The cellar was one large, open room. To the right of the stairs was a floor to ceiling steel door that belonged in a bank vault, not an upscale house. The most striking feature, however, was what I didn't see—magic.

Every mage knew the best way to enter a warded space was to undermine the spells that created the protection. If you couldn't see the magic, you didn't know what you were facing, much less how to defeat it. This wasn't something you bought off the shelf.

Bart pressed his mage stone into an indent above the handle and pulled open the thick door. Stepping back, he waved me and his grandparents in first.

We descended several feet to a concrete pad that had a table and eight chairs in the center. The steel plates that lined the walls shimmered with protective magic. Light came from an arcane ball that floated near the ceiling. He'd clearly put work into building this room.

The door clanged shut, sealing us inside. Bart stepped down and walked me to the empty side of the table. Across from us, his grandparents watch him intently. He looked tired, which wasn't a shock. It seemed like days ago we stood in his kitchen waiting for Isaac to take us to the airport to get my parents. If he hadn't scared the shit out of me with that vision, I'd have insisted we do this tomorrow.

"First, I'm sorry for being rude," Bart said. "Cael, these are my grandparents, Sally and Wilbur Pederson. Gran, Gramps, this is Cael Reinhold, my mate."

"Very pleased to meet you, Cael." Gramps stood to shake my hand. "Call me Will."

Sally didn't get up, but she smiled. "I'm glad you're not wasting time pretending you aren't meant for each other."

Sally and my mother would get on like old friends. They called bullshit where they saw it, but never stopped loving us. Bart still seemed preoccupied, so I put my hand over his. "Thank you."

"Yes, thank you." Bart squeezed once and let go. "Sorry to drag you back again, Gran. This was a first for me."

She waved him down. "Tell me what you saw."

Hearing it a second time scared me more than the first. Right after it happened, Bart was running on adrenaline, and he was very succinct in his retelling. This time he went into more depth. Sally and Will interrupted at times to ask for details, which Bart usually didn't have.

"Could you see who the mage was?" Sally asked.

"How many mages are in custody that require three vehicles to transport?" he replied.

Sally looked at Will, who shook his head. "It doesn't have to be Declan, dear, but it's a good possibility."

"I'll check if they're moving him soon," Will said.

I blinked at the exchange. Bart had said Will was a bank executive and neither he nor Sally were on the Mage Council. Who was he going to ask, and why would they give him that information? Sally seemed to think it perfectly reasonable. Bart hadn't indicated he found it unusual, but he wasn't himself and it set my hackles on edge. There was more here than Bart's pseudo grandparents coming to check on him. Even as head of the Ocular Society, she shouldn't have that kind of pull. Avie would, but Sally and Will?

"If they are, make sure they send more than three vehicles," Bart said. "And don't put Declan in the middle car."

"I presume you couldn't tell where or when this happened or you'd have told us," Will said.

Bart shook his head. "Only it was at night and in a city. I didn't recognize any landmarks."

"We have other information to help us narrow down where it will happen," Sally said.

I studied Sally without staring. Bart respected her as more than just his grandmother. I wanted to raise my concern, but Bart was already unsettled. He didn't need me to drop another bomb into the situation.

"Should we warn the Council and Assembly?" Will asked.

"Yes, but we need to do it through back channels." Sally looked at Bart. "I don't want to expose you as the source of the information. We can discuss who to contact on the way home."

Her concern for Bart should have alleviated some of my anxiety, but it was like he was under a spell. The casual way they discussed filtering information to the ruling bodies of mages and species spoke of far more than met the eye. And he hadn't questioned any of it.

How did I politely ask who the hell they really were? Nothing good came to mind and since it appeared they were almost finished with the conversation, I stopped caring about good manners.

"What's going on?" All eyes focused on me. I refused to shrink from their attention. I was right and deserved to know the truth. Looking at Sally, I asked, "Why is Will getting an update on prisoner movement . . . How is he getting it, and what are you going to do with that information?"

Bart turned toward me, an irked expression on his face. He opened his mouth to speak, and I saw him make the connection. Rather than bark at me for being rude, he turned to his grandparents.

"Yes. What *is* going on?"

I expected Sally to be irritated that she'd been accused of something nefarious. Instead, she smiled, took out her mage stone and set it on the table.

"Well done, Cael," she said. "I expected Bart to lead the inquisition, but he's still processing his vision."

"Inquisition?" Bart asked. "Gran, you're talking in riddles."

"Before I can tell you more, you both need to take an oath never to reveal what I tell you tonight."

Her stone pulsed and I sat back, holding my hands up. "I'm not agreeing until I know what we're talking about."

"Then we have a standoff." She raised an eyebrow, and if I was honest, it was scary as fuck. She had total confidence in her abilities, and she didn't care what I wanted. "Take the oath or we'll leave."

"Granny, what are you doing?" Bart sounded more hurt than annoyed. "I didn't require you be sworn to secrecy."

"I know, dear, but this is out of my hands."

She wasn't lying, but she wasn't giving us the whole truth. No surprise. You don't require an oath of silence without holding back something important. This deadlock was especially dangerous given the high-level spells she'd use to bind me and Bart.

"Out of your hands?" Bart asked. "That's crazy."

"We all answer to someone," I said.

I learned three things about Bart and his family today. They weren't all assholes, Granny Pederson didn't distinguish between her biological grandson and his half-brother, and Bart didn't play their game. This, however, wasn't a game. We needed to agree, or she couldn't tell us anything.

"What happened to, 'I'm not agreeing to anything, blah, blah, blah.'" Bart's almost-smile mirrored his emotional output. "I'm supposed to be the reasonable one."

I covered his hand with mine. Normally, I didn't do public affection. It always seemed forced, like people were shouting their status to make single people jealous. Now, however, I realized couples touched because it made them feel better and they didn't care what others thought. "You are, babe, but right now you're distracted."

Bart slipped his pinky over mine, squeezed gently, and turned back to his grandmother. "Not even a hint?"

Shaking her head, Sally pursed her lips for a second. "Not even a little one, kiddo."

We put our mage stones on the table, and Sally brought hers closer. I studied Bart to be sure he was up for the conversation. He was fatigued, but not exhausted. So long as he wasn't asked to do any strenuous magic, this wouldn't tax him. Once it was over, however, he was going to sleep. Our original plans to complete our bond would have to wait.

"Do you agree?" Sally asked.

I blinked and realized I'd been incredibly stupid. Sally was about to bind me to a powerful prohibition spell, and I hadn't paid attention.

"I do," Bart said before I could ask her to repeat herself.

He had no apprehension, so I doubled down on stupid. "I do."

Our stones flashed, and my stomach twisted into a knot. I'd been cautious when it came to magic. No duels, no experiments, and no agreeing to binding oaths without knowing exactly what I agreed to in advance.

"It's okay, Cael." Bart rubbed my back gently and soothing energy flowed from him into me. "You can't talk about what she says while the stones are glowing. At any time, you can stop, but you can't talk about what you'd heard so far."

How had he known? He continued to massage me until I took a deep breath. My tension melted away, but thankfully he kept his hand on my back. I liked the contact.

Sally folded her hands on the table and began. "The eight guardians of the Great Ward keep themselves hidden for their protection. Only the griffin, Leifr Cormaic, has continued to interact with his kind, and then only in times of great need. Isolated as they are, the guardians lack the most important weapon to defend themselves: knowledge. To address that concern, the guardians created the Society of Guardians."

Three months ago, I'd have scoffed at what I'd just heard. Three months ago, I hadn't met Bart and learned that foresight was real, or that he was my mate. Still, it was hard to accept.

"The Society draws its members from all races," Sally said. "Prospective members are approached carefully and sworn to secrecy before they're told anything. Hence the lack of any record of our existence."

Sally explained it in such detail my eyes rolled back. It made sense the Guardians created a secret group dedicated to protecting them. The scary part was they existed under our noses.

"How many of you are there?" Bart asked.

"We don't know," Will said. "Only the Guardians have that information."

Bart's displeasure with that answer crept up our link. It was the truth, but the Guardians weren't around to tell him. Sally and Will had also withheld information. They hadn't lied, but I wasn't letting my guard down.

"Why tell us now?" I asked.

"Bart's latest visions and your status as mates required we bring you both into the Society."

The first part I expected, but the second part of her answer gave me a bad feeling. "Why does our status matter? Are all fated mates invited to join?"

"Not all." She waited until I met her gaze. "The last time a human alpha mage was mated to an elven alpha mage, they became the Western Guardians. The guardians believe your bond and Declan raising a demon are connected and want you in the Society."

Her answer begged the question why, but she held up her hand before we could speak.

"You've also been summoned to the elven homeland."

Chapter Twenty-Two

❧

BARTHOLOMEW

A family jet flew us to the closest airport, but the trip still took most of the day. Cael had been pensive the entire trip. I wasn't much better. Being summoned to appear before the Conclave wasn't our choice for how to spend a weekend, especially not when Cael's parents were visiting.

For being so open, Idaho felt small. The city of Salmon, population 3117, was the nearest city to the homeland. City? That was a joke. There were more beings who went to school or worked at Utrecht. Blink and you'd miss everything.

West of the city, big replaced small—vast open spaces under a big sky. The road was the only sign that beings had been here and staring at it, I understood why the Conclave and the Shifter Assembly clashed with humans. We slapped our ugly stamp on these beautiful places in the name of progress. Ours, not theirs.

Seeing the homeland was exciting. Few humans received permission to enter, and only if they had business. The land was sacred and even well-meaning beings could upset the balance the elves had with nature. Seeing it under these circumstances, however, took the shine off the experience.

My father wasn't happy the Conclave had summoned me. He had the authority to forbid me to appear, but he chose a different route. As special envoy to the Elven Conclave, I held the title of ambassador. No one expected the Conclave to abduct me, but Dad wasn't taking chances. By agreeing to allow the Chancellor's envoy entrance, the elves guaranteed not only my safety, but also my release when our meeting was over.

Cael spent most of the flight and drive from the airport gazing out the window. I didn't need our bond to know he was anxious. Elves were free to visit anytime they wanted, but they were rarely summoned. Even when teenage elves had their magic tested, the Conclave requested they make an appointment. This was a command to appear, at a meeting, with all twelve members. The ruling body wanted to put eyes on us for a reason. We just didn't know what that reason was.

When we reached the edge of the homeland, Cael shifted into his elven form. Unlike most shifters who had to account for increased or decreased body mass, fur, claws or talons, the change from human to elf only took a few seconds. One moment he was the Cael I knew, and the next he was . . . still Cael.

He'd grown a couple of inches, gotten leaner, and his skin had less pigment, but he was recognizable to his human self. His ears weren't pointy as depicted in the media, but they were longer and wider. The part that changed the least was his eyes. They were still Cael's.

We changed into traditional elven clothes, natural fibers with no animal hides, before we met our escort. Cael wore beige cotton pants and a forest-green cotton/silk blend shirt that was open at the neck. I chose brown pants and a tan shirt because green wasn't a good color on me. Cael teased me about making sure I had the right outfit, but attention to detail was important. At least, that's what I told him.

Shoes, or lack of shoes, had been the biggest issue for me. Earth magic protected the soles of an elf's feet. All they needed was constant contact with the ground. I didn't have that natural ability, so I spent the days before we left finding a way to recreate the effect with magic.

My first several attempts were failures. Either it didn't work, or my feet felt like they were encased in concrete. Finally, I found a reference to a spell someone else had created in an old book and it worked well enough I could leave my shoes in the car.

Our escort met us with horses, and we rode for over an hour under a canopy of leaves so dense, barely any sunlight made it through. When we emerged into a clearing, I finally had an unencumbered view of the sky. The sun had dipped below the tree line, but there were hours of daylight left.

Twelve elves sat cross-legged, hovering off the ground. Arrayed in a wide circle, they remained motionless as we were led to a spot just outside the ring. My human prejudice led me to expect a group of old elves who looked so similar I couldn't easily tell them apart. Instead, they were as ethnically diverse as humans.

Something touched my hand, and I looked down as Cael threaded his fingers through mine. "We wait here until they call us to enter."

He sounded more confident, and his energy was less chaotic. Being home grounded him. Our eyes met and a rush of emotions hit me. Love, happiness, and desire were strong, but gratitude hit me hardest. I centered him, not the homeland.

I smiled and opened myself so he could know I felt the same. Before Cael, I thought I'd been happy, but I was merely content. Now I knew what true joy meant. "As long as we're together, I'm in no rush."

Scanning the clearing, I saw two things I'd missed when we arrived. The twelve floated over stones set flush with the ground. Each had a glyph etched into the surface. I couldn't see what they did, but Cael had been wrong when he claimed elves didn't use glyphs and earth magic together.

And we weren't alone. Spaced among the trees, hundreds of elves stood in silent observation. I didn't know if that was positive or not. People attended Mage Council meetings when something momentous was discussed. Elves appeared just as curious as humans.

An ancient elf stepped down and walked our way. He smiled and calm energy pushed out from him. "Welcome home, Caelinus Eoghan Reinhold. The homeland celebrates the return of one of its children." He touched the tips of his fingers to his forehead, lips, and heart, then bowed his head and spread his arms wide.

Cael released my hand and imitated the gesture. "Thank you, Revered One. It is always good to come home."

The elder nodded and turned his attention to me. "On behalf of the Conclave, I welcome you, Ambassador Hollen. I am ard ri Tadgán. It has been some years since one from your family visited our lands."

I bowed deeply and recited the words Grandpa Hollen instructed were appropriate for this meeting. "On behalf of the Chancellor, I bring greetings and well wishes to you ard ri, to the Conclave, and all elves. My father sends his personal regards and thanks you for allowing me into your home."

The twinkle in Tadgán's eyes told me Grandpa knew the proper etiquette for dealing with elves. Not that I doubted him, but it seemed a bit unnecessary. I had a lot to learn about diplomacy.

"Well said, young mage. I see your family keeps current on the delicacies of interspecies relations."

I saw no proof he was mocking me, so I answered honestly, "I'm sorry to report, ard ri, that my grandfather spent an hour drilling into me the need to follow the protocols and not cause an interspecies incident."

He chuckled first and then this proper and stately elf leader tossed his head back and laughed. Not a derisive chortle, but a full-bellied laugh that seemed out of place for somewhere so solemn.

"You surprise me, young mage. Most would have suggested it's to be expected of one in your position. I like honesty, and that your family makes its young respect the other beings you share this world with."

Cael's pride percolated through our link. Pleasing him was far more satisfying than making the ard ri laugh. "I'll need to spend more time learning your customs given my new status."

Tadgán kept his smile but raised an eyebrow. "Well said." He swept his left arm toward the circle. "Take your place and we can begin."

I nearly got whiplash from how quickly we switched from jovial to stone cold serious. For all the niceties shown, the Conclave hadn't summoned us for pleasantries. This wouldn't be a conversation either. This was a test, but we didn't know the subject matter.

As an envoy, the Conclave had no ability to command me into their place of judgement. If I refused, I'd be escorted out of view and Cael would face their scrutiny alone. The ard ri clearly believed I wouldn't leave my mate, but couching it as a command spoke to his expectations. It also reminded me to stay on guard.

We made our way to the center, and the other elven lords floated around the circle until all twelve faced us. Tadgán nodded and Cael sat crossed-legged on the ground. I'd been instructed I couldn't do the same unless granted permission, something Grandpa said hadn't happened in his lifetime.

I sat back on my heels, kept my back straight, and stared at my inquisitors. Three of the elven lords scowled at my lack of deference, but I kept my gaze steady. The Conclave's power over me was limited to what I gave them. They asked me to sit for their questions, and I agreed. I didn't agree to be a cowering supplicant.

"No respect," a fair-skinned elf with silver hair to my far right said. He glared daggers at me as if it would cause me to shrink before him.

My mouth almost moved before my brain stopped me from insulting the elf lord. My title didn't require I bow to them, and he knew that. Saying it, however, would debase my position, so I kept silence.

"You are correct," Tadgán said. He glanced to his left, waiting for his colleague to make eye contact. "You fail to show Chancellor Hollen's personal envoy the proper respect. He has graciously accepted our request to sit before our body and has taken the time to learn our protocols."

The lesser elf opened his mouth, but the elf to his right put a hand on his arm. She had tan skin and brown hair held together with flowers and combs. "Anablin, our brother is right. Would you grovel before the Mage Council if asked to appear before them? Ambassador Hollen has submitted himself for questioning, something no human has ever done."

Some on the Conclave had terrible poker faces. I couldn't hear the words, but they had a private mind to mind conversation while Cael and I waited.

It didn't matter, I'd learned I held all the power. The Conclave *wanted* me to stay. Every member thinking clearly understood the magnitude of what my father had permitted. They also knew I could leave any time.

"I stand corrected." Anablin's harsh voice shattered the silence like nails on a chalk board.

It was a terrible apology, but he'd been forced to say something. He thought he'd won with his fake remorse, but the words didn't matter so much as the context. He'd backed down.

"Apology accepted." I steeled my expression to keep any hint of smug from my face.

Anablin seethed and his eyes smoldered, but he couldn't respond or else he'd admit his apology was anything but. The elf who had tried to reason with him snickered and her reaction only added to Anablin's ire. I'd be sure to keep my wards up to avoid any unfortunate accidents happening to me while in the homeland.

Tadgán put his hands together and then slowly drew them apart. Power radiated from the ground and expanded outward from the center of the circle. It was a binding spell, akin to the ones used to compel compliance to an oath, only far more complex. The tendrils of power slithered into my core but lacked the coercive effect of a true binding. I could expel these if I wanted.

The ard ri lowered his arms, but the power remained. I would have feared its presence, but the earth magic wasn't harsh like an oath spell. This was soothing and protective.

"We asked you to appear before us because the Earth is troubled. Chancellor Hollen informed the governing bodies of the demon Ambassador Hollen slew last spring. Circumventing the Great Ward is a malignant act we'd hoped not to see even in our long lifetimes. It speaks to a powerful new evil in the world, one your mate bond confirms.

"The last time an elf was mated to a human mage, it was to create the Great Ward. Your bond, coming so soon after a demon breached the barrier, is no coincidence. Mother Earth is taking steps to protect itself, but we don't fully understand what shape the threat will take. The only thing we know for certain is you two are vital to its designs."

I snuck a peek at Cael, and he was looking at me. Reaching over, I took his hand in mine. I didn't care if it was a breach of protocol or not, I needed to feel him. No one, not the Conclave nor the Mage Council, would decide our future. We weren't pawns in a preemptive strategy the elves were planning to save the world.

To hell with protocols, I needed answers. "What do you need from us?"

Tadgán's lips quirked a fraction higher. Not a smile, but as close to a reaction as he'd give me. "To know you and Cael. We surmise much, but we want clarity."

"Our bond didn't come with instructions," Cael said. "How can we explain what we don't know?"

The members of the Conclave tried to look disinterested, but their attention was riveted on us. My chest burned as I waited for Tadgán to reveal why Cael and I had been summoned.

"By opening yourselves and letting the Earth see all that you are," Tadgán said.

Hell fucking no! was my first reaction. My father didn't trust the Conclave enough to let me appear without diplomatic protection. There was no way I'd let them root around inside my head. Cael tensed and squeezed my fingers. Did he feel the same or was he affected through our bond?

"Bart." The concerned way he spoke my name meant I was pushing my emotions into him. "It's okay."

Was it? I stopped thinking about how to respond and let Cael's calming energy ease my fear. It was his turn to appease my concern. He trusted them, but they were his people.

I quieted my thoughts and focused on him. We were an "us" now. There was no more "me." It filled my heart to the bursting point and scared the crap out of me at the same time. Everything I did now affected us both.

He smiled when I faced him. "We'll be fine. I promise. No one is going to get inside that beautiful head of yours. The Earth doesn't think in words or images. It sees your essence. What makes you who you are. There's nothing to fear."

Cael had already lowered his wards, but when I tried to feel him outside our bond I couldn't. The energy that Tadgán had released surrounded us and kept us hidden. Inside our bond I saw what I always did. The beautiful being who wanted to help everyone; the teacher who took delight when his students soared, and who sought ways to help those who didn't; the friend who never let down those he'd promised to be there for; and the lover who didn't know how to hold back when he was with his mate.

I didn't know how others saw me, but it was impossible someone like Cael could be with me if the Earth would reject me.

"I love you, too." I had no other words to respond to what I saw when I looked at him. He didn't need to hear them, but I wanted to say them. For him. Only for him.

Cael pulled our hands up and kissed the back of mine. "I love you the same."

I realized how blind I'd been. We didn't need words or actions to define what we were. If we opened ourselves to each other, it was there all the time.

Jan always said I was a distant lover. He was right. I'd never trusted anyone enough to let them see all of me. My past relationships were superficial, endorphin spiking, thrill inducing associations that never satisfied me. It made sense. There was only room inside me for Cael. No one else could've made it through.

I lowered my wards, every one of them, and faced the Conclave more naked than I'd ever been before.

Chapter Twenty-Three

❧

CAELINUS

I opened the door to the shelter we'd been given. From the outside it was a small mound, but inside it was as spacious as my apartment in Philadelphia. The stairs descended to a great room with a few places to sit, no electronics, and bare dirt walls.

Like all traditional elven homes, everything was carved from the earth. The walls and most of the furniture were packed dirt. Rock was used for the tables, wood for the bed, and natural plant fibers for the mattress and linens.

The place thrummed with earth magic that refreshed my body. It should have calmed my soul, but the Earth was unsettled. Faint, almost an afterthought, I'd detected a whiff of dissonance when Bart and I opened ourselves to the Conclave. It was why the elders had summoned us.

A rush of delight filled me as Bart walked around our temporary home. I'd worried he'd find the place too spartan, but I should have known better. To him, this was a magical wonder, something he'd want to study. Ever the scholar, this apartment was a classroom, and he was a student.

I walked up behind him while he peered intently at the wall, slid my arms around his waist and pulled him to me. The effect of his body on mine was instant. Pressing my hard-on against his butt, I smiled when Bart pushed back.

"You're so sexy when you get all geeky," I said.

Bart laughed and tilted his head back. "I'll need to be geeky all the time if that's how you feel."

I nipped his ear lobe and he moaned. "You're sexy no matter what."

"The things you say when you have this poking me from behind." Bart ground his firm ass against my cock. "Or should I say, in my behind."

I squeezed him tighter because that was terrible. "We need to work on your sense of humor."

"Seeing as I don't have one, that will be a long-term project. Might take a few decades."

"I have the time." I licked down the side of his neck and then kissed my way up. "As long as we don't have to go to any more banquets in our honor."

"It wasn't *that* bad."

Bart might be able to fool everyone with his practiced public persona, but he'd been bored five minutes after we arrived. "That's not how you felt when it was happening. You didn't even like the food."

"I thought the food was amazing."

Interesting that he didn't deny he'd been bored. "How could you tell? You barely ate anything."

Bart snorted and pulled me around so he could kiss me. "I don't like having sex when I've eaten too much."

Raising an eyebrow, I tried—and failed epically—to look dubious. Bart limiting what he ate so we could have sex jolted my already supercharged hormones. "Cocky much? What made you think we'd have sex tonight?"

I expected a snappy comeback, but I got a puzzled face.

"You . . . Oh my god, Cael." His eyes opened wider. "You don't know, do you?"

"Know what?"

He took my hand and put it on his rock-hard cock. "You were pumping out pheromones all night. I was afraid I'd have to fight half the elf nation to keep you to myself."

Through our link, I knew Bart wasn't joking, but that was impossible. I had enough control not to mark the room with my scent. "Why didn't you say anything?"

"I thought you did it on purpose to let everyone know I was yours."

My hand was still pressed to his groin, but the conversation took the edge off my lust. "I wouldn't put you at risk. Why would you think that?"

Bart took a step back. I reached for him, but my angry tone made him flinch away. "I never thought you were putting me at risk. It seemed like you were just naturally hornier in your elf form, and it was a sign we'd complete our mate bond tonight. If I'd been worried, I'd have protected us."

A full mate bond would have prevented a misunderstanding like this. We had enough, however, that he felt his rejection hurt me and he softened his aura.

"I don't think wearing my elf form changes my sexual desires, but I've never had sex while I'm shifted."

"Never?" His impish grin beat the return of his arousal by a heartbeat. "We so need to change that. It could be way better for both of us."

To the outside world, Bart was the brilliant but stuffy and staid Professor Hollen. With me, he was anything but reserved. I got all his passion and need. "No one's ever told me it's better, but couples shift to their elven form to conceive. There's a near one hundred percent success rate that way."

"So, if you fuck me in your elf form, I'll get pregnant?" He wiggled his eyebrows. "My parents will be thrilled."

Male pregnancy wasn't a thing among any of the species, but Bart almost made me wish it was possible. I'd have his children. "I think the other way around."

"Hmm," he kissed me softly, "We need to test both while we're here. Just to be sure."

The thought of him and me naked reversed my flagging lust and sent it soaring. "Yes, we do."

We kissed our way across the room; I didn't wait for the bed to pull off his shirt and lick his nipple. Biting the nub gently, I slid my hands inside his waistband and pushed his pants down. Bart groaned and pulled my head up.

He tugged at my shirt. "You have too many clothes on."

In less than five seconds, the shirt flew over my head and my pants ended up on the floor. Bart was on his knees, his lips pressed against my cock. He ran his hands slowly up my chest, tweaking my nipples when he paused.

"You're so beautiful," he said, before swallowing most of my cock.

"Oh, God." I tossed my head back as my knees wobbled and pleasure coursed through me. He fisted my cock and jerked me as he drew his lips back and forth.

Sex in elven form was different. Bart's scent was much stronger than normal; it made me harder than I'd ever remembered. Now I understood why I was leaking pheromones—I could smell my mate and I *had* to bond with him.

Bart was very good at sucking dick and tonight he was especially good. I wasn't going to last, so I grabbed him under the arms and made him stand.

"Why'd you stop me," he said with a smirk. "I was having fun."

No surprise. Our bodies were pumping unusually high levels of dopamine into our systems. "I thought of it first." I towed him with me as I backed toward the bed. "I get to go first."

"If I think of something, I get to do it?" he whispered in my ear. Sliding his tongue behind my ear lobe, he bit the soft flesh hard enough that I gasped for air.

"Yes," I panted, pulling us both onto the bed.

"Anything?" He crawled over me as we moved back.

"Yes." I flipped him around and lay on top of him. "After I do what I want first."

I covered his lips with mine and pushed my tongue into his mouth with an urgent need. Our cocks were trapped between our bodies, and I ground myself against him. He hooked one of my legs with his and wrapped me in a bear hug.

Pausing to catch my breath, I pulled back and stared at him. "You are so fucking handsome. I want to do so many things with you."

"Is this where I give you a blank check to do whatever you want?"

My brain went haywire. I didn't keep a mental list of things to do next time we had sex. We communicated well and did whatever in the moment. It was good. Bart's offer, however, suggested he wanted me to take control. "Only if you mean it."

He raised an eyebrow. "Oh? Have something in mind, do you?"

I had plenty in mind. His pulse quickened; I ran my tongue down his neck and sucked the sensitive area where it met his shoulder. "Give me permission and you'll find out."

Bucking under me, he hissed. "That's playing dirty."

Which is exactly what he wanted. I feathered his chest with kisses until I reached his nipple. Looking up, I swirled my tongue around and captured the sensitive tissue in my teeth. "I have so many other ways to torture you if you hold out."

Biting gently, I released it just before he squirmed beneath me. He threaded his fingers in my hair and I expected him to pull me up, but he pushed me down instead.

"I agree. Do whatever you want."

His body's reaction to my touch confirmed his permission. I ran my fingers down his side like I was playing a piano and kissed my way back up as he shivered. "I want to be inside you. I want to fuck you into the mattress and make sure you feel it tomorrow. Are you ready for that?"

He cupped the back of my head and answered me with a kiss. It was rough and desperate, but passionate. His tongue pillaged my mouth, and I felt it all the way to my toes. When my balls stirred, I pulled back.

"Yeah, you're ready."

His hand slid around the side of my head, and he ran his thumb across my cheek. "I'm so fucking ready."

I pressed my lips against his but kept it short—I wasn't going to last long. Reaching left, I summoned a bottle of lube from my luggage, then pushed his knees apart and knelt between his legs. I'd have to forgo some of the things I wanted to do—I was too close. We'd do those later.

I poured some of the slick liquid onto my fingers and slid my middle finger inside him. Rotating it, I moved it in and out before adding a few more drops.

"Jesus. If you don't hurry up, I'm going to shoot all over myself."

I ignored his plea. He might not have noticed, but in elven form my cock was longer. Not a lot, but he'd feel it. "You sure you can handle it? Maybe we should do this another day."

"Oh hell no." His hands pressed against my chest. He slid them to my nipples and pinched. "You don't lube my ass and then say let's wait. Finish what you started."

Classic Bart—all in no matter the role. Tonight, he was a bossy bottom and I loved it.

Pouring more liquid into my palm, I jacked myself twice to coat my dick, then I grabbed him under his knees and put his legs over my shoulders. I inched closer, moved the head of my cock around his hole, and slowly pushed into him.

He threw his head back and breathed in through clenched

teeth when the fat part of my dick breached his ring. "Keep going," he said as he exhaled.

My eyes rolled back as I slid into his warm, tight hole. "Oh shit, Bart. You feel amazing."

"So do you, babe." He pulled me down for a kiss.

When my groin pressed into him, he clenched his muscle around my cock, rooting me in place. Leaning forward to kiss him, I shoved the last bit of me deeper inside. He grunted and slammed his head onto the pillow.

"Holy fuck," he groaned through clenched teeth. "You're bigger."

"Yeah." I pulled back and thrust forward. He huffed out his breath and gasped for more. "And you love it, don't you?"

"Yes!" He buried his head against my shoulder and bit me gently. "So good."

I picked up the pace, already galloping toward an explosive release. "Shit. I'm getting close."

"Don't stop, babe." He grabbed his legs and pulled them back to give me more access. "Give me all of you."

"Oh, fuck!" I plowed deeper and faster. My balls tingled and I tipped over the edge. "I'm gonna come."

"Yeah, Cael." He squeezed his muscles around my cock. "Shoot it. Give me your load."

His filthy mouth spurred me to rail him harder. I sank as far as I could, and my cock exploded. "Fuck." I gasped for air as I fired again and again inside him.

Something inside me surged across our link. Bart's consciousness grabbed it and pushed part of himself back. My mind lunged for it and pulled it in before it could be retracted. That piece of Bart settled into my core, spreading until it reached every bit of me.

It felt like a star exploded in my head. Far from scary, it was a welcome addition that filled a hole I didn't know I had. I was drunk on Bart, and it made me powerful. I'd have lived forever in that moment. I finally knew what it meant to be complete.

When I regained a measure of control, I sat back on my heels and pushed inside him as far as I could. I grabbed his cock and stroked him as I made short thrusts.

"Oh shit, Cael." He clutched the sheets. "I'm going to shoot."

"Yeah, shoot for me." I squeezed his cock and held it for a second. When I released my grip, cum shot across his torso and a big glob hit him in the face. Leaning forward, I kissed him as he contracted and squeezed my cock with every spurt.

I tasted the cum on his lips and kissed the rest off his face. His chest heaved as he drew in a huge lungful of air. When he exhaled, I collapsed against him.

I waited until my pulse had slowed to something close to normal and propped myself on my elbows. "That was incredible." My lips touched his and we kissed softly.

"I'm definitely going to be pregnant after that."

We laughed and his ass clenched around my cock. Normally, I'd be so sensitive I'd beg him to stop, but this time it only made me harder. "That was just the warm-up. I'm not nearly done with you."

"Bring it, babe. I'm definitely not done with you."

Chapter Twenty-Four

❦

BARTHOLOMEW

Outside my office window, students enjoyed the amazing October weather. I couldn't wait to join them. In the two weeks since leaving the elven homeland, I'd found any excuse to be outside. Cael said it was a side effect of being impregnated by an elf. The old me would have turned red from that comment. Now I wanted to get naked.

We didn't hide our relationship after our appearance before the Conclave. I wasn't sure we could. There were some shocked expressions, but most of our colleagues figured it out weeks ago. There were snickers, a tiny amount of ribbing, and a lot of well wishes.

Except from Aunt Gretch. She'd called us to her office to remind us about appropriate behavior on campus. Talk about awkward. And because I lose my filter when I'm embarrassed, I asked why we would risk getting caught having sex on campus when we each lived a ten-minute walk away? Cael nearly choked, and Aunt Gretch frowned before reciting a list of people caught in the act. We promised to be good and ran from the office.

Now whenever Cael entered my office, I imagined us naked and going at it on my desk. Totally inappropriate, but so fucking hot.

"Ready, babe?" Speaking of hot as fuck. Cael leaned in my doorway, arms crossed, leering at me. His smile was so magical, I could live off the feels.

"Yes. Jan's meeting is on break. He'll meet us outside. Can you hold this while I get our drinks?" I handed him the box and loaded three steel water bottles into my backpack.

He kissed me on the lips. It was too brief, but it kept us within Aunt Gretch's "boundaries." "If I built you a giant kitchen, would you cook and feed the world?"

"Sandwiches *you* made, fruit, and leftover pasta salad is hardly *me* feeding the world."

"It's not what you made, it's the fact you did it before work. I would've ordered food and had it delivered."

Once I slipped my backpack on, I motioned for the box. He snatched it up and held it away from me. "I got it, babe. Make an elf feel useful."

He wiggled his eyebrows and I hissed in a breath. "You're so evil."

"What?" He lowered the box to cover his groin.

"That's the lamest innocent act ever. You kept the box to hide that you're hard." I had to calm down before we got outside. "Jan will never shut up about this if I show up sporting wood."

"Jan's fun. He invited us to his beach house. We should go."

It was a skillful change of subject. More so because it worked. I loved that Jan had taken to Cael so quickly. We'd had Jan over for dinner the week we got back from the homeland so I could tell him about my premonitions. He'd been skeptical at first, but he accepted they were real after I explained what Granny P. told me.

After we'd talked about my vision for a few minutes, Jan ignored the implications of my foresight and opened a bottle of wine. For the first time in my dating life, Jan didn't pretend to like my partner. They got on like old friends.

There was still no way we'd stay with him at the beach. "Sleeping in the same house with Jan and his housemates ceased being fun after the first time."

"Yes, but I've never experienced it."

"You're not missing anything." I'd never understood the allure of going in with five or six other gay guys to rent a house. I really was an old soul. "I'll buy us a house before I'd do that again."

He bumped shoulders. "I'm teasing, but it would be fun to go down one weekend before it gets too cold."

Unlike me, Cael didn't grow up two hours from the beach. This was new to him. He wouldn't say it, but he wanted to go when Jan was there. "I'll find a place for us next weekend." Someone in the family had to have a house we could use.

"Great." Cael smiled and any reservations I had disappeared.

Using his cute butt to punch open the door, Cael led the way. As promised, Jan waited against the side of the building.

"Hey, guys." Jan pushed off the wall. "Amazing weather. Great call to eat outside."

"Hey Jan." I hugged him, and he and Cael bumped shoulders. "How's the meeting going?"

"You know how it is. The Council wants what it wants, and the school doesn't agree."

Politics made me crazy, but Jan loved it. If anyone still had questions he was a Hollen, this settled all doubts.

"What's the issue?" Cael asked. "If I'm allowed to know."

Jan shrugged. "It's not top secret. The Council wants to place a team of inquisitors on campus to safeguard the grounds. Brador would be fine with the help *if* they reported to *him*. That isn't going to happen. The supervisor in charge will report to Sister Dearest."

"I didn't know you were an inquisitor," Cael said.

Jan acted horrified and "clutched his pearls." "Do *not* wish that on me. I work for the Council in the Department of Magical Training. The Council authorized the placement of the detail, and my shop makes sure it happens. Avie sent some stiff as a board assistant deputy to negotiate on their behalf, which really didn't help. I'll be here all afternoon, and in the end, I'll need to impose the Council's will on the school."

"Why?" Cael looked to me for an answer. "It's a good idea."

The whole thing annoyed me, but that was politics in general. "They're pointing the finger at each other. Avie thinks the lack of security at Utrecht was to blame for Declan raising a demon and hiding the second glyph. Brador blames her and her team for missing the second one."

"The bigger issue is Grandma Hollen," Jan said. "These attacks almost killed Bart. In case you hadn't heard, he's the golden boy of the family. Esmerelda is *not* amused."

My face burned with embarrassment. "I will cut you with a rusty, jagged knife, Jan."

"Blah, blah, blah. You've been threatening that for twenty years." He looked in the box. "What did my amazing chef brother make for lunch?"

"Turkey, cheddar, arugula, and chipotle mayo on baguettes," I said. "And Cael *and* I made them."

"Shit." Jan looked at us. "This is serious if he lets you cook."

Cael shrugged. "Mates are serious things."

"So I hear." Jan rolled his eyes and punched my shoulder.

We reached Jacobson field, and thankfully there was an available table. A nearby group of barely teens were reenacting some magical fight.

"Hey," Jan nudged me. "Remember when we tried to play X-Men?"

The wistful way Jan mentioned it was at odds with the reality. Mostly. Any fuckup you walked away from wasn't all bad. "How could I forget."

Cael grinned at me. "There's a story here."

Naturally Cael wanted to know the dirt—he perked up any time someone mentioned my past. It didn't matter it was long before we met, he always acted like he'd missed something important.

"Barto convinced me and our friends to duplicate our favorite X-Men's powers using magic."

"Whoa. Negative!" I put my bag on the table and glared at Jan. His innocent act only annoyed me more. "I showed them a pair of sunglasses I'd enchanted so I could imitate Cyclops' eyebeams. *He* said let's play X-Men."

"How old were you guys?"

I growled at Jan for bringing this up, but the kids playing triggered the same memory for me. The timing sucked, because I hadn't planned to rehash my past at lunch, but on the scale of bursting into flames hoping to die of embarrassment, this wasn't even a hot spot.

"Thirteen." Jan helped Cael unpack the box. "We were all jealous when we saw what he'd done."

"So naturally he suggested everyone else learn dangerous, body altering magic just to show me I wasn't so great."

"What happened?" Cael looked way too amused as he unwrapped his sandwich.

"My glasses melted the one and only time I tried to use them. I burned my face and had retina damage."

"Shit." Cael's heart raced as if this had happened seconds ago instead of fifteen years.

"Relax, it was a long time ago." I rubbed his forearm and sent calming energy toward him. "I was lucky. Jan tried to create claws that grew from his knuckles. He spent nearly a week in the infirmary as they reset and healed his hands. He's lucky he didn't have permanent dexterity loss."

"Mine took a while to heal, but they weren't life threatening." Jan settled onto the bench across from us. "Connor almost died."

"Connor the banjo guy?" Cael asked.

"Yeah," Jan said. "He used to get a major boner over Ice Man. Probably still does. His body temp dropped so low, he nearly died of hypothermia. And then there was Nehman."

I snickered at the memory. "I forgot about that."

"What happened to him?" Cael asked.

Jan had a mouthful of sandwich, so I took up the story. "Nehman wanted to be Beast—I have no idea why—and his spell turned his skin and hair blue. There was no fur, but the pigments had to grow out. Took a month to get back to normal. He was almost totally royal blue in his yearbook . . ."

The bright day was gone, replaced by a cool night. Jacobson Field was empty. Cael was on my right in his Northwestern sweatshirt, and Jan wore his bomber jacket. None of us spoke, we were focused on . . .

" . . . picture"

Cael grabbed my arm. "What just happened?"

Like after the first waking vision, I had to push through the disorientation and fog to stay conscious. My synapses were firing wildly, and it felt like I was mired in thick, deep mud. The ringing in my ears quickly gave way to a nausea inducing headache. I gulped air in short, quick bursts and swallowed twice to keep my stomach from revolting.

A water bottle was pressed to my lips, and I took tiny sips in between gasps of oxygen. Finally, I regained control of my body and stared into Cael's eyes. He was frightened, and if I hadn't been the one seeing things, I might be scared, too. But I didn't have time to be afraid.

"I saw us, you, me and Jan, walking this way before the fight with the demon. This is the path we take. You're still on my right and he's on the left."

"So not the same," Cael said, as if trying to convince himself it was true. "What were we wearing?"

I nodded and rubbed my forehead to ease the pressure

building just above my eyes. Slowly, the excess brain activity reversed course, and I could think clearly.

"Different yet the same." I took a longer drink. "This was minutes before the others. And you were both wearing the same thing."

CAELINUS

The good mood died after Bart's vision. Jan was visibly upset; I wanted to be, but I had to keep calm or I'd influence Bart's emotions. We'd managed to achieve a small return to normal when Avie called.

Bart loved and admired his sister, but she was used to getting her way, and he could be just as stubborn. Today was one of those times where they didn't agree.

"For the last time, Avie, I'm not moving back to Hollen Hall."

They'd been arguing about this the entire walk back. She had to know he wouldn't agree. Bart loved his family, but not their machinations. It might have been a joke, but Jan wasn't totally kidding when he referred to Bart as the golden boy. That status put a target on his back among the less influential but more ambitious family members.

"No," Bart said with a half laugh. "He ran off the moment he heard it was you. Try his cell phone."

That was no exaggeration either. Jan had practically sprinted to get back to his meeting rather than speak to their sister.

"Okay," Bart shook his head. "Bye."

He tapped the screen and stared at his phone. "Sorry. I shouldn't have taken the call."

I agreed with him, but not for the same reasons. He thought I was upset he answered his phone, but I didn't appreciate that Avie annoyed him. I knew it came from a position of love, but that didn't entirely excuse her. "It's fine. Why does she want you to move home?"

"Granny Pederson told her about my visions. *Now* Avie believes it's possible someone other than Declan is pulling the strings, and she's concerned I'm the target."

Then again, Avie trying to protect my mate was something I totally approved of. "If it's safer at Hollen Hall, why not go?"

"First, I don't need to. My protections are strong enough to withstand almost anything."

Anyone other than Bart and that statement would be bravado. He, however, had seven different, powerful wards protecting the house, plus the safe room. If that wasn't enough to hold off whatever was after him until help arrived, he wasn't safe anywhere. Plus, his house was closer to help than Hollen Hall.

"The other reason is there are too many innocent people there. If something is after me, better it come to my house than hurt dozens of people there."

Bart had clearly thought this through. I might want him to put his safety first, but in an odd way staying at his house would be safer for him. If something showed up at Hollen Hall, he'd lead the fight to save everyone else.

"You'd be safer if someone stayed with you." I wiggled my eyebrows.

Bart's smile returned. "Know any qualified candidates who want that job?"

"I might."

Chapter Twenty-Five

❧

BARTHOLOMEW

"Isaac's here." I grabbed my wallet and phone. "You sure you don't want to come?"

"Nope, I'll see you when you get home." Cael trotted down the stairs, sweatshirt in hand. "I want to get a few things from my apartment. Send me pictures and I'll give you my opinions."

Using my day off to shop for cars—without Cael—wasn't how I'd planned to spend my free time, but somehow that's what was happening. My family wanted someone to guard me, and they used my promise to hire Isaac as my driver to get around my objections.

"No, you won't. You'll just tell me it looks nice."

Cael leaned in and kissed me. "Have fun."

He gently pushed me out the door and waved to Isaac before heading back inside. The exchange had me floating. I loved how easily we'd become a couple, and that my house was now our house. He hadn't fully moved in, but we were getting there.

Isaac got out and held open my door. "Good morning. Lovely morning for car shopping."

If this had just been us looking at cars, it would have been an amazing day. But it wasn't. My meddling grandmothers meant well, but Sally and Esmerelda didn't comprehend the strength of my defenses or how much danger they put Isaac in to make themselves feel better.

"Hi Isaac. It's a morning at least."

He laughed and shut the door when I was seated. "C'mon. It won't be too bad. I only have three stops and I prescreened them all. We show up, take a test drive, tell them we'll let them know, and repeat. I've even arranged to show you the one I think you'll like best, last. That way we can talk details with that dealer without having to go back. Easy peasy."

Isaac was closer to me than half my siblings and ninety-five percent of my extended family. He also knew me better than them. "You can stop pretending. Esmerelda called."

"Oh." He made a three-point turn and headed down my driveway. "It's still a nice day, and I promise *this* won't be a hassle."

Now I laughed. Isaac didn't do drama. He and I were friends, but he wouldn't say no to Esmerelda.

I closed my eyes and relived my last conversation with my grandmother—*grandmothers*. They'd lulled me into thinking they were just trying to help, and they agreed that it was imperative I find the nexus between the two halves of my vision. Unfortunately they couldn't tell me what the connection was or how to know if I found the right one and since I wouldn't move home, they decided Isaac needed to move in with me. When I protested, they reminded me Isaac was going to be my driver and he should have a room in my house. Otherwise, he'd have to rent a place nearby.

No one did guilt quite like grandmothers.

"Everything okay?" Isaac asked.

I opened my lids and stared into his pale blue eyes in the rearview mirror. He embodied raw physical strength. I'm sure that's why my grandmothers wanted him in my house. "Mostly. Thinking."

Isaac nodded once, and let it go. If only it were that easy for me.

The fight wasn't going to happen at my house. If I didn't stop the demon on campus, it would kill hundreds or thousands before it could be stopped. It might even open a rift and bring in reinforcements. Preventing that was the most important thing, and Isaac couldn't help with that fight.

The creature in my premonitions would dwarf the one I'd killed. I wasn't sure I could take it down alone, but Cael couldn't help me like he did when I erased—

"That's it."

"What's it?" Isaac asked.

"Sorry. I was thinking out loud." I pulled out my phone and scrolled down to find the right number. Tapping the call button, I looked into the rearview mirror. "I need to stop at Utrecht first."

CAELINUS

Walking home alone, it was hard to remember what that first week was like without Bart. I thought about him constantly now and I didn't like being apart. We'd settled in so well together, it felt like we'd always been a couple. Mom would tell me that was the mate bond, but it was still amazing.

It was a beautiful crisp autumn day when I finally got off my ass and left Bart's house. I probably should have taken Bart's car, but it was too nice outside. Isaac could pick me up when they finished.

I cut through the train station parking lot and admired my apartment building as I waited for traffic to clear. The open courtyard flanked by the wings of the building made it a great shady place on a warm day. Most days it was empty, but today two older men sat on the bench closest to the street.

I'd never seen them before, but the building was big enough I hadn't run into a quarter of the residents. Staying at Bart's as much as I did further limited my contact. Bounding up a short flight of stairs, I nodded as I walked by.

"Good afternoon, Caelinus Reinhold," one of them said.

I spun around. I didn't recognize either of them. "How do you know my name?"

"Does that matter?" the other asked.

My heart seized and I reached for my stone. Bart's family worried he'd become a target. If they'd studied him at all, they'd know we were a couple. The pair stood and I studied them closer. One was a mage, and the other . . . "You're an elf."

He smiled. "As are you."

The mage side eyed him. "Forgive my husband. He delights in being mysterious. Darius Hollen." He spread his hands and bowed.

"You're related to Bart?"

"Distantly, though I've never had the pleasure of meeting him." He pointed to his husband. "My mate—Ignatius Eadweard."

It took a second for their names to sink in. Every elf knew Ignatius and his mate, but no one had seen them in twelve hundred years. Correction—no one outside of the Society.

I clenched my mage stone but left it in my pocket. Even if Ignatius was lying about who he was, he was still an elf. My kind were the preferred snack for demons. We led the fight in the last war. That did not, however, mean I should trust them.

"You two are good, but the cosplay convention is next week. Have fun."

I chuckled that the old dudes had enough time to play games, then I climbed another set of steps and nearly knocked Ignatius over.

"This isn't a joke." He pulled an amulet from beneath his shirt. "We are the Guardians of the Western Point."

I grasped the railing to prevent myself from tumbling down the stairs. "How . . .?"

Darius appeared next to Ignatius, showing me his pendant. "We wish to speak to you, Caelinus."

I stared with my mouth open. The Western Guardians? Here? It wasn't possible. "How . . .? Why should I believe you're . . . you know . . . them?"

"I told you he wouldn't believe us just because you're an elf." Darius put his pendant away. "Sally Pederson sends her regards on behalf of the Society of Guardians."

Okay. Score another reason for swearing members of the Society to secrecy. "Let's go inside."

We climbed the stairs in silence, which gave my overactive imagination too much time. The Guardians personally visiting me could only be a harbinger of something terrible. A dozen different images of Bart under attack flashed through my head.

Finally, logic reasserted control. If Bart were in trouble, I'd have felt it through our link. They clearly wanted something, but if it had been urgent, they wouldn't have sat on a bench waiting for me. Still, this wasn't a social visit.

I ushered them into my apartment and offered them a seat. "Can I get you a drink?"

"Water would be lovely," Darius said. Ignatius raised two fingers and I nodded.

It felt like a dream. The Western Guardians sitting on my cheap, prefab furniture like we were old friends. It didn't seem real. Neither did having Bartholomew Hollen as a mate and learning there was a super-secret society that served the Guardians.

This was not what I expected when I accepted the job at Utrecht.

I poured two glasses from the filter pitcher in my fridge, plastered a smile on my face and returned to my guests. "Here you are."

"Thank you," Darius said.

I plucked my briefcase from the chair and sat. "A lot of weird things have happened in the seven weeks I've been in Philadelphia, but this—"

"I'm weird?" Ignatius raised his glass and peered over the lip.

"The two of you sitting in my living room definitely qualifies as weird."

Darius laughed so hard, he had to set his glass down. "Iggy, he's a young version of you. How delightful. Please tell me Bartholomew appreciates your sense of humor."

They talked about Bart like they knew him. It bothered me. If Sally really sent her regards, they probably *did* know a lot about him. And me. "He hasn't complained so far."

"That's good," Ignatius said. "It took Dari a couple centuries before he stopped rolling his eyes every time I made a joke."

"Not a day more than seventeen decades, dear."

Despite the playful banter, their emotional colors glowed happy contentment. "Did you want me to call Bart and have him join us?"

"No," Ignatius said. "We came to speak to you alone."

That didn't sound ominous in the least. It breathed life back into my worst fear. "Is Bart in danger?"

"No more than anyone else," Darius said. "Which is terribly cryptic."

Ignatius patted his mate's thigh. "Yes, love. Even for you."

"My apologies." He rested his elbows on his knees and leaned forward. "Iggy and I have discussed this with the other Guardians so often, I forget it's not common knowledge. The Great Ward is failing and needs to be renewed."

More comforting than Bart personally in danger, but not by much. "Have you told the Mage Council? I appreciate the information, but I'm a junior professor of creative magic. You really need to speak to Bart. He's the brilliant one. He might be able to help restore the spell."

"We are aware of Bartholomew's gifts," Darius said. "Your mate is powerful, and our enemies rightly fear him. His powers will no doubt prove useful when it comes time to replace the spell, but that isn't why we're here.

"Bartholomew wants to save those he loves no matter the cost to himself. If he thinks there's a chance you'll be hurt, he'll do whatever it takes to keep you safe."

Now I was really bothered. "How do you know so much about us?"

"The Society keeps its eyes on everyone who could potentially be invited to be a member," Ignatius said. "Sally gave us a very detailed report on her grandson."

"Oh, right." They had me so off-kilter, I kept forgetting Granny P. reported to them. "I'm trying to get Bart to accept my help."

"You need to do more than try," Darius said. His stern tone felt like a rebuke. "Do not let him take on this fight alone. He will fail and without Bart, the Ward will fail, and war with the demon realm will consume our world."

Talk about high stakes. These two needed to work on their delivery. "You haven't met him. Bart won't let anyone help if he thinks they'll get hurt."

Darius set his jaw and stared at me. "If he won't accept help, then plan how to give it to him anyway."

Most people would've said "Try harder," but Darius understood Bart. Probably because Bart was a lot like him. The more I mulled over the advice, the more I approved. Mostly. It would involve keeping some part of myself from my mate. No small feat, but to keep him alive, I'd do it.

"I understand."

Chapter Twenty-Six

❦

BARTHOLOMEW

The cold front they'd promised had moved in while I was in the dealership. Even with Isaac's preparation, we hadn't had enough time to finish the sale on Saturday—Isaac's dad was head of the Hollen family motor pool, and I wanted him to negotiate the sale. By the time we finished the third test drive, there wasn't enough time to get him to the dealership. Tuesday afternoon was much better than Saturday morning to buy the car anyway.

Isaac turned right and drove my new car off the dealer's lot. It was weird to think of a 1960s classic Bentley as new. It was even stranger that it was mine. Most cars in the motor pool belonged to the family trust. This was mine and Cael's.

Now that we had the car, Isaac would be moved to my payroll and once I fixed up the third floor, he'd move into my house. There wasn't much to do, but I wanted him to pick the paint colors and bedding since it would be his home. We agreed he'd stay in Cael's apartment until the work was finished.

Cael had wanted to finish moving things from the apartment

to our house rather than go with me to get the car. Smart elf. Listening to Mr. Hale dicker with the dealer was not fun. It became a game of who wanted what more. Did we want the car at any price? Did the dealer want to lose a cash sale? Eventually, both sides had a deal they could live with, and I signed the papers.

I closed my eyes and listened to the purr of the engine. The soft hum was soothing, and it nearly lulled me to sleep. I was enjoying the feel when white light exploded inside my head, and I found myself on a street I didn't recognize.

Three gray government SUVs rumbled to a stop at a red light. The sports cars from my first waking vision appeared on schedule and surrounded the convoy. This time they focused their attacks on the third car.

Despite the changes from my original vision, people still died on both sides. Then, the rear driver side door blew off and soared over my head. Three people rushed forward to whisk away a hooded man in the back seat. Someone tugged the hood off to reveal—

The street and the mage battle were gone, and I stood on the grounds of Utrecht Academy. It was later in the evening, and much cooler. Something vast loomed in front of me. Jan was dead on the ground to my left, and Cael was on the ground to my right. He was badly hurt, and I somehow knew he was dying.

I summoned Jan's lifeless stone, and just like the last two times, something pounded on my defenses as Cael moaned and his fingers clawed the dirt.

I readied a spell I'd prepared and shouting, I raised the two stones, released my energy and—I was back in my car.

"Bart?" We'd pulled over. Isaac had twisted and reached for me. "What happened?"

"Did I . . . I shouted, 'I'll kill you!' didn't I?"

He nodded and pulled his arm back.

"I didn't mean you, Isaac."

"I know." Thankfully, I could tell he meant that. "You were flailing, like you were having a seizure. Was it . . .?"

He didn't need an answer. The worst part was how scared and helpless he looked. There'd been nothing he could do to protect me, which had unnerved him.

"Another vision. Two actually. The attack on the convoy and then the demon on campus." I found my phone and dialed Avie. I held out a tiny sliver of hope I was wrong. She answered on the second ring.

"Bart, I can't talk. I've got a crisis unfolding."

I was too late. I should've let her do her job, but if I was right, tonight was the night in my dreams. "A convoy of three gray SUVs with a prisoner in the third car is under attack."

"How'd you—"

"Who's the prisoner, Avie?" I needed confirmation to set my plan in motion.

"What?" Avie said. "No, send in the other two units. Don't let them get away!"

This was unfolding just as I saw a minute ago. Nothing she did would stop it. Somehow, whoever was behind this knew which car to attack. That was problematic, but it could wait until the demon was dead.

"Avie! Who's in the back seat of that third car?"

Someone shouted and Avie cursed. "Bart, how did you know this was happening right now?"

The question stole my voice. I'd never seen something unfold in real time. It was always an event from the future. Something else to figure out. If I survived the night. "I had a vision a minute ago. I called to warn you."

There was an explosion and more shouting. Tires squealed and I heard the exchange of concussive magic.

"Fuck a demon, Lynch, go after them!" Avie yelled.

"Who was in the car, Avie?"

"Declan."

CAELINUS

A buzz woke me from a dreamless sleep. I blinked and sat up. The theoretical magic textbook fell off my chest. Searching frantically, I found my phone before the call went to voicemail.

"Hey, babe." I checked the time; it was later than I'd expected. Bart should've been back an hour ago. "Everything go all right with the car?"

"Fine." He drew a breath, and I froze. Things weren't fine. "My vision came true. Declan was sprung from the convoy."

Nope, things went right to hell in one breath. I shook off the fog of my nap. "I thought . . . Didn't Will alert the inquisitors?"

"They moved him despite my warning."

Bart paused and I realized he'd cut himself off from me. Our link wasn't dead, but he'd blocked most of his emotions. I'd call him out, but I'd done the same to hide what I was planning. It was what Darius and Ignatius had told me to do, but I expected more than three days to fine-tune things.

"What now?"

"Isaac's getting Jan on our way home. We'll pick you up after that."

"Babe, what's going on? Why are you picking up Jan?"

"Avie suggested he stay with us until they catch Declan. Given the number of people involved in freeing Declan, she thinks it's best you and I don't travel alone."

Bart never asked for or easily accepted help. I didn't need my empathy to know he was shaken. Declan orchestrated his escape despite Bart's warning and the added security. This wasn't a lone wolf trying to raise a demon.

"Bart, we'll get through this. You and me, with some help from Jan."

"You're right. We will. We should be there in forty-five minutes."

The clinical answer was consistent with the tight rein on his emotions. I understood why he didn't want anyone to see him frightened. If he was afraid, it might cause others to panic. But I was his mate. We were supposed to support each other in everything.

Except I was closed to him. He couldn't seek comfort from our bond. Not being able to feel my emotions probably caused him to wall off his to shield me. We needed to talk in person. It would be almost impossible to hide anything if we could see and touch each other.

"I'll get their quicker if walk."

"No." The near panic in Bart's voice startled me. "My house wards have been turned on. You'll be stuck on the street."

They hadn't been active when we left for work, or when Isaac picked Bart up at school. "When did you set them?"

"After I spoke to Avie. I didn't want to come home to people hiding in or around the house." He paused and added, "I can turn them on or off from anywhere in the world."

Of course he could. Bart was that brilliant, but it didn't explain why I couldn't go there now. "I already have access to the house."

"No. Remember how I said the layers weren't connected? You need to be attuned to each one. We never got around to that. Only Jan and Avie can get in without me. It's safer to stay where you are. Declan probably has people watching my house, not your apartment."

I'd have a target on my back if I waited outside his house. "Okay, babe. I'll wait for you here."

"Thanks, Cael. I . . . I love you." For a moment, Bart's emotions flowed through our link. They were a jumble of different feelings, but before I could home in on any, his walls slammed back into place. "I need to call Jan and update him on our ETA."

I wanted to comfort him, but I didn't dare reveal my own inner conflict. If he learned what I planned, he'd stop me from helping. That wasn't acceptable.

I also couldn't let him face the demon while he was this conflicted. He wouldn't survive. We'd need to talk when we got to his house; Jan and I wouldn't give him a choice.

"I love you too, Bart. *We* can beat this."

"I'll see you soon." The call ended abruptly, and I left the phone at my ear for a few seconds. Bart had been so distant. The only emotion I felt clearly was love, but it had a bone deep ache to it. The closer we inched to his vision, the more he worried about me and Jan. It was close now; he couldn't pretend it was in the distant future.

Pushing those thoughts aside, I gathered the few things I had left in my closet. It was pointless—Isaac wouldn't stay here until the danger passed. But it would be easier to argue he should stay in my apartment if it was empty.

At the edge of my thoughts, I caught snippets of unrest. They'd pop up, faint and elusive, and then cut off in a flash, like someone noticed an open door and slammed it shut. Bart locked me out, but it was hard for mates to block each other fully.

He probably felt my fear through our link and assumed I was afraid I'd die. I had a healthy respect for demons and planned to be very careful. Bart, however, scared me. He'd do anything to shield those he loved from danger. Even sacrifice himself.

I clamped down so I didn't add to his concern. He didn't need another reason to take on this fight alone.

I worked quickly to assemble my remaining items in short order and checked the time. It was close to when Bart should arrive. Carefully, I checked our link, but it was nearly blank. The missing closeness left a hole in me I couldn't fill.

The phone rang and I jumped. Good thing we weren't tightly

connected right now—he didn't need my jittery nerves. It was Isaac. Weird that Bart didn't call himself.

"Hey Isaac. Are you and Bart here?"

"No. Bart's at the house. He sent me to get Jan and you while he gets the place ready."

A wave of nausea hit me. Bart had cut me off so I couldn't tell he was going it alone. "Where are you?"

"We're out front. Do you need help?"

Isaac had no idea, which made sense. He'd never leave Bart alone if he knew. "No. I'll be right down."

I grabbed my sweatshirt and stopped before putting it on. Bart's betrayal put me back on my heels. I needed to regroup and focus. There was no room for mistakes. I tossed the Northwestern fleece onto the bed and found my navy-blue Utrecht Academy one. Slipping it on, I grabbed the original one and headed out.

I ran down the stairs and burst out the side door. Isaac stood at the back of the car with the trunk open. He looked at my hands and pointed.

"Where's your stuff?"

"No time. Jan?" I tapped on window and looked inside. Bart's dream was happening. "Take off your coat."

"What?" Jan shook his head. "Why?"

Ignoring the question, I opened the door. We didn't have time for a discussion. "Take off your coat and put this on."

"What . . .?" Jan didn't move. "This is weird, even for you."

"In Bart's vision you're always wearing that coat. Take it off."

"What's going on?" Isaac stood beside me.

"Bart played us all. He went to Utrecht to fight the demon alone. We need to get to him before he's killed." I shoved my sweatshirt at Jan. "But first you need to take off that coat. We need to change everything he saw if we want to save him."

And ourselves.

I couldn't believe he'd kept this from me. He left for a suicide mission and never said . . . A cold chill raced through me. When he told me he loved me, he was saying goodbye.

"Jan, listen to me. Bart's going to die if we don't get there in time. We'll only get one chance, so please listen."

Jan didn't say anything for several seconds. Then he peeled off his coat and threw it in the back seat. "Tell me your plan."

Chapter Twenty-Seven

BARTHOLOMEW

It was as dark as in my visions. The feeling I'd lived through this moment before came with a wave of disorientation—my brain struggled to reconcile that there were no memories locked inside my head. I avoided following the path we'd taken in my waking dream, not that it mattered at this point. Everything was different.

I patted my coat pocket. Things would *be* different.

Saying goodbye to Cael nearly broke me. I'd kept my feelings locked down tight. He had, too, which worried me. I'd heard that mates could affect each other adversely without meaning to. Had my deception caused him such pain he needed to seal himself off?

If I survived, I'd find out the truth. Assuming he forgave me.

I had a plan to deal with the demon, but Cael would never agree to it unless he was standing next to me. My plan wouldn't work if Cael was there, and he'd never accept that answer. He'd left me no choice but to deceive him.

How very Machiavellian of me.

I forced myself to think about the fight. Contrary to what

Cael, Jan and Isaac would say, this wasn't suicide by demon—I'd taken time to prepare and planted the seeds that would see me walk away when the fight ended. But I still needed to execute.

The first time, I'd gotten lucky—I showed up before Dec was finished, and he underestimated me. He wouldn't make those mistakes again. Except, he would. I'd never told him about my visions.

A figure was hunched over the ground where the demon would appear. The illumination from the ornate light posts didn't reach the person's features, but I didn't need to see his face. It was Declan, and he was directing energy at the glyph. It was bigger than any I'd seen before, but so was the demon in my dream.

"Declan," I called softly. "You need to stop what you're doing."

His laughter sent chills down my spine. This wasn't the Declan I'd dated. Whoever was controlling him was crazy as well as evil. No sane person tried to raise a demon. A demon of just average power was nearly impossible to control. The one Dec had summoned in his classroom had been above average and would've overpowered him. This one would be even bigger.

He stopped his crazy cackling and fixed his gaze on me. Whatever enchantment he was under had robbed him of his sanity. If there was anything left of him, it was buried too deep for me to see.

"Stop? Because the great and mighty Bartholomew Hollen said so? I think not." He touched his stone to the ground and his magic fed the spells. It was almost active. "I knew the allure of this much dark magic would flush you out of that fortress you pretend is a home. Now I don't need to hunt you down to finish the job."

There'd been no spillage for anyone to detect, but it explained why they chose Utrecht. Clearly the plan had been to raise this demon and set it loose on my house. Given what I'd seen in my vision, it might have breached my defenses if it had caught me unaware.

Thank the gods foresight was real.

"If you continue with this madness, you won't leave that circle. Let me help you."

"Oh right—the golden child, alpha one mage is here to save the day." He shook his head, but I didn't need him to agree.

I palmed my mage stone, ready to act when he gave me an opening. "This isn't like you, Dec. Fight it. They're using you. You'll die before you can turn the demon on me."

The real Declan appeared for a second but was gone just as fast. "No one's controlling me, *Barty*. I'm doing this for me."

The brief glimpse of the suppressed personality reminded me not to give up. Declan wasn't to blame, but what if I couldn't reach him?

"People died to free you from the inquisitors. No one does that so you can raise a demon to exact revenge on your ex-boyfriend. Whoever organized your rescue is manipulating you, Dec. They want *you* to summon this demon because you'll die in the effort and won't be able to tell anyone who's really behind this."

Declan's expression went blank, and I pounced. A tiny beam of light shot from my hand and the spell I'd prepared struck him in the chest. His body seized and he clutched his head with both hands. Squeezing his eyes shut, he grunted in pain.

The anguished sound cut through the empty campus. Control that strong had to have been drilled deep into his soul. I knew freeing him would hurt, but I also knew Declan wouldn't want to let loose this kind of evil into our world.

A moment later, he stopped screaming, exhaled, and bent over with his hands on his knees. He kept his head down and panted as the echoes of pain faded. Finally, he looked up and our eyes met.

"Bart . . ."

A flicker of darkness expelled from his chest, and he recoiled from it. It hovered in front of him and then dropped, inches from his feet. The ground rumbled and Declan swayed on unsteady legs. His eyes opened wider and the terror on his face didn't need an explanation. He'd triggered the glyph.

"Run, Bart. It's a trap."

Of course it was a trap. But not for me.

"Please, Declan. You need to get out of there." I waved him toward me with my free hand. "The creature coming is beyond anything you can imagine."

"I can't. He's too strong."

The lines glowed a muted red. My ears thrummed with the building power. Soon they'd turn a bright, ugly crimson and spread out until they filled in every inch of space inside the circle. That was my timer. "The demon doesn't have any power over you. Just walk away."

Declan shifted but his feet remained in place. His attempts to move quickly turned frantic. "Bart! I can't . . . I can't lift my feet!"

This didn't make sense. If they'd caged Declan to be an offering, who was going to control the creature? Only the one who summoned the demon could command its loyalty. With Declan gone—

"Dec, you've got to free yourself. That thing will destroy the city if it escapes."

"I'm trying! I can't move. He won't let me." He used both hands to try to move his leg, but it didn't budge. "Bart, help!"

Despite his request, he knew I couldn't save him. If I stepped inside the lines, I'd be helpless. The circle got brighter, and the red energy inched closer to Declan. It was too late.

"Who did this, Declan. Who made you do this?"

Declan aimed his mage stone down and fired at the ground around his feet. It only accelerated the spell. "Bart, please!"

The plea tore me apart inside. I couldn't direct my magic into the circle or the demon would be able to control me. My act of freeing Declan from mind control meant his last moments were filled with terror.

"Dec. Who did this to you?" It was selfish, but I could at least avenge him.

"De—" A flash of light cut him off and he screamed as he was tossed in the air. The lower half of his right leg, from the knee down, was still on the ground where he'd stood.

A huge dark presence filled the space inside the glyph. As Declan's body neared the apex, a red arm, thick with corded muscles, reached for him. I pointed my mage stone and released a torrent of magic. A brilliant, fiery burst of energy streaked past the demon and struck Declan's torso a moment before long red fingers closed around the body. The spell consumed him and ashes slipped through the demon's fingers.

I watched as the tiny flakes of Declan floated to the ground. I'd just killed someone without hesitation. Not just anyone, but someone I'd been close to. It had been necessary, and Declan—the real Declan, not the thrall to some dark soul—would've preferred that death to being eaten by a demon, but I'd still killed him.

For the second time since the sun had set, I'd done something that should have shattered my moral center. Instead of recoiling in horror at my actions, I quickly justified them as necessary for the greater good. How had it become so easy to shed a lifetime of principles meant to guide me when things got difficult?

A roar shattered the night. The demon swatted away the last bits of the sacrifice it needed to free itself. Its head spun in my direction, and it turned angry red eyes on me. Without Declan's body and soul, it would be vulnerable if it left the circle and its connection to its power base.

The fight wasn't over but my odds of survival had improved. I didn't know how weak it would be if it stepped outside the glyph, but it had to be significant or it would have charged me immediately.

Instead, it stood still, glaring at me with crimson eyes. It was more humanoid than I'd seen in my dreams. Nostrils flared as its chest heaved with every noisy breath. The dark-red skin shimmered, like it had been covered in oil, and it wore what appeared to be armor from neck to mid-thigh. The angular face was framed by two horns coming from the top of its skull. They extended to just below the chin and curled up into points.

I didn't see any weapons, but magic pulsed like blood, coursing through its body. The tomes had very little information about the princes of hell, but this was surely one. They were few in number and rarely engaged in the fighting. Declan couldn't have summoned a being of this power randomly. This had been planned on both sides of the ward. That was a chilling thought.

"Brave human." Its raspy voice was unpleasant and harsh. "Bow to me and I'll make you my servant."

The promise was empty air; it didn't expect me to accept. It was smarter than the other demon I fought; before it attacked, it assessed the battlefield. I prayed it didn't find what I had hidden.

"You should go back before you die." I expected it to laugh or to lash out in anger. Instead, it kept its eyes on me.

Much smarter and far more dangerous.

"Come closer and I'll show you who shall kill who."

I fought the urge to walk forward and then my wards flashed white. It shielded its eyes with an arm and the compulsion was gone.

"I'll stay here."

Its nostrils flared and it let out a snarl that would put a wolf-shifter to shame. I braced for a new attack, but it just watched me. Whoever was behind this must have promised the demon it could consume the mage that summoned it. Such a deal would've granted it unfettered freedom in our world.

My actions not only denied the demon the energy it craved, but also control of the portal to use as it pleased. If it were me, I'd assume I'd been betrayed and the one who tricked me was standing just beyond reach.

I let the silence drag out. Time was my ally. Avie was preparing a tactical team, and I'd convinced Brador to bring his top people. The longer the demon stayed in place the more chance we had to bring enough people to defeat it.

But they weren't here. That scared me—or would've if I weren't already close to crapping myself. My stone pulsed and its warmth bolstered my courage.

The demon opened its mouth and I saw its large, pointed teeth. "I will enjoy rending your flesh from your bones while you scream for death, mage. You are nothing to me."

Flames shot from its mouth, and I created a concave shield of light with my stone. The curvature of my defenses sent the attack back at the creature; the fire washed over its armor, but smoke curled from a few spots of exposed skin.

Its eyes narrowed. It would never admire a human—we were beneath a demon prince—but it had to respect I was dangerous.

The demon sniffed the air. Turned left, then right, and finally settled on me. It raised its left foot, and I released the first of the spells I'd prepared. A cylinder of white light sprang from the ground and surrounded the circle of magic.

The creature pulled back and howled. "You can't hold me forever with your pathetic cage."

Despite its brash talk, the demon didn't test my barrier. Too bad. It might have hurt it bad enough to give me an opening. Fortunately, I'd prepared for that scenario.

My spell that created the white energy cage also slowly closed Declan's portal. Once the rift closed, the demon would be cut off from its source of power and be overmatched.

If Avie and Brador showed up.

Extending its hands, the demon brushed a fingernail against its prison and scratched downward. Sparks flew off the magical wall and the air sizzled, but my wards held. The demon brought his hand up and the talon that touched the energy had been burned away. It licked the end of one finger and smiled.

"You're cunning, mage. I'll give you that. But I'll find a way out." It bared its sharp teeth in a frightening smile. Dark magic pressed against the light I'd used to contain the demon. The pressure on the walls was minimal, but that was going to change fast. "What will you do when I break free, and you must face me alone?"

"Who said he's alone?"

I whipped my head around and my heart stopped. Everything I did and all the risks I took were for nothing. "Get out of here."

"No." Cael crossed to my left. "Now we've changed your vision."

My worst fear had come true. Cael thought he was going to swoop in and help, but he had no idea what he'd done. "It's been different since I got here. You need to leave. Now!"

The force against my walls increased; I added more energy to shore it up. My careful plans were crumbling.

"I'm not leaving." Cael pulled out his mage stone. "When this is over, we're going to have a long talk about trust."

We weren't going to have *any* talks on any subject if he didn't leave. "Listen to me. Your wards are inadequate. The demon will shred them and take your power. You need to leave. Go find Avie and Brador, *then* come help."

The demon sniffed the air. "An elf?" The glee in its voice seized my heart. "You brought me an elf! You are a fool, mage. Once I consume him, I will be invincible."

"You're not eating anyone, demon." Cael raised his stone to defend himself.

The creature stared at Cael like he'd done to me when he first arrived. "Come to me elfling!"

Cael struggled not to move, but the demon's voice command had taken hold. This is what I'd seen in my vision. It was going to suck the life from my mate right in front of me.

No! I wouldn't let that happen. Shifting my stone to my left hand, I held it toward Cael. "Touch your stone to mine. Now!"

Before he could react, the demon roared. "No! Drop it, now!"

"Bart!" Cael trembled as he struggled to resist. "I can't . . . stop . . ."

The fear in his voice and eyes tore at me as I watched his fingers uncurl and his sapphire stone slip from his fingers. I summoned the gem from the ground and pressed it into his hand. Touching the two stones together, I forced my mind into his. If we hadn't been mates, he would have resisted and we'd have both died. But our bond was strong, and he opened himself.

I saw that he deceived me because Darius and Ignatius warned him not to let me go alone. I saw him recruit Jan to help. Most of all I saw his love, etched deep into every crevice of his being. I knew he saw everything in me as well.

Free from our constraints, our bond linked us tight again, and I was flush with the strength that came from the connection. I was stronger than ever because we were greater than the sum of our parts. Extending my wards, I blocked the compulsion and Cael stopped trembling.

Cael's fingers clutched his stone, but his eyes never left mine. "Wow."

"Exactly." I felt so full I thought I'd burst.

A third presence entered our joined minds. *«At last!»*

"Did you say that?" Cael asked.

The Orme Seax felt hot against my back, and I reached around to grab it. "No, but I know what did."

CAELINUS

The voice in my head had a familiar touch. I didn't recognize it, but it wasn't the demon. Bart sounded very confident, and I might have been, too, except he pulled out that overly decorated knife he'd shown me weeks ago.

He'd said he thought it was sentient, but it hadn't spoken to him.

"Your elfish Viking blade spoke to us?"

"Yes, and it all makes sense now."

I was glad he understood because I had no clue. "You lost me."

"No time. You need to shift. And take off your shoes."

The demon roared. Bart grunted, and the jewel in the pommel pulsed a harsh, angry blue, like it had been offended by the creature's actions. Bart's face showed the exertion I could feel as he raised his stone.

"What's happening?"

"It's trying to break my containment. The spell was only designed to hold long enough for help to arrive, but something's wrong. They should both have been here by now." Bart turned his palm face up so he could look at his mage stone. "Where's Jan?"

When we linked, I'd seen snippets of his memories, the strongest, most recent ones still stored in his frontal lobe. Bart would have seen the same in my mind. "One o'clock. Coming through the trees."

"Shit." Because we were still connected, I felt him reach out. If I'd tried, I probably could've heard their conversation. I also felt his anger followed by an uprising of relief. "This is why neither of you should've come."

He shouldn't have snuck out on us. I didn't have clean hands, but if we were keeping score, he did it first and his deception was worse. To me at least. "What's wrong?"

"You lumbered into this fight without protecting yourself from a demon's voice. If he'd staggered out of the forest without talking to me, he'd have been susceptible to the demon's commands."

So maybe my deception wasn't as bad as his, but it was bad enough. Jan and I had been fools. We'd have died if not for Bart.

"Cael, I really need you to shift."

I felt his frustration. We'd come to help, but I didn't listen to him. He had a plan, something Jan and I charged into the fight without. I shifted, kicked off my shoes, and struggled to get my socks off.

"Hurry!" I heard the strain in his voice. "I can't keep it contained much longer."

A burst of emerald energy struck the demon, rocking its head back. Bart used the distraction to release a spell. Slivers of golden light shot across the space between us. It slithered through the shimmering energy containing the creature and exploded into hundreds of silky strands.

The filaments of magic stretched and wound themselves around the thrashing demon. For every thread it broke, five more encircled it; alone, no one line could hold the massive being, but thousands of them did the job.

I peeled off my socks and my skin touched the earth. It was harder to make full contact in the city. There was too much cement and metal underground. By design or chance, however, this part of campus had a nearly perfect connection. I drank deeply and felt the soaring high it gave me after being apart.

The hilt of the seax was pressed into my hand.

"Take this," Bart said. "And give me your stone."

He had his hand out, but his focus was on our foe as it struggled to free itself. Jan continued to attack from behind, but his blows didn't seem to have an effect.

"It's going to break free at any second. I'll engage it so you can use the seax to kill it."

Bart's voice in my mind lacked its vibrant feel. He was burning himself out. I needed to help him but . . . *"How—"*

"Don't ask questions, just listen. The blade needs earth and mage magic. It worked against a lesser demon without earth magic, but it won't against one this powerful. I'll give you the mage magic, but you need to give it what it really needs."

I'd been scared when we arrived, but I'd had confidence we'd succeed. Now I wasn't so sure. Everything was happening so fast.

Mental communication, like reading, was much faster than talking, but sometimes you needed to read out loud for it to make sense.

"It's okay, Cael." Bart's calm voice soothed away the building panic. *"When I hold out your stone, touch the pommel gem to it and give it your earth magic. Then let the blade tell you when to release the energy. Easy peasy."*

"Lemon squeezy."

The demon heaved and the threads burst apart. Ichor seeped from a hundred cuts, and it was angry now. It completely ignored Jan's assaults, which was astounding since any one of them would've take out most mages. Its vitriol was squarely on Bart, which was exactly what he wanted.

Bart struck it with a white luminous blast that staggered it for a moment. Jan timed his attack perfectly and the demon lurched like a drunkard. Recovering, he glared malevolently at Bart.

"Well played, mage, but I have your scent. I'll find you. I'll strip the flesh from your bones slowly and delight in your screams of agony before I end your miserable life."

Breathing heavily, Bart tensed. Magic welled in the stones in each hand. *"Get ready,"* he said.

Jan struck again, but the demon didn't flinch. It remained motionless for a moment, and then shock registered on its face. Looking down, it growled, but this time it sounded different. Still angry, but now desperate. It scowled at Bart with such hatred it would stay with me for years.

"You think you've won?" It thrust its arms out and the prison buckled. Bart winced, but the walls held. Barely. "If I can't leave, I'll take you with me, mage!"

"When the barrier fails, I'm going to hit it hard. That's your chance."

I heard, *"Don't screw up, we'll only get this one opportunity"* at the end, even though Bart didn't say it.

The luminous walls bulged again, but Bart must have shut it down. They disappeared without exploding or bursting apart.

Before the demon could react, Bart hit it hard enough that it took two steps back.

"*Now!*"

He thrust his left arm out and I touched the seax's blue gem to my stone. Earth magic filled me to the brim, and I waited for the signal.

The demon brought its arms in front of it and stopped Bart's attack with one of its own. Sickly red magic vied with violaceous in a push/pull battle. The confluence of two streams created a blinding event horizon.

«*Release me!*»

It took a leap of faith to do what I'd been told. If the seax dropped to the ground, there wouldn't be time to pick it up and start over. The image of the blade releasing a massive burst of energy flashed into my mind and I understood.

I released my hold. Earth magic poured out of me and into the weapon; blue/green energy shot across the space and struck the stunned demon just under its arms.

I saw fear in the creature's eyes as it tried to move its right hand down. Bart used my attack to increase his, preventing the demon from defending itself from the seax's energy.

The armor glowed where my magic struck. A blue/green hue spread slowly over the reddish black from the point of impact until the center melted away. The circle widened and the demon roared in pain as my earth magic burned its body.

Still wailing in agony, the demon thrust its arms forward and discharged a massive burst of power. Bart's knees buckled, but he stayed on his feet. He was, however, burning himself out fighting the creature and supplying magic for the seax.

I was about to separate the blade from my stone when Bart and the consciousness in the seax screamed *"No!"* into my head.

"Don't let up," Bart said. "*If you do, it will kill us all.*"

I refused to let my only choice be to let Bart sacrifice himself for everyone else. The problem was, I didn't have any idea what else we could do.

Over the demon's shoulder, I saw Jan firing energy from his stone, but the monster was so intent on killing Bart before it died it had no impact. The image of Jan firing at the seax flashed through my thoughts. The blade had told me how to save Bart.

"Jan! Stop attacking the demon and send your magic into the blade."

"Are you crazy? I'm trying to stop it from killing Bart."

"It's going to kill him if you don't do what I say. I need your magic to replace Bart's so he can use all of his to defend himself."

I forced the image the seax showed me into Jan's head and prayed he wasn't too stubborn to listen. My heart sank as he kept blasting our enemy and ran to his left. Before I could curse him for a fool, he shifted his aim and green energy slammed into the blue gem of the seax.

Flush with power, I pushed Bart's hand down. Through our link, I felt Bart acknowledge the change. Swinging the hand with my stone up, he held it next to his. He was still close to burnout, but now he could use the magic he was feeding the seax to shore up his shield.

Reaching deep into the ground, I pulled all the earth magic I could find for one final assault. Jan wasn't as strong as his brother, but he wasn't dividing his power. The magic he gave me more than made up for what Bart had supplied.

The demon's face twisted into a snarl and its aura fluctuated. It was failing, but it still had enough to take Bart with it before it died.

A hatred welled inside that wasn't all mine. The Orme Seax thrummed in my hand, and I had a thirst to avenge someone I didn't know. I channeled that emotion into my attack. Pouring everything I could through my body, I shoved it into the blade.

The jewel in the pommel took Jan's energy, mixed it with my earth magic, and doubled the strength of the fire coming from its point.

"Leave my mate alone!" The words tore unbidden from my lips as the renewed assault rocked the demon.

The demon immediately stopped its attack on Bart. Every muscle in its body tightened. Reddish black magic radiated from its torso, swirling around the wound, pushing against the spread of blue-green light. Panic set in. Impossibly, the demon was thwarting my attack. A moment ago, it had been on the ropes, but that just proved how powerful its attack on Bart had been.

The brief smile of hope vanished from its face when a new burst of purple magic struck its chest. A small, tight circle of pure energy paused for a moment at the armor, and then punched its way out the demon's back.

The wail of the dying being hurt my ears, but the seax refused to let me falter. Bart's strike broke the demon's concentration and my earth magic raced across its body like paper that finally caught fire. The remaining armor peeled back, followed by skin, muscle, and bone until there was nothing left but ash.

I whooped and punched the sky. Across the circle, Jan let out a triumphant shout. Bart lowered his arms, met my gaze, and collapsed.

Chapter Twenty-Eight

BARTHOLOMEW

Angry voices woke me from a peaceful sleep. How incredibly rude. Couldn't they find some other place—a place far away from me—to have this argument? I tried to ignore them, but then I heard a voice I recognized.

"He raised a second demon right under your nose, and you prevented us from entering the grounds!" Avie shouted. "You almost got my brothers killed!"

"Don't try to pin this on me!" Brador yelled. "If *you* hadn't let him escape, this never would have happened."

I forced my eyes open. Most of my senses had returned. A pair of hands radiated warmth against my bare chest. Who ripped open my shirt to . . . Right. Healer.

"Excuse me." My raspy voice was barely a whisper. I tried to sit up, but the hands kept me down.

"Bart!"

The shouts came from multiple directions. I heard Cael's first, followed by Jan, Avie, and people I didn't recognize immediately. My mind was waking from its fog. I was cradled in Cael's lap, and he was stroking my hair gently. Tilting my head back, I met his concerned gaze.

Soothing energy flowed between us, washing away most of the exhaustion. Healers did incredible things, but they couldn't match the power of a mate bond.

"Hey, handsome," I said. "Thanks for coming to find me. You were amazing."

He wavered between relief, joy, and anger. I understood them all. "You scared the shit out of me. I don't know whether to kiss you or punch you for your stupidity."

It was my turn for an emotional whirlwind. "That makes us even."

In his elven form, his face wasn't as expressive, but I didn't need my eyes to know what he felt. Later we would need to talk about trust, but there was a more immediate issue.

I pushed up slowly and the healer shook her head. "Sit still, Mr. Hollen, you have a bad case of magical depletion."

Maybe I did when she found me, but I had a lot of practice using large amounts of magic. My body recovered quickly. And I had Cael. "Thank you for your aid, healer, but my mate's touch has helped me recover enough that I can speak to the others."

Cael and Jan helped me up like I'd collapsed from magical depletion. I hated being seen as weak, but truth was, I might have face planted the cement if they hadn't been holding me.

"Mr. Hollen." The healer, an older woman with steel-gray hair, wore a do-not-fuck-with-me expression that demanded my respect. "You're not released from my care. After you speak to the Deputy Inquisitor General, you are going to the hospital for a complete examination. Are we clear?"

"Yes, healer. I promise to cooperate."

"Who are you, and where's my brother?" Jan put the back of his hand to my forehead. "Do you think he hit his head and doesn't remember who he is?"

Humor was Jan's go-to crutch. The fight and my passing out

had scared him, and he wasn't ready to deal with things yet. "I'm reading the room. Would anyone let me say no?"

Jan snorted and rubbed the top of my head. He knew how much I hated that, but he did it when I'd fucked up and he didn't want to pile on. I'd have to talk to him, too, but first I had to find out what had happened.

Gently, I freed my arms and walked over to Avie and Brador. They'd stopped yelling, but their body language hadn't backed off an inch. I held up a finger to stop any questions.

"Where were you? Both of you?" They both shrank from my gaze. "I almost died because neither of you showed up as agreed."

It was harsh but justified. The three of us agreed I'd try to stop Declan from raising the demon, but if I failed, they'd bring help. Fast. I bet my life on them because Avie and Brador were extremely reliable. For neither to come to my aid was alarming.

"My strike team and I were here, but we were locked out." She didn't hide her fury. "When we tried to reach him, he was 'away' handling an emergency."

To his credit, Brador didn't cede an inch. No small feat given Avie's anger.

"You were locked out because we had a perimeter breach on the west side of campus." He looked pointedly at Jan and Cael.

"No," Cael said. "We used my credentials and the southeast entrance."

Avie crossed her arms. "You're through, Brador. When I'm finished, you'll be lucky to spend your life in jail."

"I'm not afraid of you Avelina."

If I wasn't suffering from severe depletion, something I wasn't going to admit at the moment, I would've stayed out of their power struggle. With the healer hovering ready to swoop me off to the hospital, I didn't have that luxury.

"Stop!" Everyone stopped talking and looked our way. Instinctively I started to ward us from unwanted ears but caught myself. "Avie, can you keep anyone from listening?"

Avie didn't like being told what to do, but all Hollens understood the need for private conversations. She surrounded us with a magical bubble. I waited for her to nod before I began.

"I've only got a few minutes, so let me tell you what I learned so you can look into it when I'm needlessly taken to the hospital." No one objected, so I continued. "First, Brador is not the enemy. If he'd wanted me dead, he could have made sure the demon ate me. There wouldn't be enough left to figure out his deception.

"Second, Declan wasn't working alone. I know." I held up a hand to stop Avie's protest. "I know you're skeptical, but I have more proof now. I used a spell and broke the control over him, but it was too late. The glyph had been activated. He tried to get me to run before he died."

"He could have been acting," Brador said.

"To what end? If he wanted me dead, telling me to run wouldn't help. But there's more. Whoever was behind this created the glyph to restrain the person who activated it. Declan was supposed to feed the demon. And since I'm quickly running out of time, it wasn't a miscalculation. Inside the circle, you'll find the lower part of Declan's right leg. The portal opened with such force, it severed his leg at the knee and flung him into the air."

Avie and Brador looked toward the circle, where a pair of inquisitors were examining the last remaining bit of Declan, and I waited until what they saw sank in. They turned back to me.

"And last, Declan didn't create that glyph. It's centuries old."

CAELINUS

Jan and I sat in the corner as Bart's family gathered around the room while he slept. He'd been right about not needing to be hospitalized. The doctors confirmed what the medic said on scene: severe magical depletion. Nothing a few days of no magic wouldn't cure. The doctors wanted to observe him for at least twelve hours before they discharged him.

Hearing that, Bart promptly closed his eyes and went to sleep. He woke up briefly when his parents and grandparents arrived, but he'd used so much magic he didn't stay awake long.

Gretchen arrived just before lunch along with Bart's younger brother, Leothius. After making sure her nephew was going to be all right, she announced Bart and I were barred from campus until further notice. Part of me wanted the time off, but then I remembered my students—our students—and it didn't sound so great. We'd figure out how to rescind that sooner than later.

Over the next few hours, I learned Bart's mother, Miriam, was a hoot. She and Jan kept a running commentary about the parade of extended family that rushed breathlessly into the room, tried to act concerned, sent a message to someone, and left without waiting for Bart to wake up. If they thought they were impressing Bart's parents or grandparents, they should have stuck around to hear how that conversation went.

The private room was as big as my apartment, which was only a slight exaggeration. Hollen Memorial Hospital had a top floor set aside just for Bart's family. The Hollens didn't miss a trick.

Esmerelda Hollen reentered the room holding a younger man's arm affectionately, with Owen, Bart's youngest brother, close behind. She'd been visibly upset when she arrived but had calmed down after speaking to Bart.

"I thought you and Leo went to get a cup of tea, Mrs. Hollen."

"I told you to call me Esmerelda." She kissed my cheek, knowing full well I'd never call her by her first name. "I asked Leothius to get it for me when I saw my other grandsons arrive. Have you met Owen and Roderick?"

I'd seen Owen on campus, but we'd never formally met. Roderick, however, was almost a total mystery. Bart talked about most of his siblings, but Roderick's name hadn't come up often. We shook hands and I escorted Esmerelda to an overstuffed armchair.

"I see the sycophants still come out for tragedy," Roderick

said, sitting next to his grandmother. "How many know three things about Bart?"

He appeared close with his grandmother and brother. Given how little he was talked about, I'd envisioned Roderick as an outcast. Something else to talk to Bart about in the future.

"Be nice, dear," Esmerelda said, in a tone that didn't disagree with the assessment. "Appearances *are* important."

"Especially when there's a high probability they'll make it on the news," Owen said.

I chuckled and we chatted for a while about nothing. I quickly learned Roderick didn't talk about where he lived or what he did, so I stopped using that as a topic for small talk.

Bart's brothers were genuinely concerned, but his grandmother was scared. She'd tried walling it off, but she couldn't hide it from my empathy. I grabbed her hand and squeezed gently. "He's fine, Grandma. I promise."

Using "Grandma" instead of Mrs. Hollen had been her request. I'd had trouble with it, but at that moment she needed Bart's mate to tell her everything was okay. Some of the tension left her body and she managed a thin smile.

"Thank you."

Roderick rubbed her arm and mouthed "thank you" over her perfectly coifed head. She didn't release my hand, and the four of us sat silently with our own thoughts.

Through our connection, I knew Bart wasn't really asleep. I didn't blame him for wanting to miss the shit show that was his extended family, but he was close to his brothers, and I knew he'd want to see them.

I patted Esmerelda's hand. "He's awake but doesn't want to deal with all the sycophants."

Owen snorted, but Esmerelda shushed him even as she smiled and rolled her eyes. Armed with a purpose, she became the force of nature Bart had described. Within a minute everyone who wasn't a sibling, grandparent, parent, or mate had been asked to leave. Some of the cousins, aunts and uncles grumbled, but they moved quickly as Esmerelda and Miriam shooed them toward the door.

"He's awake, isn't he?" Miriam asked. I nodded. "He did it as a boy. Taught Jan how to do it, too. Not that it ever fooled us for long."

"Long enough, Mother." Bart opened his eyes and sat up. "And it was Jan who taught me. I was always the good child, remember?"

"Hmph." Miriam looked at me and shook her head.

Bart had a lot more energy than when we arrived. Seeing his brothers helped, and watching the affection between them helped soothe my own frayed nerves. I was part of this family now, just as Bart was part of mine. Despite all the stories about the soulless Hollens, away from the paparazzi they were a normal family that cared deeply for each other.

Leo arrived with Grandma's tea, and I used the temporary lull in conversation to speak up. "Could Bart and I have a few minutes alone, please?"

I felt Bart's affirmation for some privacy. There was trepidation mixed in, but he wanted to have this conversation as much as I did. We locked gazes and waited for the others to leave.

The door closed, but we didn't speak immediately. We'd both done things we shouldn't. I could argue he started it by planning to go without me, but my sins were much worse.

"I'm sorry, Cael. I—"

"Me too, Bart." I sat on the bed and took his left hand in mine. There were burns from using my stone that hadn't been healed. They'd needed to wait until he was stronger.

"Can I go first?"

I knew why he asked, and I wouldn't let him go there. "Only if you promise not to try to take all the blame."

He smirked and put his right hand over mine. "In that case, you should start."

I brought his injured hand to my lips and kissed it. "I know you think what you did was worse, but I kept something from you as well. Darius and Ignatius, the Guardians of the Western Point, came to see me last week."

The guilt I carried bubbled from inside. Everything Bart did was meant to keep me alive. He desperately wanted to make sure his visions never came true. Instead of trying to keep him safe I'd let him walk into danger so I could swoop in and be the hero.

He rubbed his thumb across the back of my hand. "What are they like?"

"Huh?"

"The Guardians. What are they like?"

I'd just confessed how I'd betrayed our trust and he asked about Darius and Ignatius? Didn't he understand? I'd allowed him to face the demon alone. If we'd been late, he wouldn't have survived.

"Cael." Bart squeezed my hand. "If I'd died because I went alone, thinking that would keep you alive, how would you feel?"

"What kind of question is that? I'd be heartbroken and furious."

"Then we're equally at fault. I wanted to keep you safe, you wanted to save me. We both had good intentions, but we were both wrong." He struggled to sit up, but he did it without any help. "If you think what you did was so terrible you need my forgiveness, then you have it. Completely and without conditions."

My heart felt on fire it was so warm. I already loved him beyond my words to describe and he found a way to make me love him more. Water welled at the edges of my eyes, and I felt a tear run down my cheek.

I released his hand and dove in for a hug. He was right. We'd both wanted the same thing, we just did it the wrong way. This couldn't define us. "I forgive you, too."

He didn't say anything, but I felt part of me disappear. Far from scary, it was the most beautiful thing I'd felt. We'd finally let go of ourselves and became one. The way we were meant to be. No me or I, just us.

"I love you, Cael. I promise to work together no matter what." He kissed my cheek. "We're stronger together. You proved that last night."

Inside he was glowing with a light I'd never seen before. It took me a moment to realize it was us. I didn't look, but I knew I shone the same.

When we'd met, I'd been drawn to him. He called to me in a language I couldn't understand. Now, I was fluent. We were mates. Forever.

"Love you too, *Barry*."

Epilogue

BARTHOLOMEW

Behind the shades, dawn had arrived. I gently lifted Cael's arm from around my chest and rolled out of bed. We'd finally got our weekend at the beach, which we turned into a full week. All it took was a demon prince being set loose on campus; Cael, Jan and me almost dying; and the Mage Council canceling classes for two weeks while an army of inquisitors from around the world searched every inch of the campus.

I'd been as quiet as I could, but when I returned, he was awake.

"Morning, love." I kissed him but didn't get back in bed. Our private getaway was about to become a family gathering and we had things to do before everyone arrived.

Cael smiled as he stretched. "You're really going to start working? No one will be here for at least seven hours."

He was adorable when he tried to ask for sex without asking. It didn't work. Otto was always early, and he was traveling alone. He also hadn't had a vacation in two years, so my money was on him showing up before lunch.

"You can stay in bed if you like, but I need to order the food so it can be at the airport when Jan, Leo, and Owen take the helicopter."

"Where's the fun in that?" He threw back the sheet and seeing his naked body almost made me change my mind. "Thank you for making that happen, babe."

"Of course." I tore my eyes off of Cael and pulled on a pair of comfortable cotton pants from the dresser. "I'm excited to meet your brothers."

Cael pressed against my back and slid his arms around me. He didn't say anything, just held me. Standing in our bedroom with the sound of waves crashing in the background made this too perfect a moment to rush. I'd always loved the ocean and spending our first vacation together made it even better.

"It's blows me away sometimes when I realize you're not just Bart."

I laughed, thinking back to when we met. "Will I ever live down Barry?"

Cael hugged me tighter and kissed my nape. "That's not what I meant. I think of you as Bart, the professor, my mate, the guy who cooks these amazing things for us and half the faculty. But you're also Bartholomew Hollen."

I knew we'd get here one day, but I'd hoped it would be farther into the future. "That doesn't sound like a good thing."

He breathed in deeply and settled his head on my shoulder. "Actually, it's a very good thing. People are comfortable around you. You treat everyone like an equal, even though we're not. Then you do something like get us this house, and that reminds me you're Bartholomew."

We'd managed to avoid the different worlds we grew up in mostly because I didn't use my wealth around him. The limo was my extravagance, and he wrote it off as necessary to keep Isaac around to help protect me. Taking him to the beach couldn't be rationalized.

"Was the house too much?"

"No, but it's amazing. We're on a private island in a house three times the size of your already large home. We need the helicopter that's on standby at a local airport to get here. Those aren't things average people can do. Most days I get Bart. This was Bartholomew."

I wasn't sure if I should be happy I succeeded at keeping my life average or worried he'd always be uncomfortable around my family's wealth. It wasn't the ideal occasion to discuss this, but there would never be a perfect time.

"Let's get dressed and I'll make breakfast." I resisted the urge to block how anxious I felt. We'd agreed never to do that again, but I'd already made him worried. I spun and pulled him closer. "Nothing's wrong. We just need to discuss something we've been avoiding."

I left to get coffee and tea started while he got dressed.

My promise of breakfast was empty. The family had closed up the house for the winter, so there wasn't much in the pantry. All we had was the coffee I'd brought and some popovers I could warm up. The shopping list needed to be my priority.

I'd just put the kettle on and started the coffee when Cael joined me. "We don't need to talk about this."

We'd touched on some of the family business the first time Cael met Isaac. I didn't need a mate bond to know it made him uncomfortable. Things had changed, and we needed to have the conversation.

"It's fine, and overdue. Everything I own is ours; you at least need to know what we have. I told you that most of the Hollen family assets—houses, cars, planes—are part of the family trust. Grandpa Hollen controls that. There's a pecking order for using anything, which has led to a few angry moments."

"I'll bet."

"My personal wealth comes from that trust, but the Byzantine formula for who gets how much is beyond complicated. If I try to explain your eyes would roll so far back, you'll never find them."

He laughed. "It can't be that bad, can it?"

"Worse." I tapped the buttons to set the oven temperature and took the pastries out of the refrigerator. "But we can talk about that when I can show you numbers. To simplify it, I got a lump sum when I was born, like all my siblings. It went into a separate account run by the trustees who manage the family trust. Every year they deposit my share of the family income into the account. I'm not sure how much is in there, but you're a very wealthy elf."

"I can't think of your money as mine."

I understood that this was new, but that was the mindset that nearly got us killed. We were mates. There was only us and ours. As I thought how to respond, I realized I was making the same mistake.

"You're right. You can't buy anything with my money. We can buy things with our money. Next week we can work out how we make financial decisions." I took down two mugs, put a tea bag and hot water in one, and handed it to him. "Until then, just think of it as ours."

He smiled and found a spoon in the drawer. "Considering we're on an island in the Atlantic Ocean with no place to spend money, I'm good kicking this discussion down the road."

It would take time for him to get comfortable with the idea, but this was a good start. "Excellent. Now, let's get dressed and take our breakfast to the porch to watch the sunrise."

Late October mornings on the coast were chilly. We wore two layers under our sweatshirts, but there was still a nip. I didn't care, I loved the sound and smell of the ocean. If I could be a shifter, I'd want to be a dolphin or a shark. A merman would be cool. No one had ever met one, but if we were wishing, why not?

Cael sat bundled under a blanket. I suggested we go inside, but he insisted he was happy on the porch. Unfortunately, we'd need to go in soon, but I kept pushing that off another five minutes. If I didn't stop Otto would show up, we'd still be preparing things, have no food ordered, and he'd assume we'd been having sex all morning.

A loud thump, like a dump truck dropping its payload, gently shook the house. We jumped up and had our mage stones out before we spoke.

"What was that?" Cael asked as if it happened all the time.

"I've no idea."

The house was shielded by a strong ward, but nothing had activated it. I walked to the end of the porch and swung my stone in front of me as I turned the corner. I stopped so quickly that Cael bumped into my back.

"Holy shit," he whispered. His pulse quickened and he gathered his power. "Is that a dragon?"

It was, but it shouldn't be standing on the lawn without triggering the defenses. I understood his guardedness. Dragons and elves had an adversarial past. As two of the higher beings, their struggle for influence among shifters led to the elves leaving the assembly just after the Great Ward was created.

Two beings, an elf and a mage, jumped off the dragon's back and put a hand on its neck. They paused as if in conversation, and the dragon shook its massive head. The pair nodded and headed our way.

"Is that . . .?"

"Yes," Cael lowered his stone, but didn't release his power. "You wanted to meet them. Now's your chance."

"Good morning, Caelinus," the elf said, pulling his cloak around him. "I keep forgetting the spells that keep us warm don't extend beyond Glaphyra's back."

They climbed the stairs as if they'd been invited and hadn't come to visit riding a dragon. Not that I wouldn't have invited them, but manners were still a thing.

"Why are you here? And how did you get onto the island without tripping our wards?"

Then again, manners were overrated when someone showed up unannounced with a dragon that agitated your mate.

The mage laughed softly. "He is *so* like you Iggy. Always asking more questions before hearing the answer to the first one. I'm still a Hollen, the wards recognized me and let me pass."

His answer shouldn't have surprised me as much as it did. Darius and Ignatius, the Western Guardians, knew we were at the beach house and had flown here on a dragon. Nothing crazy about that. "Are you going to tell us why you're here, or is it too early in the morning?"

"I love the beach," Darius said. "The ocean has been crashing against the shore for millions of years. It will continue long after we're gone."

Ignatius rolled his eyes. "He gets so philosophical when we go to the ocean. I much prefer the mountains."

They'd refused to answer my question twice; they clearly didn't want to tell me why they'd showed up, at least not yet. If they'd been anyone other than the Guardians, I'd have told them to leave. But they were Darius and Ignatius, and they weren't a threat, so I changed tactics. "Can I get you some coffee?"

"Oh my, yes please," Darius said. "But Iggy prefers tea. Real tea, not that fake herbal stuff that's so popular lately. Green is his favorite."

Cael chortled. "I'm not sure we have green tea. We haven't had time to shop, so you'll have to make do with whatever's in the house."

"Whatever you have will be wonderful. Just make sure your coffee beans were grown in Columbia, ground to the proper size, and the water is poured evenly at just the right temperature, because Darius is quite particular."

Darius gave us a long-suffering look but didn't respond verbally. The playful push-and-pull might be a window into how Cael and I would be in a hundred years or so. Seeing the genuine affection they had for each other after twelve centuries made me warm inside.

"We'll be right back."

The house was well-stocked with assorted teas, so we were able to make Ignatius his preferred green. Darius, however, had to make do with the excellent Vietnamese coffee I'd brought from home.

Guests served and decorum and proper hospitality obligations met, I sat next to Cael on the loveseat and decided to try again. "Not to be extremely rude, but we're expecting our siblings to arrive today. Was there something we could do for you, or is it coincidence you chose today to visit this particular beach house?"

"And why did you fly here on a dragon?" Cael directed this at Ignatius.

Darius laughed. "Don't sound so horrified. It's infinitely more enjoyable than a plane or helicopter. There's nothing like feeling the air on your face as you cut through the sky."

"Or when you're plummeting to earth because they forgot you were there and did a barrel roll three thousand feet up." Cael shook his head. "No thank you."

"Don't be so narrow-minded," Ignatius said. "One, the animosity between our species ceased to affect me when I became a guardian. Not surprisingly, when shown the proper respect, dragons are excellent friends. They wouldn't barrel-roll with friends on their backs. And second, there's this thing, it's called magic. It helps you stay on their backs *and* breathe at high altitudes."

Darius wagged a finger at his mate. "Be nice, Iggy. The boy has probably never seen a dragon, let alone ridden on its back."

Ignatius's lecture had little effect on Cael's distrust. He also didn't like the idea of flying on a dragon's back. I might have been a bit less apprehensive than him, but I wasn't eager to ask for a ride. The more immediate issue, however, was that we now had three more guests.

"I'm about to order food for the week—if you three are going to join us, I'll need to order extra." I paused and looked at the pair. "Although I won't be able to feed a dragon. If she isn't comfortable shifting, she'll need to hunt for herself. There isn't room on the helicopter for that amount of food."

"That's very considerate of you, I'll ask Glaphyra." Darius smiled. "She wants to meet you two, so I think she'll accept your invitation."

The way he said that made me uneasy. Everything about meeting them unnerved me. Most beings thought the Guardians and the Great Ward were myths. There were no records of the Guardians ever going out into the world. They kept hidden for good reason. They certainly didn't ride on the backs of dragons to a beach house to have coffee and green tea with other beings.

I checked with Cael, but he shook his head. "Why does she want to meet us?"

"I thought that was obvious," Ignatius said. "You're going to take our places, and she's in charge of our protection."

"We're . . .?" Cael sputtered before I could speak.

"The Great Ward is failing." Darius set his coffee down. "There are two options—we can bring it down and recast it, or we can create a new one before the original fails. The first option would open our world to invasion. The second requires we find replacement guardians."

"No." It came out before I could stop myself. I shook my head and repeated, "No. I'm not interested. Go find someone else."

"There is no one else," Ignatius said. "You and Cael will need to take our place, or the world will be plunged back into open war with the demon realm."

"There are always other options," Cael said, echoing my rejection.

"In truth, there are not." Darius sounded almost sorry. "About sixty years ago, the eight guardians noticed the Great Ward required more and more energy to maintain. We met with the heads of the higher beings and the mage chancellor and set in motion the search for our replacements."

"One of the most important requirements is that the pairs be mates," Ignatius said. "How else could we ensure they'd remain together for centuries to preserve the ward? We also determined that the four pairs would need to be similar if not the same as the originals. The mages represent humans and provide the magic that sustains the integrity of the ward. The other four beings each had qualities vital to keeping the barrier in place."

"Just as Ignatius and I were the first pair chosen, so, too, are you." Darius folded his hands in his lap.

The way he said it burned me. No matter what they said, we had a choice. I'd been a slave to my visions for too long. No one would tell me I *had* to do anything.

"Tell whoever chose us we're not interested."

"There's no one to tell. The world chose you," Darius said.

"The Earth?" Cael asked. "You want me to believe the planet has the ability to sift through every being and pick four pairings?"

"The eight of us, along with the earth magic of the higher beings, released a spell to bring the four pairs together," Darius said. "It was the same spell Katarina and Adelais cast before creating the Great Ward."

"Then you should cast it again," I said. "This pair isn't interested."

"Whether you like it or not doesn't change the fact that you were chosen," Ignatius said. "Our planet is far more sentient than you believe. It's doing what it must to preserve all life."

It wasn't as crazy as it sounded. How else could we explain fated mates without something beyond what we can see. Human cultures embodied this in a god or gods. Beings refer to it as the Earth Spirit. Whatever it is, we should expect it to react in a way to save us.

Understanding didn't mean I liked the result. We would have to sacrifice our lives and all we hoped to achieve for the greater good. We'd nearly died saving everyone. Someone else could step up this time.

"We'll need to think about it," Cael said.

I obviously wasn't as good a being as my mate. "You're okay with this?"

"That's not the right word." Cael took my hands in his. "I love you beyond my words to express. If the Great Ward fails, you and everyone else I love is at extreme risk of death. I plan to spend my life making you as happy as I can, so if this is what it takes to make that happen, we'll make it work."

"Before you both skip off into the credits of a vomit-inducing romance movie, you're not being locked in a tower forever with only bread and water." Ignatius drew a swat to the arm from Darius. "What? It's true."

"His sense of humor makes my life so wonderful, but it can at times be a bit crass." Darius gave his mate a stink eye. "There'll be sacrifices, but there will also be new things that open to you."

"Like flying with a dragon or riding a unicorn," Ignatius said.

Neither of those were incentives to give up our lives. Cael and I were professors, we trained the next generation of mages to be better than the last. Losing that part of ourselves would leave holes that could never be filled. "Will we be able to teach?"

"I don't know," Darius said. "The world was very different when we assumed the roles, but the risk is still the same. Once the Ward is renewed, you will be targets for anyone trying to bring it down. You can't have a publicized schedule."

"On the other hand," Ignatius said in a slightly more upbeat tone, "technology and modern transportation create opportunities not available twelve hundred years ago."

The attempt to give me hope failed. We'd be exiled to a remote, heavily warded compound, with no chance at a normal life. Unlike the current guardians, who assumed their position before the internet and could occasionally go out anonymously, we were already minor internet celebrities.

"Babe?" Cael rubbed my hand until I met his gaze. "You know we can't say no."

His touch tamped down my anger. He didn't like having this forced on us, either, but his thinking was clearer than mine. If the Ward failed without a replacement, forget a normal life or teaching the next generation. There wouldn't be a world left at all.

I closed my eyes and exhaled my frustration. "I know."

"This isn't what I want either, but I promise we'll find a way to make it work." He squeezed my hand. "The important things are we'll keep the world safe, and we'll be together."

His love poured through our bond and all the anger and irritation at someone else controlling me again burned away. Our love was stronger than anything we'd face, so long as we confronted it together.

"Together." I nodded and kissed the back of his hand. Pushing to my feet, I pulled him up. I knew there was a lot we didn't know, but it didn't matter. I'd been given this amazing being to share my life with for a purpose. The price didn't matter so long as I had Cael.

"Let's go meet Glaphyra."

The End

Thank you for reading! I hope you enjoyed this first book in the Mages and Mates world.

Bart and Cael have found their forever mate, but the Great

Ward still needs three more pairings. Pre-Order *It Spells Trouble* and find out how Jannick meets his mate and mends his shattered heart.

Available May 23, 2023

It Spells Trouble; Mates and Mates Book 2

And, if you haven't done so already, sign up for my newsletter to learn more about the next books in the series, cover reveals, and other news.

Gallorious Reader News Sign Up:

Acknowledgments

It takes a village to do so many things and writing a book is no different.

Macy Blake - my younger big sister who has encouraged me and given me her most precious gift - her time. Thank you for everything.

Meghan Maslow - I owe you too many thank yous to list, so I'll go with the most important - thank you for being an amazing friend.

Lynda Lamb and Lorraine Fico-White - thank for your wonderful editing skills.

Kitty Munday - for being a great proof reader and a better friend.

Alexandria Corza - your talent brought my cover to life and makes me smile every time I look at your work.

To Mike and kiddo - I don't want to know a world or a day without you both brightening my life. It is my great joy to spend my life with you both.

About Andy

Andy Gallo prefers mountains over the beach, coffee over tea, and regardless if you shake it or stir it, he isn't drinking a martini. He remembers his "good old days" as filled with mullets, disco music, too-short shorts, and too-high socks. Thanks to good shredders and a lack of social media, there is no proof he ever descended into any of those evils.

Married and living his own happy every after, Andy helps others find their happy endings in the pages of his stories. No living or deceased ex-boyfriends appear on the pages of his stories.

Andy and his husband of more than twenty-five years spend their days raising their daughter and rubbing elbows with other parents. Embracing his status as the gay dad, Andy sometimes has to remind others that one does want a hint of color even when chasing after their child.

Also by Andy Gallo

If you enjoyed *Break the Spell*, be sure to check out my other stories.

Mages and Mates:

Spell it Out: A Mages and Mates Prequel

Break the Spell: Mages and Mates Book 1

It Spells Trouble: Mages and Mates Book 2

Harrison Campus: A contemporary MM Romance series:

Better Have Heart: Book 1

Better Be True: Book 2

Better to Believe: Book 3

Better Be Sure: A Harrison Campus Novel

Better For You: A Harrison Campus Holiday Novella

Harrison Campus Box Set

Learning to Breathe: An MM Urban Fantasy Series.

A World Away: Leaning to Breathe Book 1

It Spells Trouble
MAGES AND MATES, BOOK 2

Buy or Read in Kindle Unlimited

Mage Jannick Pederson thought it was a simple assignment: help the gryphon leader find some missing human children and then go home. A noble cause, even if he didn't much like the abrasive jerk. So why didn't someone tell him he'd be working *closely* with the leader's son instead? That hot piece of perfection could make even happily-single Jannick give up his no-strings-attached ways.

Gryphon shifter Conall Arwan has simple goals for his life: get his PhD in pediatric shifter social work and stay off the radar of his disapproving father. When his father orders him to work with a hot but arrogant mage to find missing human kids, all Conall sees is how it pushes back his graduation date. Again. And even if the mage unexpectedly turns out to be not *so* bad—and maybe even a little sweet—there's still no future for them. Conall's dad has plans for him and they don't include getting involved with a sexy, infuriating mage.

But fate has other ideas.

It Spells Trouble is a 75K word fated mates romance with a hearty dose of steam and a guaranteed happily-ever-after. This book is part of the Mages and Mates series and includes a plot to destroy the world, a desperate decision with far-reaching consequences, and one pissed off gryphon father.

Each book in the series can be read alone, but they are better read in order.

Harrison Campus Box Set Collection
AN MM COLLEGE ROMANCE SERIES

Buy it or Read it on KU:

This box set includes all five books in the Harrison Campus series (four novels and one novella). These slow-burn, low-angst stories prove opposites do attract, and follow the emotional highs and lows of five couples falling in love and finding their HEA.

Better Be Sure: An Out for You MM Romance (Harrison Campus Book 1)

Jackson Murphy bet his legacy that he can bring a guy to his fraternity formal. The guy he loves, Ed Knowles, isn't out and won't come to the dance. Does Jack follow his heart or hold onto the last link to his deceased father?

Better Have Heart: A Rivals to Lovers MM Romance (Harrison Campus Book 2)

Isaiah Nettles counts on winning the Gage Scholar program to help his family. The only thing in his way is Darren Gage, the heir to the Gage fortune.

Darren Gage plans to become the Gage Scholar to win back his father's affection. Then he meets the competition and things get complicated.

Better Be True: A Fake Boyfriend, Roommates to Lovers MM Romance (Harrison Campus Book 3)

Nico Amato is in love with his roommate. His all-American, jeans and t-shirt roommate who thinks Nico is too much. When Luke needs a fake boyfriend, does Nico refuse? Nope. He's in so much trouble.

Luke DeRosa has it bad for his roommate. His flamboyant, oversized personality roommate who does everything big. They kind of guy who finds Luke boring. When Nico needs a fake boyfriend, Luke should refuse. How does yes come out of his mouth?

Better to Believe: A Brother's Best Friends, Nerd/Jock MM Romance (Harrison Campus Book 4)

Coury Henderson has it all worked out: Pitch well his senior year, get drafted, play pro baseball. Falling for, Liam, his best friend's super smart, younger brother, isn't compatible with those plans.

Liam Wright has crushed on his brother's best friend, Coury, since he was twelve years old. Not that he'd ever have a chance. Jocks don't dig nerdy guys like him and Coury barely knows he's alive. So why can't he stop hoping for more?

Better For You: A Nerd/Jock, Forced Proximity MM Romance (A Harrison Campus Novella)

Charlie O'Leary agrees to work at the library before going home for Christmas. He needs the money. Staying with his secret crush, Evan, is a bonus. But hot, rich jocks don't go for nerds like him.

Evan Turgon needs help. He has five days to finish a paper he can't wrap his head around. Lucky for him, his cute, straight-A, fraternity brother Charlie is staying in the house. Too bad smart, cute guys always think he's stupid.

❦

Buy it or Read it on KU:

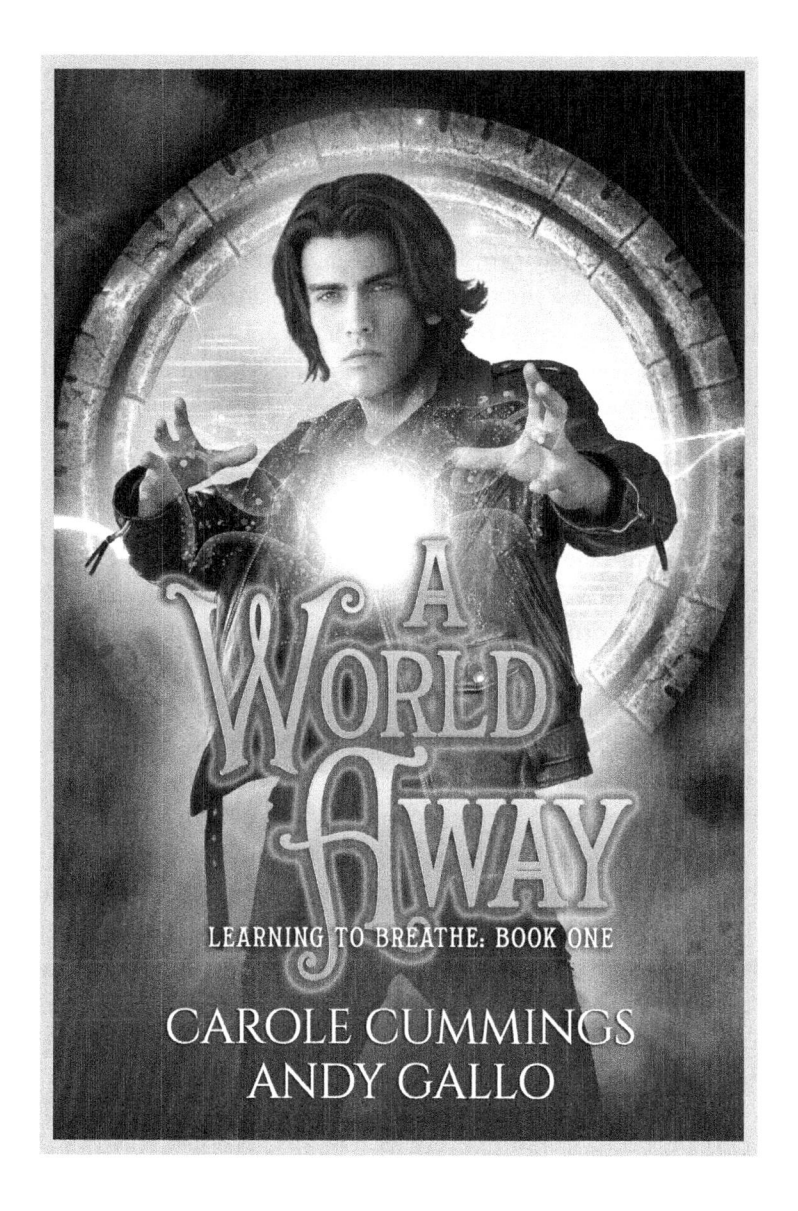

Buy or Read in Kindle Unlimited

We're not alone. There are an infinite number of universes and no two are the same.

Nathan Duffy knows how to keep things locked down so tight even he doesn't know they're there. Like his childhood trauma over the near-catastrophe he almost caused when his power manifested. His adolescent resentment over the near fatal injury he still hasn't really accepted. His futile not-so-platonic love for his best friend Cam. And that one pivotal moment when the love and the power had merged to save Cam from the accident that left Nathan unable to walk. Nathan figures losing the use of his legs was a fair exchange for Cam's life. He just can't ever let Cam know why.

For Cam Almenara, life has been an ongoing cycle of questioning reality. What if his mother hadn't died when he was ten? What if that drunk driver hadn't almost killed him and Nathan? What if Nathan's powers hadn't protected Cam at the cost of Nathan's ability to walk? What if Nathan had never convinced himself that Cam's feelings for him are nothing more than attachment and survivor's guilt? And what if Cam can never convince Nathan otherwise?

When Nathan is suddenly stricken by seizure like nightmares, his power slips its leash—*again*. Fearful his rogue abilities will hurt —or worse, kill—Cam, Nathan comes to the conclusion that it's him or Cam. Nathan knows who he'll choose. Trouble is, so does Cam. And he's just as willing as Nathan is to make the ultimate sacrifice to save the best friend he loves... and prove they belong together.

A World Away is 130k friends to lovers, slow burn romance with a guaranteed happily-ever-after. This book includes parallel universes, a chance to see "what if," extreme selflessness, and two very snarky main characters who can't seem to see they belong together.

NOTE:

A World Away was previously published as *Relativity: Lateral Parallax Book One.* There is a new 8K plus ending that shows what happens when they allow themselves to act on their feelings.

Buy or Read in Kindle Unlimited

Fantasy by Andrew Q. Gordon

Champion of the Gods
BOX SET

**It took the Seven to create the world, each to rule their own.
Until one wanted to control it all.**

Buy it or Read it on KU:

In the Great War of ancient times the God of Death sought to rule the world. He almost succeeded, but the Champion of the Six, destroyed the bridge into the world and closed the Eight Gates of Neblor. Some thought forever.

But he returned.

His servant, Meglar, surprised his enemies and all the great wizards who opposed him. The Six chose a new Champion to save the world. Young and untested, Farrell struggles to unite those who oppose the God of Death. With each confrontation, however, his task seems ever more impossible.

❦

What readers have said:

If you like beautifully designed worlds, riveting action, and a story steeped in magic, you'll love Andrew Q. Gordon's **Champion of the Gods,** *an epic fantasy series of magic, swords, and sorcery.*

"Mr. Gordon's world-building and character creation are definitely on par with that of Tolkien." -Len Evans, Amazon Reviewer ★★★★★

I am left wanting more details and stories from this incredible universe Andrew Q. Gordon has created. -Brax, Amazon Reviewer ★★★★★

This complete set contains all five books in the Champion of the Gods series. Over 2500 pages of magic, heroism, and fantasy adventures. Save 50% versus buying the individual books by reading the entire series in this special bundle deal!

❦

Included in the Box Set:

The Last Grand Master (Book One)
The Eye and the Arm (Book Two)

Kings of Lore and Legend (Book Three)
Child of Night and Day (Book Four)
When Heroes Fall (Book Five)

❦

Buy it or Read it on KU:

Purpose:
AN URBAN FANTASY THRILLER

But it or Read it on KU:

Forty years ago the Spirit of Vengeance—a Purpose—took William Morgan as its host, demanding he avenge the innocent by killing the guilty. Since then, Will has retreated behind Gar, a façade he uses to avoid dealing with what he's become. Cold, impassive, and devoid of emotion, Gar goes about his life alone—until his tidy, orderly world is upended when he meets Ryan, a broken young man cast out by his family. Spurred to action for reasons he can't understand, Gar saves Ryan from death and finds himself confronted by his humanity.

Spending time with Ryan helps Will claw out from under Gar's shadow. He recognizes Ryan is the key to reclaiming his humanity and facing his past. As Will struggles to control the Purpose, Ryan challenges him to rethink everything he knew about himself and the spirit that possesses him. In the process, he pushes Will to do something he hasn't done in decades: care.

But it or Read it on KU:

Printed in Great Britain
by Amazon